A Split Second to Midnight

by

Joe DiPietro

1663 LIBERTY DRIVE, SUITE 200
BLOOMINGTON, INDIANA 47403
(800) 839-8640
WWW.AUTHORHOUSE.COM

This book is a work of fiction. People, places, events, and situations are the product of the author's imagination. Any resemblance to actual persons, living or dead, or historical events, is purely coincidental.

© 2005 Joe DiPietro. All Rights Reserved.

No part of this book may be reproduced, stored in a retrieval system, or transmitted by any means without the written permission of the author.

First published by AuthorHouse 07/29/05

ISBN: 1-4208-5977-3 (sc)

Printed in the United States of America
Bloomington, Indiana

This book is printed on acid-free paper.

Author's Note

In this manuscript, segues to contemporary physics concepts are paraphrased to allude to "science fiction'" concepts for powering Alexander's light speed star ship. The reference work for these concepts is Stephen Hawking's book, "A Brief History of Time."

Chapter 1
Astrophysical Discovery

  Early in the 21st Century, the International Confederation for Aeronautics and Rocketry unto Space (ICARUS)--the global alliance of all the major economies, interested in exploring space, built and deployed the first true NASA managed space station. It was placed in orbit some 240 miles above earth, and over several years it became increasingly larger and more ambitious. From that space platform an endless procession of scientific discoveries continued to unfold as earthlings made their first sustained attempt to transcend the bonds of earth. The spirit aboard the space station was one of open scientific curiosity, sometimes almost childlike in its purity. It was a democratic environment, free from earthly politics, dedicated to the pursuit of cosmological investigation.

  Yet for several decades after the deployment of the space station, there was one major discovery that generated notoriety and piqued curiosity. It was what scientists call an "anomaly"--something that seemed to defy all known explanations. There were many young scientists, all with ICARUS flight training, who wished to identify the anomaly. There was competition to find, explore, classify, categorize and explain the anomaly. It was often "seen" from the ICARUS space station on a path or orbit, perpendicular to the asteroid belt and yet just beyond that belt. Many scientists had theorized about its nature but no one on earth ever isolated this new 21st Century celestial phenomenon.

The light from the anomaly was sporadic and inconsistent. The telescopes on the space station discerned the sparse shimmering presence of light from the anomaly every thirty-six days, for thirty-six consecutive days. When it disappeared for thirty-six more days and reappeared thirty-six days later. About all they could say for sure is that the anomaly was a group of seven celestial events orbiting the sun at about 91% of light speed. Light from the anomaly was sparse, shimmering, and frustratingly ephemeral for space station astronomical observers.

Then, in 2036, a team of ICARUS scientists came up with a plan to intersect the orbit of the anomaly of The Seven (as it had come to be called). At the time, there was no thought of coming close to it -- it was simply a plan to get a photograph, to be in a position to photograph the light source. A flight of four of the most powerful ion-rocket-powered and sophisticated planes went off in pursuit of the phenomenon. The pilots were among the most experienced but the scientists on each plane had never before been on such an adventure. Obeying the commands of earth-bound ICARUS commanders and influenced by the scientists intent on gaining an optimal photographic angle, the pilots over-rode their own knowledge of their rocket planes' limitations at the scientist's request to get a better photographic angle, when their on-board telescopic lenses provided the scientists on earth a view of the anomaly that was far superior to any previous space station photographic information.

What happened then caught the scientists totally by surprise. When they saw the seven celestial events they appeared to be seven cylindrical tubes, each sixteen miles in length, each four miles in diameter. Each cylinder had a dome on it; the dome was a docking bay. Both ends of each cylinder were covered by what appeared to be great massive crystal windows, four miles in diameter. The ICARUS scientists could look through the great crystal windows to see trees, terrain, buildings, mountain ranges.

The seven celestial events--those sixteen-mile long cylinders--moved at 91% of light speed. Acting on instructions from the scientists, the ICARUS ion rocket planes gave frenetic chase, then went out of control when they attempted to accelerate for optimal views of the interior of the celestial cylinders that accelerated at a far greater speed than the ICARUS rockets. Due to the great confusion caused by the scientists' surprise and `conflicting commands from ICARUS flight control, three of the ion rocket planes crashed into the asteroid belt.

Only one survived to return to the space station. This was the plane piloted by Stefano Colona, the lead probe--like a forward observer in a military operation who called in artillery. He had tried to warn the ICARUS team on earth but they insisted that their computerized program showed the planes were still in a safe trajectory. Only his own stubbornness emboldened Stefano to resist the pressure from both the ICARUS commanders and the scientists on board.

On returning to the space station, Stefano was devastated by the loss of his colleagues and at first he went through a period of self-blame: how might he have better communicated with those commanders who called the shots? But gradually he came to accept that he had long been bothered by various aspects of the ICARUS operations. For one thing, he resented that ICARUS chose to remain a para-military culture. As the forward observer, Stefano--on-site, nearest to the anomaly and the asteroid belt--should have had fail-safe authority to call the photographic angles of the astronomers in space. Instead there was a hierarchical protocol of earth-based para-military commanders who insisted on running the operation from the ground with their limited visual cues from space-based cameras, scanning limited horizons.

But what finally bothered Stefano the most were the attitudes and motives of the people who had come to control ICARUS. Early in the 21st century, the breaking down of so many of the old travel and trade barriers led many foreign investors to approach NASA. Foreign lobbyists from prosperous economies, who loved traveling to and doing business in the USA, took the position of not wanting to re-invent the wheel and compete with NASA. Instead they lobbied heavily for a commercial NASA -- open to investors, domestic and international, for the lucrative unexplored world of our solar system. To this end, NASA set up ICARUS.

What riches were imbedded in the other eight planets? This had become the primary question behind the activities of ICARUS. Most specifically, based on many scientific expeditions, who was going to gain mining rights on the moons of Jupiter? The technology to exploit the solar system was at hand. The promise of new, unparalleled wealth for many, riches and power beyond all expectations, led to the emergence of a new type of people around the planet--popularly called "Neo-Californians," for the metaphorical "Neo-Gold Rush" of the 21st century. For some, the excitement of being a Neo-Californian, with their imagined states of unbelievable wealth, was so intense that many were concerned about others getting the drop on their imagined claims. ICARUS became the focal point of an incredible amount of pressures and plotting, of strains and scheming. What had begun as a noble scientific adventure was becoming just another commercial venture.

At first there was nothing solid, nothing real, only great investment in mining futures, great expectations, and the search for the chosen technologies. And at the center of this almost frenzied speculative race was ICARUS. There were Neo-Californians puffing out their chests all over the planet because they claimed to have "contacts" at ICARUS. Bragging rights for public shares of ICARUS was a favorite topic of the Neo-Californians, many of whom would rather seek their imagined fortunes than deal with real problems at home.

Stefano Colona had long been aware of this. Growing up as a young Italian he had a highly idealized view of NASA and the USA. When through a family marriage he was able to gain American citizenship, he was overjoyed that he could have a straight route to ICARUS. He applied himself to his studies, mastered all the skills necessary, and became one of the youngest ICARUS pilots ever. But his disillusionment after the tragic crash also led him to become one of the youngest ever to retire from ICARUS.

It was a most difficult decision because his entire life had been a preparation for and dedication to the goals of ICARUS. In retiring, he felt a total collapse of his personal ideals and aspirations. Although he did not totally abandon his desire to identify the anomaly that had killed his colleagues and ruined his career, he now redirected his energies and passion to another goal--what he regarded as the injustice done to his parents and himself.

Chapter 2
Archaeological Discovery

They stood face-to-face--Arlee and Zohar. She, Arlee, headed a guild, far older than any medieval guild and unlike any guild in human history, a guild that demanded extraordinarily high standards from its members--all females. Each was a Mother Acolyte, and Arlee was the Mistress of the Guild. All were descended from one of the more mysterious peoples to have ranged the earth.

Around 4000 BC, then living in the Zagros range that stretched along the border between Iran and Mesopotamia. Arlee's people had a matriarchal society. They worshipped fertility symbols associated with The Supreme Mother Goddess. With invasions from Indo-European peoples causing constant alerts to protect their towns and villages, these people's sense of well-being was diminished. Arlee's people desired to maintain their homeland, yet they were torn between devotion to their leaders, who inspired them to stay, and fear of invasion from their neighbors that motivated them to migrate.

The Zagros people had a highly technical culture for their time. Emerging as a new social and economic force in their society, some men had adapted the reaping knife and sickle handle into wood-working tools and saws. This gave their society an advantage over nearby peoples, who were still confined to a basic agricultural way of life. Economic need and a certain amount of resentment led these surrounding peoples to present a constant threat to Arlee's society.

Meanwhile, to complicate matters, ecstasy-producing hallucinogens had been introduced to Arlee's society by traveling Dravidian Shamans from southern India. The Dravidians encouraged these Zagros-range dwellers both to improve their technologies and to fight the invaders. Although these drugs had somewhat clouded the judgment of the Zagros dwellers, the mixture of these two cultures had led to an extremely sophisticated society--one that on many levels was rife with tension. Arlee herself was the daughter of a high priestess of the Mother Goddess and a Dravidian spiritual leader, and she embodied much of this tension in herself.

Facing her was Zohar, the master technologist for The Guild. One of the more innovative of the early Zagros people, he was responsible for maintaining the technical standards of living for the members of The Guild and, by extension, for the culture's general citizenry. Their technology had developed beyond anything known to the contemporary continents of the Earth in the 21st Century. And aside from advanced technology, they lived in an open political system devoid of pressure groups, lobbyists, corporate politics, international politics and wars.

Arlee was impatient with Zohar who was unaware that diverse civilizations currently flourished on earth. Privately she thought about the latest episode with Earth-based astronauts chasing after the biospheres with their inadequate manned space probes. She was thinking: "One of their planes did get away. And they may soon penetrate our fields. It is only a matter of time before they will find a way to improve their space craft and attempt to probe our biospheres. Eventually finding out about us in this Technosphere." But all she blurted out was, "All the more reason for you to proceed quickly with developing Technosphere II."

"What reason, Arlee?"

She knowingly nodded, "You'll see, when you get there."

Zohar, due to his intense focus on problems at hand, managing the biospheres, was unaware of many events in the solar system; events that Arlee attended to with curiosity, not action. Now, tough, she was feeling threatened, feeling a need for action.

Zohar spoke. "It is one thing to develop a new Technosphere to avoid further interaction with the big eyes, Mistress Yin" (as he always addressed Arlee). "But to ask me to transfer Technosphere into an artificial galactic orbit so that you might experience the continued sensations of artificially induced nirvana--that is too much to ask! We've established Technosphere for you and a handful of your chosen women, The Guild. The men and women technicians and workers in the biospheres have been content to work, live, and procreate there. But I am not sure how they would react if they knew you and the Guild had gone off into a totally different level of being. I fear they will think you have simply...escaped into outer space." Zohar could not resist a sly sarcasm in his last remark.

"To speak to me in terms that are...unwarranted, unfounded, and unproved...this is only a reflection of your inability to reach inner peace, the goal of every member of The Guild who trusts my every intuition, Master Yang." Arlee's voice did now betray more than impatience, although Zohar could not actually see her.

Standing face-to-face in the Technosphere presented problems as they related to human interaction, speech, the spontaneous exchange of facial expressions. The Technosphere was in an orbit beyond Pluto--by Earth standards a wide sweeping orbit. Arlee was faced in the direction of the orbit, a forward vector in any moment of time and motion of Technosphere. At 96% of light speed, the light from her face did not reflect back to Zohar in a full spectrum due to the light dispersion variables involved with approaching light speed. The orbit, however, from Arlee's point of view, needed complete alteration. To attain near-light speed, she declared that Technosphere must be moved from an artificial sun orbit into an artificial orbit about the perimeter of the Milky Way Galaxy which was the contention of their discussion.

Zohar faced the direction of her voice. She wanted 99.9% of light speed, (or, the threshold before entropy, becoming pure dispersed energy), and she thought that she knew how to attain it. "We can only approach light speed by moving beyond the galaxy to a much wider orbit. And attaining light speed means experiencing higher levels of nirvana by engaging all of the DNA switches that release the entire spectrum of endorphins."

"But, Arlee, when we were on earth moving at the speed of earth's orbit, we had reality, ambition--a reaching and striving for the higher life style. We've utilized the technology obtained from the 'Big Eyes' to adapt their biospheres, to our ecological needs, to escape impending starvation from an emerging tribal rivalries.".

The technology was developed by the Andromedan "Big Eyes," then passed on to Zohar who took more than his share of credit for the developments. He studied human DNA biology, biochemistry, ecology, agricultural science, herbal science, and physics with the "Big Eyes," masters, of DNA engineering. While others feared them, Zohar embraced them. Whatever his other limitations, Zohar was intellectually ambitious.

"I'm tiring quickly, Master Yang," she intoned, "leaving my higher state of consciousness, forcing myself to speak logically, only brings me down, down, down from nirvana as I quickly approach your zero state of consciousness...consisting of fear, uncertainty, and doubt. The purest state of my mind is toward natural bliss, nirvana."

"And at your own expense, Mistress Yin. Because uncertainty and doubt are at the core or your wishes for an altered orbit and a new Technosphere. Can't you be reasonable?"

She smiled at him, although he could not see this, anymore than he could see her black skin in this light. She was naked before him, as vulnerable as the moment of her birth. Through the ensuing Earth millennia, tens of thousands of years of her near-light-speed travel, she mutated into something more beautiful than ever beheld on earth. Her cranium expanded; her eyes widened to beautiful almond shapes with varied blue hues shading the periphery of her great pupils; her generous head tapered from her large cranium to a gracefully pointed chin. Her body was lithe and graceful; her firm breasts pointed from a round base at her chest; her hairless body contained only a trace of her genitalia.

Her bodily functions mutated as a result of living in Technosphere at near-light speed. The helical structure of her DNA strands were altered by their synergy with the virtual effects of universal energy, causing her mutated nervous system to regulate previously unknown DNA switches to differentiate her into an altered human structure.

But living in the Technosphere at 96% of light speed had done something else for her: she had come to believe she was omnipotent. "We know, Master Yang, that light-speed travel attunes our beings to the full scope of cosmic rhythms, lifts us above the subjective experiences of the base point of zero--consciousness on earth. We have attained higher levels of consciousness, greater than zero. I don't want to discuss those in the biospheres who are comfortable and content doing their daily work, harvests, and acts of procreation only to await their inevitable deaths. I am the empress of these colonies. I am the priestess of the human mind. And you will build Technosphere II to my specifications!"

Suddenly Zohar's voice, demeanor and very being changed. "Arlee, darling, come back with me to the biospheres and learn the true meaning of sensual love. No one has died in the biospheres...yet. And no one fears death; they only look forward to rebirth. Yet death is inevitable."

She smiled, "You're certain, are you?"

"Never mind death for now. Help me build Technosphere II large enough to house any citizen, of the seven biospheres who wishes to join you. We might convert a biosphere into Technosphere II. I can't do it on my own. Be with me. Love me. Enjoy the pleasures of my touch...to learn, to love me again; return to earth with me to find the necessary metals and materials to build Technosphere II."

"Love thyself, Journeyman. Raise your self-experience to my level. Knowing what I know, I will not live and die in the colonies...when I can lead our people to the promised state of mind. It's not selfishness or greed from which I speak, but only the nature of things...survival, infinite survival, of the fittest of wits."

The problem of seeing her complete facial expression due to the diminished light in Technosphere was unsettling to Zohar. "But from the seven colonies, our biospheres, the citizens need to learn to trust the wisdom of The Guild Members who live at the highest planes of consciousness!"

"Yours is not to reason why. For you to entertain any thoughts of The Guild Members revisiting the lower thresholds of the mind is ludicrous."

His voice resonated with amplified sound and reason, "Arlee, it's not the colonists who manifest delusional thinking. When this Technological Bliss, which I've constructed for you, eventually fails, so will your artificially induced state of bliss."

"Master Yang, Journeyman, the technology will not fail. You will construct Technosphere II--and not from a biosphere, which is not a technological fit. We've been through all of that...before. Build Technosphere II to the specifications of The Guild. And as Technosphere II orbits the galaxy at ninety-nine point nine percent of light speed, in due time The Guild will transcend this mortal universe and cast off their mortal coils of life and attain the heightened states awareness available only to us who constantly exist in this mortal state of nirvana."

"And that's the rub now, isn't it? The mortal state of nirvana can only be found by the priestess of our culture. Not even The Guild shares your enthusiasm for infinite bliss. And who will help me in constructing Technosphere II when the natural resources do not exist in the biospheres. And the inhospitable planets of great heat, storms and gravity will kill the citizens of the colonies and then..."

"And nothing, Zohar. I command that you return to our own once hospitable planet...Earth. Obtain the natural resources necessary to build Technosphere II. And don't worry about the Andromedan Big Eyes...for we all know the truth about you and our exodus into space."

"To the foolishness of your drugged mind. To the foolishness of your addictive state. There's no immortal state of nirvana to be attained. Your mind's in a constant state of producing endorphins. And I've never told you this, Mistress Yin. I never invented light speed tachyon wave drivers. The technology was given to me, us, as a method of escaping our beloved mountain domains and moving to that new land. I studied it. I negotiated for the migration vehicles of the Big Eyed visitors to our planet; now, those vehicles are the biospheres. In their foolishness they trusted me. Remember that the technology arrived here from another galaxy. The inventors probably died in the rain forests from exposure to insects due to my incompetence and... "

"And your low state of self-esteem, Zohar. You studied the technology; you brought us here and I will guide you to your higher state within. Not as you promised to guide me when I was a virgin on Earth and you thrust yourself on me. Don't delude yourself into believing that the 'Big Eyes' died. They only stroked your fragile--"

"The consummation of our love was wonderful; the closest thing to nirvana that I've ever experienced. And your father, the arrogant high priest of our paradise, had no direction to lead us. We got here through my wit, guile, anger and sheer stupidity to think that I might embrace the technology of a culture far advanced to our own. The foolishness that lives in men's hearts cannot be corrected by light speed travel, only amplified into greater delusional thinking."

"I'll listen to no more of your frustration. Follow my orders, Journeyman. Revisit, relearn the technology. Return to earth for the natural resources. Figure it out! Build Technosphere II. Find the beings who put us out here!" At that she vanished into the angles of light and shadow, leaving Zohar more frustrated than ever.

Chapter 3
Family Conflict

By the year 2046, ten years after his early retirement from ICARUS, Stefano was working as the marketing VP for LiteWave Technology, based in Alexandria, Virginia. Its president, Alexander Petrov, was Stefano's cousin. Alexander was the son of the founders and still principal owners of LiteWave Technology, Maria Colona Petrov and Sergei Petrov. Stefano's mother, Carla, and Alexander's mother, Maria, were sisters.

Sergei Petrov, a Russian scientist, had married Maria Colona in the early 1990's, when the Soviet Empire was disintegrating. Sergei spent several years in Italy due to the fact that Italian physicists were doing some of the most advanced work in high energy physics. Sergei went to Italy as an idealistic scientist, with little interest in practical applications of his work until he met Maria -- already as a young girl, the ruthless pragmatist.

Maria had gone to law school and while there had an affair with Paolo Treviso, a dashing young man who had a minor reputation as an Italian football star. She introduced Paolo to Carla, undeniably the more beautiful of the two, and Paolo then began an affair with her-- eventually fathering her son, Stefano. On Maria's advice, though, Carla refused to marry Paolo.

Maria was so strong, so pragmatic, that her sister, Carla, mistook leadership for love. Carla always felt safe and protected by her big sister. Their close relationship caused Carla, who idealized her relationship with Maria, to take her advice on most things. In particular Carla totally trusted Maria when it came to the world of money and finance. Maria convinced Carla that because Paolo would probably never make big money she should not marry him. More than that, she promised Carla that if she gave Stefano the name Colona that she would see to it that he never lacked for anything in life.

Maria assured Carla of her sincerity by giving Carla several large chunks of money, eventually totaling millions of dollars, which were from the Colona legacy, worth in excess of a billion dollars. This fortune had been inaccessible until Maria and several shrewd legal friends of hers, young professionals from Milan, found several loopholes in Italian laws dating back to the Middles Ages. As a test of their newly developed legal skills, Maria and her colleagues exploited little known estate laws for their semantic vagueness. There were several very large real-estate holdings, in the Colona name, in Venice and Milan, which had never been passed to succeeding generations. They had been held in proxy by the Vatican for many centuries. Maria and her legal friends found ways to circumvent laws against willful perpetuity and circumvented the proxy power of the Vatican.

Paulo had no money to speak of and it seemed better to Carla to receive several million dollars to support Paulo and Stefano rather than to marry Paulo and incur the wrath of Maria. Yet the money in Paulo's opinion should be half Carla's, because she was the only other living heir in this case. From Maria's point of view there were no heirs, this was just a once-in-a-lifetime windfall based on her own legal expertise.

Despite the fact that Maria gave some millions of this money to Carla, she never lost her particular distaste for Stefano, because Stefano was a continual reminder of his father's infidelity. In his early years, due to the closeness his mother felt for her sister Maria, Carla filled Stefano's head with ideas that Maria was altruistic and would share her good fortune with the other members of her family. But as he grew older, Stefano was told by his father Paolo of his Aunt Maria's true character. Ultimately, Stefano was left confused about family, loyalties, and money -- left, in fact, with all the age-old frustrations of a bastard.

Meanwhile, Maria had married Sergei Petrov, the starry-eyed optimist who excited her on many levels -- visceral, sexual, intellectual, emotional, even spiritual. Determined that she and he should be players on the world stage, she convinced Sergei to become an entrepreneur in America, where she believed she could also protect her money better than in Italy. They moved to the land of lobbyists -- suburban Washington D. C.

Maria gave a substantial amount of money to Sergei Petrov to start his own company during the electronics computer inter- networking bonanza of the 1990's. LiteWave Technology was formed with a massive influx of cash. Although it did not bear the Colona name, it was her organization and she was determined to make sure that the Colona family thrived in the USA. She made sure her son Alexander became president. And when Alexander's cousin Stefano left ICARUS, she realized the value of his reputation and even encouraged Alexander to invite him to join the firm. Overcoming her own personal feelings about Stefano, she sponsored him as an immigrant. After she saw that Stefano had some of the very talents that Alexander lacked, she encouraged Alexander to make him a vice president. All her money, however, could not buy off Stefano's desire for retribution.

Chapter 4
"I Hate Regulated"

In the summer of 2046, at the LiteWave offices in Alexandria, Virginia, Stefano reflected, as he anticipated Alexander's entrance for a briefing, probably a short meeting. Stefano was still notorious in the minds of many as a great, but if slightly aging hero, in the chase of the anomaly.

Stefano had made mental and emotional adjustments over the years since he had chased the anomaly. He grew bitter over the lack of understanding coming from the Petrov clan. He felt that he had a stake in the Petrov fortune -- due to his father's help and assistance to Aunt Maria in securing the Colona fortune. Stefano loved the excitement of space travel, but as long as the Petrovs were left to their own devices, while Stefano was out chasing around the solar system, they would never give Stefano his just due.

"Just" in his eyes only, because Alexander Petrov never gave Stefano a second thought as a co-owner, even major share holder, of LiteWave Technology. So Stefano accepted that he would have to earn his ownership gradually through stock options which was the master plan marinating in Stefano's mind. He was out to get the stock options--his own way, quickly, by hook or by crook.

Stefano became Americanized over the years and dropped his romantic Italian accent in favor of traditional American speech patterns. In his ICARUS/NASA days Stefano was a bright young man full of creative ideas and initiatives; he thought in terms of short range objectives with long term strategies. He also had a way with words. Now he applied his talents to marketing and sales. His easy manner and facility with words had gained him the position of marketing manager for LiteWave Technology. His contacts at ICARUS/NASA made him very attractive to Alexander, as the man to launch LiteWave into new markets -- transportation, based on anti-gravity technology.

Stefano planned to leverage his contacts at ICARUS/NASA to get what he wanted: revenge for Maria's not sharing the Colona fortune with his mother, Carla; revenge for Maria's stopping his mother from marrying his father, Paulo; revenge on the Petrovs for treating him as a bastard son.

Alexander had a steady gaze on Stefano as he entered the office. Stefano spoke first. "So what do we call the market for your brave new technology, Alexander?"

Alexander looked Stefano directly in the eyes. Opposites in some ways, they did share a common trait--intensity. "I want your support, Stefano! I want you to handle this for me. My time needs to be focused, channeled into the final phase of releasing this new technology to market."

"Okay, but you must first help me, Alexander. Give me that fancy catch phrase to launch your anti-gravity technology into the Neo-Californian market place."

Alexander gave Stefano a disbelieving glance; they had discussed this so many times before. Stefano was the marketing ace, the rhetorician.

"Don't look at me that way, Alexander. I know that you hate Neo-Californians. How about...Virtual Transport?"

"Too suggestive of other technologies. How about something catchy, something pretentious...like, The Tachyon Twister."

Stefano shook his head negatively. "You've told me too many times that you don't have a clue on how to develop tachyon technology."

Alexander winced, "Of course I don't. But if I did, I'd have the most elegant technology ever conceived...and really attain light speed."

"And what's so important about attaining light speed?" Stefano asked. The practical value of anti-gravity ships was Neo-Californian mining on the moons of Jupiter; returning valuable natural resources, new compounds, from the moons of Jupiter was what all the hype was about. Compounds too heavy to move in volume by ion rocket transports from the intense gravitational fields of those moons--that was a real economic benefit to pay for developing anti-gravity technology.

Fascinated by his own world of technology, Alexander jumped up on the desk and spread his arms back like the wings of a rocket plane. "You, Stefano, you were the master of the swept-wing when you were at ICARUS." Alexander made motions and sounds to accommodate his display. "Rockets shooting from space stations and flying to the moon, the planets. How long did a trip to Jupiter take in an ICARUS ion rocket plane?"

"About twenty-three days at 950,000 miles per hour. We had to use all of those old NASA orbiting routines; orbiting the earth, while testing all systems, before launching toward the outer solar system. And that took a couple of days. Plus other factors kept our speed down." Stefano paused for a moment as he thought of his experiences with ICARUS, then asked Alexander, "How long to Jupiter in the LiteWave vehicle?"

"Stefano, I knew that you would ask that question. In our new vehicle?...two hours tops! You just can't accelerate toward light speed and not decelerate. At light speed, from the sun, forty-four minutes to zip by the earth and Jupiter, a couple of meaningless outer space planets on the edge of the wild uncharted Milky Way Galaxy." Alexander smiled at Stefano. "So, cousin, you're quite comfortable in deep space?"

A strange, intense look manifested over Stefano's face, as his mood altered quickly, "Yes, cousin." At that, Stefano's eyes and voice seemed to move into another, more ethereal sphere. "And there was a time when calling you cousin meant something. Affection. But anyway." Stefano suddenly came back to where he had been. "Where was I? Deep space. Yes, where I learned my true animal nature and felt the best about myself. Looking at this earth from afar...a celestial floating ant colony without mercy and feelings. I learned that earthlings are egocentric beings who call anything beyond the earth outer space." Again, Stefano's eyes and voice took another turn, but this time into a sphere that frightened Alexander. "Earthlings who ignored my knowledge and requests... earthlings, Yankees, caused those planes to crash."

Alexander stared deftly into Stefano's eyes. "The primitive human mentality cannot admit fault. Instead, Stefano, ICARUS bureaucrats create comfort zones, rather than dealing with true change!"

"I hate denying my animal nature--libido, Alexander! I hate pretending to be logical, regulated, bureaucratic, governmentalized. Your anti-gravity vehicle will never see the light of day with all of these bureaucratic asinine government regulations. But still ICARUS up-and-comers, Neo-Californians are betting the ranch on new promising technologies, like yours, for deep-space mining."

Alexander looked fretfully into Stefano's eyes. "And I sense that it goes deeper than that. Don't I?"

Stefano stood up and reached across the desk to grab Alexander's collar. "Of course, it goes deeper; there's a lot that needs to be corrected around here. I have been loyal to you, Alexander, but now you're asking me to be...your hatchet man. Out with the old, in with the new."

Alexander ripped Stefano's hands from his shirt. "Stefano! You'll make it happen. From LiteWave's traditional markets--photon computers, circuit logic, and networking--you're the one to get us to virtual particle drivers. You will fly the first LiteWave vehicle for ICARUS. You'll sell it to them. Only you can do this--you who survived the anomaly disaster!"

Stefano and Alexander were now standing side by side. Alexander put his arm around Stefano's shoulder and looked into his eyes, "You'll succeed, Stefano. You'll figure it out. You're a marketing animal. You can make things happen for me. And I expect it from you. You'll persuade ICARUS and its Neo-Californians to buy our technology. And most critically...for the government, to certify it."

As they moved toward the door in a lazy cadence, Stefano's eyes locked onto his cousin's eyes, "Alexander. Can you handle my bargain? Can you deal with what I want from you?"

Alexander was puzzled by Stefano's sudden turn but chose to reply jokingly, "Who's in charge here?"

"You. For now. Don't push me. Keep your expectations in check. You're on a roll. But caution: don't roll over the edge." Stefano was not joking.

Alexander acknowledged, "You're threatening me? At this late date? If you've got something on your mind, please, get it out into the open."

Stefano removed Alexander's friendly arm from his shoulder. "Alexander. You've got too many moods and aspects to your character.

That's your flaw. Your spoken messages aren't consistent with the emotional signals that you send me. I can't read you. Do you read me?"

Alexander's head snapped back. Was this Stefano talking? When Alexander's assessment of Stefano was about the same -- too moody, too rangy in his thinking, too arrogant in his approach too heady, too aggressive; "Cousin, you're just too, too..."

"Too what, Alexander? Too obedient, too subordinate to talk back?"

Alexander decided that to go further with this would be to go over the brink, so he drew back. "Just do your thing. Make it happen for LiteWave Technology. And I'll back you up completely. It's your marketing project. And that's what you're best at. And that's why you're here."

They stood in the doorway; as Stefano opened the big glass swinging door, he gently backed out one step at a time. Tears swelled in Stefano's eyes. "And that's all, that this is? Business, cousin?" He pronounced 'cousin' sarcastically.

Alexander was surprised, "Isn't that enough?"

"You've been working too hard for too long, Alexander. I'm here in this family business for more than just marketing. Aunt Maria knows that. Haven't you ever discussed the Colona money in this business with her? Don't you know your financial origins?"

Alexander pulled Stefano by the shirt in an effort to get him back fully into the office, "Stefano. I don't want to hurt you. We've been through all of this before. Years ago. Why now? Why are you bringing up your financial interests in this company. That's all been resolved. Set-up through Maria's good fortune."

Stefano pulled Alexander's hand from his shirt, "Yes? Resolved to your satisfaction has it, Alexander? You should speak to my father, Paolo, on that subject. He'll clue you in."

At that, Stefano turned on his heels and marched straight out to the parking lot. Alexander was left shaking his head in a mixture of incomprehension and unease.

Chapter 5
Fever Greed!

Stefano felt no uncertainties. He was distinctly unhappy about his meeting with Alexander, when he went out to his car, a six-speed sportster, and sped to the LiteWave compound in Deep Creek, Maryland, the site of the firm's chief manufacturing facility. Stefano went into his office and got on the phone with a former colleague at ICARUS, Doctor Charles Tong, from Hong Kong, a leading Neo-Californian. Tong had been a part of the NASA team that moved from the government sector and went over to ICARUS with its public stock offerings. It was a very cozy arrangement for evaluating new technology: at NASA, they were able to nationalize technology under the USA flag; once nationalized, the same technology could then be sold for profit, and re-licensed, by the publicly held ICARUS. Under that arrangement, Doctor Charles Tong and similar investors were able to reap huge profits from the burgeoning market economies around the world who had Neo-Californian fever. They wanted to stake their claims on the moons of Jupiter. They wanted to speculate on the public offerings of ICARUS.

From his Deep Creek office, over his video phone, Stefano spoke. "Well, yes, Charley, I've got Alexander right where I want him. He trusts me. Thinks that I'm unhappy about my stake in the company. He can't see it coming. He doesn't know what I know. He's been too busy developing the technology, rather than managing it."

Tong was on his phone at ICARUS in Florida. He was an older gentleman, in his early sixties. Black horn rimmed glasses and a black art deco cigarette holder were his trade mark. He took a long deep puff on his cigarette. "Well, Stefano. He's clue less. Convinced that you're disenchanted...but that things are going along smoothly?"

"Too smoothly. The bastard's overconfident. But he's put the rumor on the street that he's bringing his younger sisters into the company. Because they have advanced degrees in finance and marketing. I guess that I will be working for them--based on family ties, not titles."

"So then, Stefano, why do I sense anxiety in your voice?"

"Charley, maybe I've overplayed my hand with Alexander. I don't want to make him suspicious to the point that he starts looking under rocks."

"Never. Never. He's too...too fascinated with technology. I know the man. Play your hand correctly and you will prevail. Don't permit simple paranoia to defeat you."

"The sisters might be the secret to my success. Use their animosity toward Alexander, always to cover my tracks."

"Tread lightly, carefully in such matters. They can and will blow up in your face. Ultimately working against you, Stefano."

"You don't know them like I do." Stefano was convinced that he could outsmart all of Maria's family. Somehow, someday, Stefano intended to corner the financial rewards from selling Alexander's virtual particle driver technology to ICARUS, to be re-licensed around the world to build anti-gravity mining ships.

ICARUS was not in favor of Alexander's approach: a mass, broad and sudden introduction of virtual particle drivers to build anti-gravity ships to replace runway ion rocket planes and ships for commercial travel. Alexander abhorred Neo-Californian discussions; get rich quick schemes -- mining the moons of Jupiter!

Alexander took aim at the commercial travel market place for making examples of cost savings. A commercial runway rocket plane delivered three hundred passengers from New York to Hong Kong, non-stop, for fifteen hundred dollars round trip. The trip, New York to Hong Kong, took seventy-eight minutes under the best of traffic conditions, without having to do multiple earth orbits in a holding pattern.

Alexander saw things differently. An anti-gravity commercial passenger vehicle would deliver a thousand passengers, in greater comfort, with less risk, without the stress of earth orbit, for a thousand dollars round trip -- New York to Hong Kong in twenty-six minutes.

ICARUS wanted a planned phase out from rocket planes to anti-gravity vehicles. They were out to protect the big corporate entities who stood to lose; market share, jobs, prestige, and lost prestige was the worst kind of psychological entropy for big dinosaurs like Boeing Rockets, and Lockheed-Martin's RVL's. The military value of anti-gravity ships was tantamount to dominance; moving troops and equipment, in mass, in moments, except for staging time, had the greatest strategic and tactical value for the dominant market economies and their alliances--NASA-supported AirBus, Boeing, , Lockheed-Martin's Re-usable Launch Vehicles and other less notables, like Bell AeroSpace, and SpaceShipOne's unique offerings.

Stefano developed his own agenda; the Stefano way -- shoot from the hip, observe the fallout, react to the new situations, to get to the goal of owning and controlling LiteWave Technology. The most logical part of his agenda was to sell LiteWave Technology secrets to ICARUS to raise the necessary capital to purchase LiteWave Technology stock offerings to improve his voting position, possibly gain a seat on the board of directors -- not at all to the liking of Alexander or his parents, Maria and Sergei Petrov.

Charles Tong finished the telephone conversation. "To prove your sincerity with me, Stefano, I want all of the flight manuals. All of the CAD/CAE computer drawings for the LiteWave anti-gravity vehicle's design. Most important, the virtual particle driver."

After ending with a few pleasantries, Stefano turned off his video phone, looked over his calendar of appointments on his computer, and then went back out to his car. He figured that he still had time before Alexander would be arriving home.

Chapter 6
Risks-Rewards!

Technologically, the 21st Century was a natural continuity from the 20th Century, a time when all the important engineering processes and scientific information from the former century were synthesized into systems for the design and manufacturing of sophisticated products. Computer Assisted Design and Manufacturing Systems in the 21st Century reached levels of sophistication to make it possible for a computer expert to manufacture a space ship while knowing very little about manufacturing processes.

Alexander Petrov was one of those people--an engineering wizard capable of understanding form and function to the point of working his computer-assisted manufacturing installation to an optimal level. As he set off in his electric-powered automobile for the Petrov family home, from their Virginia headquarters, he found himself giving thanks, as he so often did, that he was living in the 21st Century.

Yet with all of the technological advancements in the 21st Century, the lives of the average industrial workers in 2046 weren't appreciably different from the lives of the average industrial workers in 1946. Certainly the subjective lives of individuals hadn't changed appreciably. People still felt the same emotions as in the age of Shakespeare. Like Iago, in <u>Othello</u>, a villain was still a villain; opportunistic, the villain still found his moments, to seize, to advance his selfish hatred of others. And no one in the 21st Century really knew, any better than in previous centuries, what evil lurks in men's hearts and minds.

The Petrov family and entourage lived in a rambling French Colonial mansion in Deep Creek, Maryland. It displayed many roof angles, peaks, and skylights, while the front facings of the various units were made up of tall angled glass sections. From the outside, the mansion appeared as a sparkling shimmering fantasy capable of fulfilling the dreams of many less affluent people.

Just as in the 20th Century, "affluence" was a governing component of the 21st Century. Those who could afford it had it all.

All of the political bi-partisan wrangling in the 20th Century had led to both successful and unsuccessful projects. After decades of funding issues, for instance, Amtrak built the American version of the bullet train, an elevated transportation system that used magnetic levitation. The train tied all of the East Coast and West Coast corridors together. And the affluent ones, business moguls, had arranged things so that the Amtrak right of ways passed very close to their newer sophisticated commercial structures, which gave the affluent cities that colloquial space age look with various local and long distance bullet trains stopping at their sites. The "Maglev Bullet Train" sustained speeds of 300 miles per hour for commuter and long distance travel. For travelers and commuters, it was low cost and convenient. As for air transportation in the 21st Century, jet planes had given way to the rocket plane, which then gave way to the ion rocket plane. Which--if Petrov had his way--would soon give way to the virtual particle driver, anti-gravity transportation. Humans were on the threshold of the real space age.

Some of the less successful projects of 21st Century space age, spawned through bi-partisan bickering by American politicians, were the urban Eco-Sphere projects that were intended to place people in utopian, toxin-free, carcinogen-free, urban environments. But since the Republicans and Democrats could not agree on what a utopian Eco-Sphere was, these projects--after being built and losing funding from continuous bi-partisan bickering-- became hell zones of crime, drugs, and disease. However, from a distance, these urban Eco-Sphere ghettos appeared to be a truly space-age collage of spheres and domes with their own internal transportation systems consisting of air pressure-accelerated vehicles in vacuum tubes. People traveled, at their own risk, four- and eight-passenger Eco-Sphere vehicles, but their lives were not really going anywhere special or far.

So the 21st Century, like the previous century, was enjoyed by those who were willing to take risks and earn great rewards from their risk taking. Those who failed at risk taking might be found living in an Eco-Sphere.

But not the Petrov family. They took their risks. Maria Colona had taken great risks in her career to amass a great fortune.. Now anyone who passed through the entry to their Deep Creek, Maryland French Colonial mansion might be tempted to immediately ascend the long, curved sweeping staircase to the upper floors, where the private thoughts and secrets of the family and entourage emerged with great expectations. In those rooms dwelled desire, wanton self-fulfillment, ego gratification. Changing self-perceptions propelled each person toward their imagined higher planes of existence. All had their hidden agendas.

In her bedroom this Friday afternoon, Maria awaited Alexander's return for the weekend. She enjoyed her discussions with her son about the role of women in the sciences; inevitably, though, such topics segued to Alexander's life style -- the workaholic. She wanted him to change; she didn't want him to continue in his father's footsteps or to pursue foolish notions.

On this Friday afternoon, Maria was particularly perturbed with her nurse and wanted Alexander (when, he arrived) to administer her insulin shot. Maria had a migraine headache and was angrily addressing the nurse who was disenchanted with the pedestrian duties of attending to Maria. Painfully postured on her bed, Maria snapped at the nurse, "Just go, go, go--we'll find another nurse; there are many more pleasant women out there who are seeking employment. What you receive for your work...it's sinful."

The nurse glared at her. Loathing Maria's personal attack, she said, "Sure, sure, that gorgeous son of yours is very charming, enchanting to women, and he cares about his mother. I can be dispensed with on Friday afternoon when you're anticipating his arrival. Yes?"

Wearing a cold compress over her eyes, Maria replied "He'll take care of me. He always does."

The nurse darted an angry comment, "But who's going to take care of him? Who's going to protect that man from all of the sharks around him?"

"Don't attack my family. You're just the hired help."

"Family, Maria? Stefano's always sneaking around here. Andrea's sullen and lonely because Alexander's too busy for her. He's got his mummy, you know. And Sergei's usually fantasizing by the fire place; filling Alexander's head with wild notions...who knows what? If your son survives his sisters looking for a way to emasculate him, he deserves a lot of credit. He'll be a hell of a man in my book. Someone able to overcome any obstacle."

"Two weeks severance. That's all you're getting. Now get out!"

"Okay, okay, I apologize. You'd better let me administer your insulin shot. Just in case your little honey doesn't appear on his white steed in time."

In great pain from her migraine Maria sat up, "Insolent bitch! Get out and leave me alone!"

"Okay, okay, I don't have to take this. I'll collect my check on Monday. Just warn Alexander that Stefano's after his wife."

"No more of your insolence, nurse--leave! leave! Before I have to throw you out!"

About the time that this was taking place, Alexander was setting out to drive from the company headquarters to the family home on the lake front at Deep Creek, Maryland. Alexander's wife, Andrea, was in their bedroom, when the phone rang. Drying herself with a towel right after showering, she dropped her towel and went to the phone. "Hello?"

It was Maria's nurse. "I'll be leaving for the weekend," she said. "Please, see to it that Alexander's mother receives her insulin shot." Just then, the door to her bedroom began to open and Andrea was distracted from hearing the nurse's words.

"Oh yes, yes, whatever, dear, I'll take care of it." Andrea paused as the bedroom door crept open; with surprise on her face, she didn't hear the nurse finish by saying,"...within two hours." Truly distressed by Maria's tone, the nurse, even though she had been fired by Maria, decided to leave specific instructions pertaining to Maria. The nurse knew that Maria's family could administer the day's insulin shot.

Meanwhile, Andrea was surprised as the door opened to reveal Stefano. He had come knowing that Alexander would be later than usual getting out of the LiteWave offices in Alexandria. With as light a touch as she could, she said, "You're shameless, just entering my boudoir without as much as knock."

Stefano was tall, slim, dark, with dark curly hair, and emotional brown eyes. He darted his passionate piercing eyes about her body, "You're like a statue of Venus--demure yet feminine, naked yet self-effacing. And that's very erotic when a woman is as beautiful as you are."

She motioned to him to close the door and, without even pretending to pick up her towel, went towards him. "Stefano. What could you be thinking coming into my room like this?"

"I see things. I observe like an owl lingering in the shadows before dawn when I hear the birds cooing. I move in the cover of darkness."

"That's not an appealing image--darkness. I want the excitement of night and the bright lights of the city."

He drew her close to him. She looked up into his eyes. She quivered. "I'm so, so..."

"Lonely, of course. Being married to Alexander, there can be no other way."

"But it the business, his research--stop touching me there. Don't arouse the animal in me, Stefano...."

* * *

In the gazebo at the front of the house, Sophia and Jessica, the younger sisters of Alexander, were dressed in their summer bikini wear. Sophia, the svelte sister with firm breasts, stood leaning on the gazebo and stared out at the lake. "Alexander's been running the family business for some time now. And directing the research, too. We need to talk, Alexander and I. How can I be integrated into the excitement of the family business?"

Jessica was attractive in her own way. Like her sister, she was well proportioned although shorter and stronger in appearance. Both had luxurious long dark hair. Jessica's face was capable of stern, almost pained expressions, while Sophia's facial features were soft and set on a slim oval-shaped face with extremely large green eyes and very long lashes. She had long, dark arched eyebrows, like Alexander's. Her lips were full and generous, while Jessica's mouth was more severe. Sophia's beauty was striking in a conventional way. Jessica's attitude was striking in an exotic way.

Jessica asked, "What do we need to discuss?"

"Not us. Alexander and I. We need to discuss the future."

Jessica made a tight-lipped expression, "Not us? Then who? I'm just as much a part of this as you are. Don't deny me."

"Denied? You? Many overtures were tendered in your direction, Jessica. But you were too worried about your love life. And you don't love men, Honey. You abuse them. My turn now. Let Alexander tender an offer in my direction."

"And the men just flock about you, Sophia. With all of those men, why is an offer from Alexander so imperative?"

Sophia turned and looked serenely into Jessica's eyes, "Since I got this damned MBA in finance, what good is it? I need to become a part of something."

Jessica gave a little smirk and flick of the eye brows, "Now that you've partied your ass off, it's time to have your way with Alexander. Is that it?"

"Having my way with him? An interesting choice of words, Jessica." Sophia became quite passionate in her tone. "In fact, I think that there's something quite screwed up about me. I've had an incestuous dream or two about Alexander. He is the most beautiful man that I've ever seen. Maybe ever was."

"Right, stupid, and that's why everyone wants a piece of him. Men and women alike. People just want Alexander to pay attention to them. He matters. And everyone who meets him feels that way. And that's what really irks me about him. Boy gorgeous, boy brilliant. What a combination. And he's so in tune with himself that it's all quite natural. But, Sophia, I never thought you were capable of such perverse thinking. Let alone admitting it?"

"I'm sick. I admit it."

"Some women love a man. Some women love men. You love men, Sophia. You've been to bed with so many of them. And now you're fantasizing about our brother. Immoral. Sick. Crazy. Decadent. Debauched. But knowing you, I think I understand."

"Alexander understands me. I'll be a valuable resource at corporate. He's told me that he wants my financial know-how at LiteWave. He believes in me..."

***

Unheard by the sisters, Alexander had just arrived at home, pulling his car, a sleek tear drop, to the rear garages. Feeling unusually chipper for a Friday afternoon, after a week of especially hard works, he had gone straight to the family den to see his father, Sergei Petrov.

Even though it was a summer afternoon, Sergei was staring into a log fire. Like his wife Maria's, his health was failing. He had high blood pressure. His moods were seldom good. He suffered from anxiety as he watched his once beautiful wife's health fail. Increasingly he came to focus on Alexander as the bearer of his dreams and his family into the future. So it was that within seconds Sergei was engaged in a heartfelt discussion with Alexander.

"You've got to come to understand the tone, Alexander--the tone of life. The meaning of loving things that are far away...pathos. It's the Russian dream. It comes from the motherland. It spawns in the hearts of millions, daily. Not rational--no. But the rational mind must learn to accept it, Alexander. Pathos. That's what led us to fulfill our dreams here, in this country. I arrived here with the fall of Gorbachev. It's why you must succeed. But the LiteWave milieu, that ugly business culture prevents real success. Son. My son. We must build it. Build it and then, only then, will they understand it."

Sergei rocked assiduously in his rocking chair; his mind raced; his desires were intense, vibrant. Yet his body was old, worn, tired. It was the inevitable dichotomy: the ravages of age were catalyzed by the still active insatiable desires of youth. Having the unconscious love of things far away, unreachable, having the desire to see and be a part of them, the father drove the son to fulfill the great expectations of Sergei Petrov, a Russian immigrant, an electronics wizard who founded LiteWave Technologies, with his wife's money, during the information explosion of the late 20th century. Then he was in his late twenties; now he was in his late seventies.

Sergei looked up at his son and gave a happy little grin with the flick of his head. He continued to rock as the fire blazed. He motioned his son to come closer. By whispering in Alexander's ear, he gave his message the sense of an emotional plea. "Build it! Fail, and the world will fail crossing the threshold of confusion... of disaster!"

Alexander saw it in the past with his grandfather. The generation about to pass on had a propensity for predicting the demise of current generations; yet, Alexander was unable to sweep away the fear, when his father spoke those words. "Dad. Build it? Just build it? Not a trivial task. The prototype is built. I have it!"

Sergei was direct in his speech, as he stared into the fire. Alexander hated it when his father just stared into the fire and didn't look at those around him. "It makes you angry, son. When I stare at the fire. But I think much better when I stare at the fire. You must change things... now, before the end changes it forever."

"How, Dad?"

"First. Eliminate the nepotism that goes on in the company. Just cut it out. That bum Stefano, your mother's nephew. He's the first one to go. What value does he bring to LiteWave?"

"Revenue, Pops. Lots of money. He owns the marketing department and the sales force."

"And you, Alexander? He owns you because of revenue? Forget that Neo-Californian up-start. Be a dictator. Take control. Now is the time. There's not much time left."

"For who, Dad? For you? Or for me?"

"Death is my friend. I don't fear that. But they're out there. Alien cultures who passed the message to us...reorganize, or perish."

"Dad. Have you ever met anyone from an alien culture to make such a compelling statement?"

"Okay. I have. Right here at the lake. When you were a boy. I often rose late at night to gaze at the stars. I saw lights dancing in the sky. They frightened me. They stopped dancing and dove toward me. I was petrified. I was totally in awe of the unknown. Soon, I began to fantasize that they wanted me. Night after night they came. I watched. Night after night." There was a long protracted silence, as Sergei attempted to pique Alexander's interest.

Alexander had heard this story many times before and as usual chose to ignore its significance. Instead, he deflected by asking, "So, what about your fear? How did you deal with it?"

"Quite foolishly. Like a child I attempted to hide beneath the trees, as if they couldn't see me. I dreaded meeting them face-to-face when they would abduct me and treat me like a lower animal of little significance. I lived in fear. Yet I wanted to know more. Deep down inside I admired these creatures from distant places in the universe. It's all a part of pathos." Again there was a long protracted silence as Sergei rocked in his chair.

"So night after night you're beneath the trees and you believed that they were aware of you. Playing with your psyche, your pathos."

"Of course. Yes, that's what I thought. When one night, to my surprise, several larger vehicles rendezvoused with them. And they went off into space together. The lead ship moved on a continuing serpentine motion and the others followed. It looked like a long lazy space caravan." There was a long silence.

Alexander smiled. "So, Father. Were they monitoring you as you feared?"

"In retrospect, of course not."

"Then just what were they up to?"

"The earth is a crossroads. A watering hole. It's known by space travelers as a crossroads. The earth is uniquely positioned on the edge of the Milky Way Galaxy. It is published on intergalactic maps. We are unique because of our relationship to the twelve famous constellations with Sagittarius at the center of our galaxy. We are the galaxy of knowledge. And we were told not to eat from the tree of knowledge in the Old Testament--or lose our souls."

Alexander smiled, "Mister Petrov. What's the message here? Become religious?"

"The way things are going that wouldn't hurt. But no, that's not my message."

"Then, Dad, what's the message?"

"Those ships were monitoring space. Moving back and forth to home on the signal of the arriving master vehicles for the rendezvous."

"But the question remains. Are they interested in us?"

"Yes and no. Yes they want us to succeed. No, they've got their own lives to live."

"And why should I release to the public what I've built?"

"Because as a species we're expected to succeed because of our unique place in the universe--visible from twelve very famous constellations."

"Please, Dad, no distortions, no dissertations on astrology tonight. But there's still the burning question in my mind. Did you make contact? Did you?"

Sergei gave a long stare into Alexander's eyes; then soulfully Sergei turned from Alexander and stared quietly at the fire. He stopped rocking. He sat. He chose not to respond. Alexander nodded his head negatively. As on other occasions when he had asked Sergei that exact question, Sergei chose to become silent, pensive.

Alexander decided that this was the end of the conversation. With a gentle pat on his father's shoulder, he got up from his seat and headed for his bedroom.

* * *

Although both Andrea and Stefano were driven by their animal need for sexual release, two other types of motivation were at work in the bedroom. Andrea's motivation was to fulfill her emotional need for attention--indeed, there was a time when she fancied Stefano. Meanwhile, Stefano wanted to gratify his ego by proving to himself his mastery over Alexander. Stefano was out to gain dominion over all of Alexander's property--including Andrea.

In Andrea and Alexander's boudoir, Stefano and Andrea had progressed to passionate love making. Suddenly, to Stefano's surprise, he heard footsteps and a door close in an adjacent chamber room--many of the rooms were interconnected like hotel suites. Quickly Stefano abandoned the moment; moving efficiently, he grabbed his clothing from the floor and Andrea also quickly got out of the bed and began to rearrange he hair. Intuitively he guessed that exiting directly to the main hall was in this instance the most propitious outlet. It was!

Except that as Stefano scampered down the hall, Maria emerged from her room, staggering from a diabetic episode. Andrea had failed to act on the nurse's advice that she needed her insulin shot. Right where the two perpendicular halls met at the top of the staircase, Maria collided with Stefano. For that brief moment, as they tottered at the top of the stairway, only Stefano held her from falling.

In her pain she looked at Stefano who was totally naked. She knew immediately that he was rushing from Andrea's bedroom. "You..you bastard! First you want his company. And now his wife?"

"I can see that this discussion has no future, Good-bye, Aunt Maria." Without a chance to brace herself, Stefano released her and she plummeted down the curved staircase. From the base of the steps, it might have appeared to an onlooker that she performed an acrobatic feat in doing a handspring off the steps. It was her effort to break her fall, but when she came to her feet and tumbled forward, her neck snapped as her head crashed on the lower steps. Her head bent backwards, as her body came to rest at the bottom of the staircase. She died instantly. After glancing down at her for a split second, Stefano stepped into a nearby bathroom.

Andrea, still naked, had gone to secure the door, but first peeked a look to see if anyone saw Stefano. He had vanished into the bathroom and she had no way of knowing that Maria had just tumbled to her death. She shut the door quickly, quietly.

At that very moment, Alexander arrived in their boudoir from the side door and saw Andrea's emotional excitement. Alexander was immediately aroused and playfully tossed her on the bed. He kissed her passionately. "Good god, Andrea, I've never seen you like this. So surprised to see me..."

Andrea was suddenly overwhelmed by the presence of Alexander, usually so emotionally distant from her. In her moment of confusion she cried, "Alexander! I love only you! Please? let's make love, now!"

Chapter 7
The Anomaly

The seven biospheres were on a tangential orbit to the asteroid belt, between the asteroid belt and Jupiter. They were designed to absorb all electromagnetic energy generated by the sun; therefore, for the sake of energy efficiency, the biospheres reflected almost nothing and were also hidden from earth's astronomers, who were unable to detect them in space until the manned ICARUS/NASA space station of the 21st Century discovered the "anomaly."

The Technosphere, meanwhile, was in an artificial orbit beyond Pluto, where its wider sweep gave it a still greater speed (96% versus 91%) than that of the biospheres. It, too, was undetectable by conventional methods. No one on Earth nor on the ICARUS space station was aware of the presence of Technosphere.

Zohar had left Arlee in the Technosphere and returned to his home biosphere, one of the seven biospheres in orbit just beyond the asteroid belt. He was in a state of confusion. Build Technosphere II? In earth time, many thousands of years had passed since he first adapted the biospheres from the Andromedan Big Eyes' migration vehicles. And he was the first to admit that the Technosphere itself resulted from the insights of Arlee, who attained an understanding of the cosmos and cosmic energies beyond that of any of the biosphere citizens--including himself. She had tapped the spiritual insights of the Dravidian Shaman spectrum of hallucinogens, while still maintaining her ability for keen analysis and understanding.

Zohar spoke with his father, Shazan, in an opulent garden in the first of the seven biospheres. First in orbit around the sun, it had six biospheres trailing it, all in the same orbit and trajectory, at about one thousand miles apart. The energy- efficient, self-sufficient, biospheres were cylindrical in shape; each cylinder was four miles in diameter and sixteen miles in length. While the biospheres rotated on their longitudinal axes to create artificial gravity, they also rotated on their central width axes. Each cylindrical biosphere was transparent at each end.

The anomaly of seven rotated in unison once every forty-eight hours. As one end of a biosphere turned into the sun, there was sun rise, followed by about twelve hours of light to dusk, then sunset, followed by about twelve hours of darkness. During the hours of darkness in the biospheres they were undetectable, from the ICARUS/NASA space station, due to the anomaly's angle to the sun and its angle and distance from the space station. They were also protected from detection by traveling through space at 91% the speed of light.

Depending on the apogee of their orbits, the biospheres were filled with variations of light--white light only, white light and rainbows, streaming colored light, but always beautiful to behold. This magnificence raised the collective contentment of the citizens who learned to behold and appreciate beauty. Each cylinder rotated on its longitudinal axis to create the centrifugal force necessary to emulate gravity, at exactly one G force. The citizens stood on the wall, to them the ground, of their biosphere cylinder. With all of the lush growth in the spheres, even with the tight diameter of four miles across, there was no sensation of spinning.

From a distance, the biosphere's reflected no energy, except some light which was absorbed through the ends facing the sun. From the ICARUS/NASA space station, that light appeared to be glittery, faint and inconsistent with anything else in nature. The light was so shimmeringly beautiful, so often ephemeral, that ICARUS/NASA space station astronomers were unable to isolate it. And when the seven biosphere's made enough orbits around the sun, after their shimmering light had been observable, the light became non-apparent, as the biosphere's were in their night time phase. However, NASA was developing a table for predicting when to observe the shimmering light anomaly. Wealthy private citizens now paid large sums to visit the space station and observe the anomaly, among other celestial attractions.

Moving at a rate of about 91% of light speed around the sun, meant that metabolic bodily functions of the citizens were altered, (as metabolic optimization occurred due to hastened DNA evolution), and aging slowed immeasurably. Was death inevitable? Death was believed to be inevitable. In fact, no one had died in the biospheres since their inception thousands of earth years earlier. While earth moved at 138 miles per second, the biospheres moved at 169,260 miles per second, and Arlee's Technosphere moved at 178,560 miles per second. Now Arlee wished to move at a rate of 184,140 miles per second in Technosphere II.

Earth-based scientists themselves had calculated that somewhere above 90% of light speed, bound energy--that is, matter--behaves differently. Analogous to the Richter Scale for measuring earthquakes--where every tenth of a percent on the scale means a 100% increase in shaking--every 1% above the 90% of light speed threshold, means significantly greater subjective changes in the behavior of matter and biological life forms (also, effecting the perception of time). Above all, the synergy among metabolic structures--DNA and the rest--is so altered above 91% of light speed that it can be regarded as a magical threshold for biological change. The truly knowledgeable had come to think of it as metabolic optimization.

While the citizens of the biospheres had in fact experienced metabolic optimization, they didn't mutate into anything more than very attractive healthy human beings. But Arlee, having been living at about 96% the speed of light, had mutated to a degree almost beyond recognition.

Zohar was as human as ever in attitude and appearance, and to some extent even in his sense of limits. "I wish that I had never met the Andromedans, Father. To this very moment I regret it. To have the guilt...even tyranny?...of The Guild permeating my very being is more than I can tolerate. Arlee was so beautiful here in the spheres. And when Arlee came up with the mathematical notations to express her cosmic insights, I smiled and encouraged her. Life was so beautiful. Now the guilt that I'm experiencing, after visiting her at The Guild, stifles me. And I feel hatred and anger at her insidious delusions to go on living forever."

Chronologically in his sixties when he left Earth, Zohar had silver hair, striking blue eyes, and an extremely fit physique that improved since he and the members of his people had left Earth behind and moved into the biospheres. Zohar forgot much of the engineering involved in the propulsion systems. He felt impotent to design a propulsion system for the proposed Technosphere II. Nor did the biospheres provide the natural resources required for such an undertaking.

"You see, Father, Arlee and her father encouraged me to betray the Big Eyes. Her paranoid father never trusted them. But ultimately, due to my lack of understanding of life and the cosmos, I betrayed myself in the name of...eternal life, now becoming eternal strife. Where did it come from?"

"What's that, Zohar?"

"This notion of eternal life. Where does it come from? And why is it so important to The Guild? I would end this mortal life right now if I didn't feel intense guilt as a traitor to the believers. Yet to perpetuate this disgusting notion of immortal life is abhorrent to my very being -- let death ensue, and don't fear the rhythms of earth. I have to be a natural man, not a fool in the pursuit of foolish notions, based on euphoria. I've never been addicted to inducing euphoric feelings. I reserve my right to be euphoric only as conditions dictate. And I reserve my innate right to die. While Arlee wants to go on forever living with and in this artificial technology. Unattended, it will eventually fail. I don't intend to be their watch-tower slave. And when the trip back from euphoria ensues, as Technosphere II fails, falls into deceleration, pure hell will consume the wretched souls of The Guild. It will take millions of earth years for deceleration. But subjectively...in all likelihood...a very long agonizing time. Those fools think they'll live forever. And they've bestowed the guilt of their wretched futures on me."

Shazan was extremely old. He had left Earth in his eighties. "You resent their hold on you. You resent the drudgery of being their whipping boy for notions that you don't hold sacred. You've been a rebel since you were a boy...and now, your anger's only tempered with age. You rebel against eternal life; it's only another way of not conforming to the wishes of The Guild and established cultural authority. Never in my wildest imaginations on Earth could I have conceived of such an Eden as this and the pleasure it brings me. The biosphere where the animals roam; the biosphere of eternal gardens and beautiful birds; and on and on it goes. Why not enjoy this long period of pleasure and seek simply the knowledge of The Guild? We've gotten this far. Who knows what's beyond, Zohar? Reflect on your anger."

"Thank you, Father. But there's more that I need to confess."

"Another time, Zohar. It's time to attend to my garden and enjoy the beauty of nature. I still hold the writings of the Big Eyes as sacred; they've instructed me in the development of hybrid strains of bees. They knew so much about establishing these biospheres and maintaining the homeostasis within the spheres, each of which takes on its own character as we manipulate the variables according to our own likes."

Zohar recalled his initial encounter with the Big Eyes from the Andromedan Galaxy. They were in search of biological hosts and species for experimentation in the Milky Way Galaxy. For purposes of agriculture in the Big Eyes' home galaxy of Andromeda, they sought hearty biological specimens (carbon-based foods: cellulose, grains, nuts, flowers, herbs, sugars, and proteins) that might be suited to their environments in an era of vast population explosion in that galaxy. At one time in their history these particular Andromedans were beings quite similar in appearance and chemistry to humans. They explained that simple fact to Zohar: at one time, their species was manlike, with eyes like a human's, oxygen- breathing, carbon-based beings.

"Yes, Father, the biospheres are quite elegant. And I love each of them. But I don't love the Technosphere. And I can't remember how we built Technosphere. I forgot!. It came from the writings of Arlee--another student of the Big Eyes, who are ultimately at the root of my agonizing guilt."

"What is the problem?"

"I no longer have a clue. I just have psychological pain. How did the Big Eyes construct the massive cylinder walls? Metallurgy? Tachyon wave drivers? Even I have experienced too much happiness and euphoria to go back and revisit that trivia. And when we built Technosphere, we didn't have to return to earth for natural resources. Now, no one in the biospheres wants to fire-up the metallurgical foundries. We've depleted the necessary minerals needed to operate the foundries."

"Go back to earth, Zohar. Learn to live again. So that you'll no longer feel guilty about betraying your social responsibilities."

"As always, you're correct, Father. I'll take a tachyon wave gyro vehicle back to earth and search for metals--after revisiting the writings of the Big Eyes. If the tribal wars ended in the destruction of men, then there'll be no one there but the plants, the birds, the bees, the beasts, and an occasional mountain lion. A lion I can handle. But I can't live with constant psychological pain."

Zohar thanked his father for his sage advice and then went into one of the many retreats located around his biosphere. He no longer needed to be convinced that he should go back to earth--he only wanted to think about how he should best proceed on his mission. There was quite a different time line between that of the biospheres, moving at 91% of light speed, and that of the earth moving at 500,000 miles per hour -- galactic speed. So although Zohar reflected for several months of his time on how to accomplish the wishes of Arlee and build TechnoSphere II, several years were passing on earth.

Chapter 8
Family Turmoil

A year had passed since Maria's death. Shortly after that, Sergei's condition began to decline. He lived with constant headaches, heart palpitations, and insomnia. His company, LiteWave Technology, continued to flourish, but the major disappointment of his life was his failure to find applications for the little- understood concepts he had envisioned--virtual particle and wave, virtual effects, and such. He had passed the banner to the next generation -- primarily, Alexander--and now simply stayed at home sitting by the fire. However, he was not always treated by all his family as the respected patriarch.

On this weekend as on so many others, the family had gathered at the mansion in Deep Creek, Maryland. Somewhat against their will, Jessica and Sophia were there. They continued to blame Alexander for their mother's death. Almost always he had administered the Friday afternoon insulin shot -- except for that fateful Friday.

Their French Colonial Mansion with many rooms, vaulted ceilings, sky lights, had all of the amenities -- wet bars, Jacuzzi's, marbled bath rooms, soma beds, exquisite eclectic furnishings. It had everything, except for love.

Andrea was upstairs in her bedroom waiting for Alexander to escort her down to join the others. She was unsure whether Stefano was expected to appear, but she didn't want to find herself alone with him. As it happened, he was not there. But somewhat against their will, Jessica and Sophia -- were there. To that day, they continued to blame

Alexander for their mother's death. Almost always he had administered the Friday afternoon insulin shot -- except for that fateful Friday.

Yet Andrea felt if anyone was to blame, it was she herself. She was the one who failed to act on the nurse's phoned message. As much as it pained her to know that Alexander was blamed by his sisters, she was ill to speak up because she was afraid that it might come out that she was distracted -- at that crucial moment, she had been making love with Stefano. Her guilt, however, had one good result: she made sure that she never again placed herself in a compromising position with Stefano who might seek to make love with her..

Further, Stefano had his own reasons for no longer seeking her out again. Although he soon realized that Andrea had not witnessed his role in Maria's fateful fall, he had decided that having sex with her was too easy a way to gain cheap petty revenge. He realized that the true retribution he wanted was something far more profound than just sexually controlling his cousin's wife. Now he was sure to never place himself in a position to be alone with Andrea. Thus both Stefano and Andrea, for their own motives, intended to avoid each other.

In the area between the living and dining rooms, there was a full-scale bar. Jessica and Sophia had hired their favorite bartender to make them special drinks for the weekend. By late Friday evening, Sophia, the baby of the family, had already had too much to drink. She spoke to Larry, the bartender, "You wouldn't--well, no, you wouldn't understand, families can be very cruel. Unintentionally. But nevertheless, very cruel."

Larry, the young bar tender, was attracted to Sophia, "Well, Honey, I'm not cruel. I understand. Your family's quite difficult to deal with. So say whatever you have to say."

She was watching Alexander as he moved toward the door. "Here's my big brother, Alexander. He'd like a lady's drink. Fix him a Long Island iced tea."

"Fix her a cup of coffee!" Alexander called out as he exited the room.

Sophia spoke to Larry, "Look at him. He's gorgeous. He's arrogant. He's in control. Wouldn't you say that Alexander is someone special?"

Larry tried to size Alexander up verbally. "Well, your brother is a stunning gentleman. Actually he's quite unusual, Sophia. He's got an athletic demeanor. Yet he's got great facial features, unlike a lot of jocks. I hate to say it. But that guy's got charisma; he just lights up the room without doing a thing. That's God-given. But that man's got problems."

"Problems, Larry?"

"Sure. With all of his money. With all of his style. Too many people seem to want a piece of him."

Sophia smiled, "It's sophistication. He's got that animal confidence. He's got that God-given intelligence. He pisses me off. I hate him."

"Are we talking about your brother? Or is the booze talking? You can't be jealous of a man. A woman, yes. But not your own brother."

Sophia was slinking over the bar and looking into Larry's eyes, "Listen, Cutie -- you are cute, Larry--I can say whatever I want. I can do whatever I want. I'm a Petrov and we damn well do as we please. I think that you're interested in me, else you wouldn't take my crap."

He leaned back. "Missy, let me pour you another one. And I'll take the keys tonight. Because you can't be out driving around in your condition."

Alexander had reappeared next to Sophia and she leaned in his direction, "You're the cruelest human being, Alexander. You've taken over the company. You don't advise me of anything that goes on with you and Dad. I hate you. Do you know that? Because believe it or not, you're cruel!"

Alexander shook his head negatively, "Cruel, Sophia? That word has so many meanings."

She thought of a time when Alexander took her to the museum to see a display of van Gogh's work, where she wanted to be in the intimate company of her brother in order to share the experience. "I wanted a big brother that day, Alexander. But you had to go off and leave me. I hated it. I hated being left alone."

Alexander was clueless. What was she talking about? "Probably Dad needed me for something that day."

"Sure. So you drove me fifty miles to the museum in DC. Dropped me off. Drove fifty miles back home. Then fifty miles back to the museum to get me, then back home. Lovely, Alexander."

Alexander looked at Larry the bar tender. "Never leave a woman waiting, not even your sister. Whatever I did, Sophia. I'm sorry. I apologize for that oversight, Sister."

"Too little, too late, Al. I always loved and admired you. And you treated me like..."

Alexander felt the anguish; he responded emotionally, "Sophia. I always supported you with Mom and Dad. I persuaded them to let you attend UCLA. Three thousand miles away."

"You can say anything these days. It's what I feel in here that counts. Save the wasted words."

Alexander looked over to his father who sat in front of the fire in the adjacent living room, "Dad," he called out, "would you tell her that I always supported her?"

Sergei didn't respond. He stared quietly at the fire. Eventually he waved his hand to suggest that he didn't want to be bothered.

Sophia looked over at Dad, "And that sums it up, Alexander. Please, don't bother him. He's too busy thinking about something, something that he'll never achieve. What a creep. Him and all of his old tech talk. How did he ever succeed? The two of you, confident in your own ignorance. I'm probably better off omitted from your circle of ignorance. Technology for technology's sake."

At that moment Jessica appeared." Give him hell, Sophia. The bastard deserves it. Last year he was too busy for Mom and she fell to her death. What were you and Dad talking about that entire time? Probably something like...like the finer points of Hawking's Virtual Effects?"

The old man got up from the couch and sauntered over to the group. His hair was white, his back was stooped. "When women are capable of understanding and perceiving the universe for what it isn't, then they can enter my circle of ignorance. It isn't now and never will be...what it appears to be. That's why Hawking's so important. He saw the universe for what it is...finite, without boundaries."

Jessica was inflamed. "Still speaking in allegories! Plato here and Alexander Socrates there, were having another one of their esoteric discussions when Mom crashed and broke her neck! Jerks!."

"Figure it out for yourself, Jessica!" Sergei snapped. "Perception. It's all perception. What women perceive in their immortal state of controlled social conscience is quite different than what men perceive in their mortal state of trying to figure just how the hell this universe is really constructed."

Jessica replied, "So, sure, Plato, continue speaking in allegories and your business won't be real much longer. The only reason LiteWave's still on the map is because of your sales team. Led by your infamous nephew... Stefano." Having blurted out his name somewhat unexpectedly even to herself, she turned on her father with a subdued seriousness. "You have no reasons for picking on Stefano."

Sergei walked back to the couch and held his head with both hands. "My head's going to explode if I don't have something to eat. Send that bartender home and let's go out for dinner."

Sophia was close to tears. "If Mother were here, he wouldn't talk that way to us. He wouldn't. He used to speak about his free-floating vehicle negating the forces of gravity...which, will never happen. Not in a million years. A million years. Impossible, Plato."

Sophia continued, "Somehow men, not women, believe that there are other beings, other forces, other life forces beyond the earth. Even if there were, these things have no relevance to us. No relevance at all. It's a moot point. Alexander, live in this world. It's the only one we've got."

Jessica summed it up for Alexander, "Quit searching for technologies with no relevance--ruining your life like dad. Get with the program. Enjoy life; get to know your sisters rather than spending your time on frivolous virtual effects research. Why were we kept out of the company. What's that all about, Dad?"

Sergei suddenly smiled and shocked everyone. "You know, as children, as babies, each one of us are born as perfect entities. Each person is perfect unto himself. It's when we relate to each other that we become diminished by the original sin of socialization, enculturation that leads to desire, egotism, avarice, greed and jealousy. Or for others, even worse--life leads to cowardice, sloth, and mendacity. But always remember, none of my children were ever lazy. And I'm proud of that fact."

Jessica's attitude became something between cynical and earnest. "Now that's a compliment if ever I've heard one, Plato. And we're not stupid either. Sophia and I will have our day yet. LiteWave needs a woman's touch. Right, Sister?"

Before Sophia could answer from her now inebriated fog, Alexander, always the diplomat, called out, "Father has invited us to go out to dinner--let's go!"

Chapter 9
Sibling Rivalry

Another year passed, during which Sergei, increasingly more depressed by living in their Deep Creek home after his wife's death, moved in with his sister, Tatiana. She had followed him to America after his success with Maria, and perhaps because only she could reach his long-buried Russian, Tatiana often consoled that sad old man. He continued to suffer from heart palpitations and migraines and he worried constantly about his children's growing adversarial relationship, which even he sensed Alexander was failing to deal with realistically. It was while staying with his sister that Sergei suffered a massive stroke. As it came at a time when Alexander was totally engrossed in his research, Jessica and Sophia chose to keep news of the stroke from him until they could use it to their own advantage.

Sweeping changes had been made in the reporting structure of the corporation. Jessica and Sophia were increasingly in charge of all of the business aspects of the organization, including penetration of the board of directors. New alliances formed. Alexander doggedly pursued his goal of converting his virtual particle drivers design into a practical vehicle.

Alexander now had a research facility in the Deep Creek area. He vacated the twelve building campus in Alexandria and opted for the country. The boys--Alexander and his new side-kick Stefano--were totally involved in a new type of research, lighter than air transportation vehicles -- using virtual particle drivers. They had mastered computer technology and at this stage were running computer simulations: what if this? what if that? what if this and that? Life was pleasant. Money was no problem.

They broke for lunch. It was June 21st, the first day of summer. A storm was brewing, as they looked up to the heavens from the floor of their research facility. Alexander had designed this new research and manufacturing facility; it was open to the air: the roof, a dome, was retractable. The building was round, 350 feet in diameter. When the roof was retracted, the ambient humidity was maintained at 46%; ambient dust was held to a minimum. The manufacturing facility was a miracle of 21st-Century architectural technology.

Cheerfully Alexander looked up, "Better close the roof. If it rains heavily, we might experience some moisture on the floor."

Stefano was a tall, strong, gaunt man who had grown accustomed to playing a deceitful role as Alexander's best friend, "Sure thing, Al. No problem. It's done!" As soon as he had pressed the necessary buttons, he turned back to Alexander and called out, "I'll race you to the house for lunch!"

In a moment, the first stage, a foot race, was on. They ran out of their lake side research facility and hopped into their wave runners. It was four and a half miles around a dog leg right, from one finger of Deep Creek Lake to another finger, where the family compound was located. They seemed oblivious to the thunder, lightning, and rushing gusts of wind that raised swells on the lake. The daily wave runner race was in progress, and they flew over moderate swells and became airborne only to smash back down on the water to do it again.

As hail-laden winds pelted his face, Stefano twisted his neck to look for Alexander in the growing tempest. It was an unpredicted storm, after temperatures hovered around ninety-nine degrees for several days. Stefano howled like a wolf, as he charged through the waves in the dark rain. "I'm beating you bad, Al."

Down at the gazebo, unexpected arrivals, Sophia and Jessica, who had just started lunch, ran to the house for cover. The sisters were wearing their formal business attire. They were accompanied by a lawyer, an influential member of the board of directors of LTI, LiteWave Technologies, Inc. They all observed Al and Stefano as they raced to the dock. They chatted among themselves, while all eyes were on Al's movement, as he ran up to the house and embraced Andrea, who stood on a covered stone patio. Andrea's expression was a little pained, as she discreetly pointed toward the house. Feeling cordial, smiling, rain soaked, Al went directly to the house to say hello to the board member, Eric. Al considered him his friend and did not notice Eric's slight coolness toward him.

"This is a surprise -- Sophia, Jessica, Eric. Have you come to discuss our virtual particle driver certifications for NASA?" Standing around the bar in a family room, all three of them exchanged glances. Stefano, after carefully docking the wind runners, had joined Andrea to one side. Both took great pains not to appear interested in each other--not too difficult since all eyes were on Alexander. For a moment, no one said anything. Sophia in her demure manner took a long deep breath. "We've got some news for you, Brother."

Alexander knew something was up. "Oh really. And what news might that be?"

Jessica stood and removed her business jacket. She scowled. "It's the way that you're spending the stockholders money that concerns us."

Alexander confronted them with a glare. "I'm afraid that this is no concern of yours as managing director. Funds were allocated for this research before I left my post as chairman." With that comment, all eyes turned toward the entrance drive of the house. The rain subsided. A massive rainbow emerged. They all observed a long limousine pulling up to park.

Two people emerged from the car. One man, in a smartly tailored suit, toting a light leather bag, came toward Alexander. Another man, dressed in medical fatigues, removed a wheel chair from the rear of the vehicle; then, the man in medical fatigues struggled to load an old man from the limousine into the wheel chair. Alexander stood to observe the old gentleman; with fear in his heart, he hastened out the door to the limousine. Alexander shouted at his loudest, "What? Why? How come no one told me?"

Jessica addressed the others. "Reality--what it does to a little boy!"

Alexander leaned over his father in the wheel chair. Tears streamed down Alexander's face, as he knelt to hold his father in the wheel chair and seemingly oblivious to Alexander's emotions. "Dad, Dad, Dad--if I had known, if I had only known I would have been at your side."

Jessica came outside and responded, "He can't hear you, Alexander. The stroke left him incompetent...incapable of any form of speech, expression. It's just like Mom. You just didn't care enough to be there for her. And with Dad, you never even asked."

Alexander wiped the tears from his face, "Incompetent? Isn't this an unseemly moment for legal terms?" Then Alexander stood and wheeled Sergei down to the gazebo--the rain had stopped. Jessica, Sophia and Eric followed him at a slight distance, while Stefano and Andrea remained on the patio. "Incompetent? Incompetent?" Alexander was shouting. "You bastards came here like this--in this style? To pull your version of a coup? Get the hell out of here and leave Dad with me. And take your insidious stupid lawyer with you."

The sisters stood around the table at the gazebo; each in her own way was cold. They calmly executed this highly calculated moment. Jessica spoke with a stern expression, "I just can't believe how quick you are to assess a situation, Al. No, Brother, this is more than a coup. It's a done deal. You're out and we're in." In that moment of speech, she motioned to Eric to deliver a document directly into Al's hands.

Sophia tapped her spiked heels as she nervously walked about the gazebo. "You might remember, Al, that Dad had an ethic about protecting the interests of the minority stock holders." As she spoke, she nervously wheeled Sergei off the gazebo and back toward the limousine.

Jessica chimed in. "Like us, Al, you are too young to remember the excesses of the 1980's and 90's when CEO's issued themselves whopping salaries and stock options only to rob the stockholders of their earnings per share...only, to bail out in golden parachutes. Well, Dad and his co-founders put some bylaws in the charter of LiteWave that no one individual might allocate funds to any one project to the detriment of the stockholders. Virtual particle driver research for certification, your research facility, the family compound, even your jet skis, wave runners or whatever, are an expense to the stockholders that the board had to review and reject. There's no current transportation technology being deployed for mass production that can support the application of research costs for virtual wave drivers. To us, it's still theoretical. Let's face it, you're a dreamer, maybe hopefully, maybe hopelessly, ahead of his time."

Al was so angry, that he was unable to speak. He could only gasp.

Jessica was pleased. Her face reflected arrogant contentment at Alex's inability to respond. But it was Eric, thinking he might lighten the confrontation, who chimed in, "Alex, I can't say that I've ever seen you at a loss for words."

In a moment, Alexander lunged toward the smartly tailored lawyer and hit him squarely in the jaw with a round house punch. He grabbed Jessica's chair, while she was still in it, and hurled her and the chair into the lake. Then he grabbed Sophia, who had just come back to the gazebo, and heaved her into the lake. Andrea and Stefano applauded somewhat nervously from their position on the patio.

Jessica and Sophia swam to the dock and pulled themselves from the water but Al went the short distance to the dock and pushed them back into the water. Then when Eric tried to climb from the water, he pushed him squarely in the face back into the water. Alexander shouted, "Okay, Ladies. You've won this round. Having our father declared incompetent could only have been your idea."

Holding onto the foot of the ladder at the dock, in her soaked business suit, Jessica addressed Al. She pointed a finger up at his face. "By some little known bylaws, your assets can be frozen. I wasn't going to do that to you, even though I wanted to because of what you did to Mom, but now you've forced my hand. Right now your stock options are frozen; you can't sell a single share, you'll be penniless."

As she climbed the ladder from the water, Al looked into her eyes. "You're still frightened. Scared of a brother who loves you? What is this insanity that you're into? I love my sisters who are only overreacting to... imagined fears. In one breath you say my assets can be frozen. In the very next breath you say they are frozen." With that summation, he pushed her back into the lake for the third time.

"Bastard," she shouted. "You'll never set foot on LiteWave property again. I'll see you penniless for all of the injustices you've visited on your baby sisters, your mother, and your father. Arrogant bastard! You never intended to help us by bringing us into the family business. You used us so that you could continue to control everything by proxy. The company--and that's now me and Sophia--won't permit funds to be skimmed for virtually...who knows what? You've never read the bylaws of the original charter. And I'll be damned if we'll ever let you see a copy of them. You're out!"

Stefano, who had come down to the dock by this time, thought he might break the tension with a teasing joust. "Skimming funds for research, Alexander? That's a no no! But, girls, let me handle the NASA issues. Don't fret when success is at hand."

Alexander did an about-face, then returned Stefano's teasing with his own. "Cash skimming, Stefano? Aren't those sales and marketing tricks? Aren't you the master of that, Stefano? Just be forthright with them. Tell them that I need funds for a hostile take over of NASA's public corporation."

At that, suddenly the situation seemed to implode. Jessica and Sophia went storming up to the house, followed by Eric. Sergei was driven off in his limousine. And when Alexander and Stefano joined Andrea on the patio, the three of them broke into laughter and went in to lunch. Not any of them, however, could say exactly what was going to come out of this.

Chapter 10
Plots His Revenge

Alexander was nobody's fool. While he spoke of LiteWave breaking into new markets and revolutionizing transportation, he had already built a prototype vehicle in his highest security building at the Virginia facility. The problems with releasing it to market arose from the government's procedures for certification of the nuclear fusion power core, and other less critical, more easily solved navigating issues related to computerized pilot "heads-up" displays relating to accelerated speeds, far beyond the capability of any current ICARUS ion rocket vehicle. Alexander was ready, but he hadn't shared that information with anyone. Except Stefano, who unknown to Alexander, was out to seek personal gain from the invention, through his contact at ICARUS/NASA, Charley Tong.

In the year that followed the violent confrontation at the lake, when Alexander attacked his sisters and the lawyer, he moved his prototype anti-gravity interstellar space vehicle from the Virginia facility to the Deep Creek facility. It was an elaborate undertaking to get it to Deep Creek unnoticed by the interstate highway commission. He was willing to fly it there, but the risk of being seen was not worth the potential problems involved.

Alexander was masterful in varied areas of computer science, and computer assisted design and manufacturing. Thus he had seen to it that his vehicle was conceptualized, plotted on paper, stored in computer memory banks, and capable of being reproduced hundreds and thousands of times through computer assisted real time manufacturing. Everything except the special glass canopy, for the cockpit, was manufactured under computer control. Therefore, anyone holding the computer information, with the proper manufacturing equipment, could reproduce the LiteWave vehicle.

During that same year since that explosive incident at the lake, Stefano, with his alternative agenda, managed to smooth things over among family members, primarily Alexander and Jessica. A smooth running family organization was clearly better for Stefano, both to attain his monetary goals of controlling LiteWave stock and to calm matters down in order to focus on his revenge with the Petrov family -- primarily, Alexander.

In the new manufacturing facility, where the sisters never looked, rested Alexander's interstellar space ship, moved from Virginia. Designed and fabricated in previous years, it utilized technology based on Hawking's Virtual Effects. The zero gravity ship was fabricated from composite carbon materials (more durable and flexible than high alloy steel, harder than high carbon steel), on a titanium frame to withstand incredibly high temperatures and intense impact. The whole vehicle was covered with a shimmering titanium coating, a spray-painted substance.

The ship was modest in size. It was designed to take up to twelve passengers into deep space, but it was not intended for intergalactic travel. The ship, at rest, was fairly round and flexible at its "equator." Beneath the skin of the vehicle was the equivalent of a large skeletal gyroscope for stability. Why did the ship spin on its central axis? It spun to mitigate variations in the fabric of space based on the gravitational bend, or warp, of space at any given point, vector of travel. The gyroscopic effect served to maintain the ship's balance -- anywhere, regardless of the topology of space.

At the equator of the ship, mounted into the exterior equatorial frame, were virtual particle drivers that served as retrorockets. However, they did not use traditional rocket fuel; they were powered by virtual particle rockets. In an anticipated need for defense, the virtual particle rockets alternately fired virtual particle torpedoes -- high energy destruction. At the base of the vehicle were the primary omni directional virtual particle drivers that accelerated the vehicle and could theoretically reach

99% of light speed within minutes. However, accelerating toward light speed was an unknown that would require scientific research through future piloting of the craft.

Inside the cockpit, there were "captain's chairs" mounted to the floor--twelve of them, mounted in a circle, on the circular periphery of the cockpit, facing outward with their backs to the center of the floor. Designed for passengers rather than crew, the chairs were covered with a specially treated charcoal-gray leather and each captain's chair swiveled on a 360 degree radius. The cockpit, thirteen feet in diameter, usually remained stationary at the top of the gyroscopic skeleton. The pilot's chair, the co-pilot and navigator's chairs, were in the center of the cockpit and elevated three feet above the twelve passengers' chairs on rotating turrets.

There were doors in the floor of the cockpit that led to the galley for sleeping quarters, food, and hygiene. At the center of the galley floor, sixteen feet in diameter, was a round table, six foot in diameter for food storage, microwave and infrared cooking, eating, and disposal. Around the periphery of the galley were ergonomically designed sleeping chambers; completely sealed, they maintained ambient moisture to maintain the skin and lungs with 29.86 psi air pressure. Inside each sleeping chamber was a zip-up permeable body stocking, spring suspended, to hold the resting passenger in place, regardless of speed, gravitational forces and other physical circumstances. The sleeping chambers also served as hygiene chambers for the elimination of bodily wastes; the body-stocking also served as a bathing mechanism.

The ship's skeleton contained 37,000 gallons of recycled, constantly purified water; while maintaining sixty-eight percent relative humidity, the technology made all 37,000 gallons of condensed water available. The total amount of water and vapor were fixed and did not change. Water was the most critical factor for deep space travel in this closed-loop micro-ecological design; without water, any traveler in space will perish.

The crowning effort of the space ship was the dome--the cockpit cover. It was the most costly part of the vehicle's design. Alexander did not understand all of the chemistry required to create this newly synthesized PPG Industries glass; it was transparent, permitted the entry of white light, yet it filtered out deadly x-rays and other deadly band widths of electromagnetic radiation. Moreover, it was a self-tinting glass that protected the occupants from unbearably intense light, creating deadly high temperatures. It was the crown jewel for which Alexander had paid untold sums.

The roof of the manufacturing facility was at this moment retracted. It was night time. Alexander and Stefano had engaged the ship's rotating mechanism to test the gyroscopic effect. Remotely, from the ship's exterior, they controlled the revolutions per second of the ship's body, while the virtual particle drivers were engaged for zero gravity at the base of the ship. Stefano set the ship to weightless, went over and gently lifted the 170-ton vehicle up with his hands; carefully, cautiously, he moved under the ship and carefully balanced it on his index finger.

Alexander applauded. "Never, never did I think that the day would come when even you could one-up Atlas by placing the globe on your index finger instead of your back."

"Of course not, Alexander. My back's been broken by the Stygian Witches; Jessica, Sophia, and..."

"Who's the third?"

"It's of no matter." Stefano said, as he lifted the vehicle far over his head. "But, Alexander, when are we going to show this contraption to NASA? It will fly you know. Certified or not it will fly. Stop worrying...."

Chapter 11
Coming To Earth

Several days passed. It was dusk at the gazebo. Stefano, as usual playing his role as Alexander's best friend, was attempting to cheer Alexander up. Andrea was in the house preparing a snack. Stefano and Alexander had their feet up on the table; side by side, they were admiring the sun set.

"You know, Alexander. There's more to life than research and industry. Come on, pal, admit it. There's more."

Alexander's eyes watered; tears of emotional pain streamed slowly from his eyes, "Much more than I'll ever know. And that's a law! Thinking that I understand what it means to be a big brother to Sophia and Jessica...impossible."

"Oh, I can still see you last year when you knocked that cocky, very tailored lawyer, on his ass," Stefano bellowed out with the roar of a lion. "Kill all those slick dishonest lawyers--plumbers with words, they relieve the constipation of our twisted, choked minds. With mental defecation we become...wise?" He smiled at his own twisted humor.

Alexander bellowed even louder, "Medieval notions of business ownership, a legal profession lording over us...we the people."

At that moment, Andrea came to the gazebo with a tray of fresh coffee and pastries. "Such a gorgeous sunset." Whether it was the mood of the setting or what, she had never looked more beautiful.

Breaking his personal vow not to show interest in Andrea, Stefano threw his arms around her and swung her around, "We're broke. What are we going to do now? What are we going to do now? Let's run off to the islands."

"What are you doing?" Alexander asked with surprise.

"Proposing to your woman. She needs some attention! You've ignored her for ten years."

Alexander nodded, "Take her. Take her. She needs it badly. And I know you love her madly."

For the moment, Stefano had to look away. He loathed Alexander's control over Andrea and him. His emotional tone shifted capriciously. Still looking away in anger, he spoke emotionally, "Maybe I do love her, Alexander."

Andrea pulled back from Stefano and glared painfully at Alexander. "Actually, Stefano, that's his problem. He brought the entire world down on his head, because he won't focus on me, the one who really loves him. Presumptuous of me to speak up, Alexander? Just a woman you know."

Alexander confessed, "To deal with complex people takes more wisdom than I'll ever have, Andrea."

Stefano cleverly chose to twist the conversation in another direction. "You're brilliant, Alexander. Just blindsided by those two conniving sisters of yours. But what I'll never understand is how they rationalized that Maria's death was your fault. There's something very mysterious and unfair about that entire situation. Right, Andrea?"

Looking skyward at dusk, Andrea felt the chills radiate through her body. Suddenly she called out, "Look there. What the hell is that?"

Andrea and Stefano instantly were looking in amazement and Alexander also stood to observe the event. Hovering silently over the far end of their property was a vehicle quite similar in appearance to Alexander's. The exterior frame, or shell, appeared to function like a gyroscope; the mechanism--rotating, spinning in the center--was a shimmering metallic sphere. But unlike Alexander's vehicle, it was the bottom of the frame, the part of any toy gyroscope that makes contact with the ground, that contained a massive brightly lit circular "cockpit." This cockpit alone was twelve feet in diameter and spewing out gradients of white and colored light.

Alexander observed it closely, "Stefano--look! It has similar gradients of light to our virtual particle driver--still to be certified for government and commercial use."

Zohar, meanwhile, was maneuvering his space craft in order to get a better view of the Deep Creek area. It was the area of North America where Zohar's people had lived after having been transported there from the Zagros range of southwest Iran. The alien Andromedans had selected Zohar's people because of their unique cultural advancements in developing technology, towns, and an early monetary system. Zohar's people had even built dams and an intricate water distribution systems in the Zagros range. When they first met the Andromedans with their space ships, Zohar's people felt them to be deities of great influence, omnipotent intelligence, from another dimension of the astral plane. The Andromedans warned these people of tribes invading from the west. These hordes were predicted to destroy Zohar's people and their advanced socio-economic culture.

Meeting with the elder group of leaders of this matriarchal society, the Andromedans persuaded this specific group of Zagros range city dwellers of 5000 B. C. to move to what would become known as North America. The people wanted forests and streams where they could build dams, so they picked present day Maryland, the Deep Creek Area. The Andromedans transported them to North America in the first phase of an Andromedan experiment to move an optimal group of earthlings into an artificial milieu created by the Andromedan scientists -- the biospheres, known as the ICARUS/NASA 'anomaly.'

And now Zohar was returning to Earth for the first time in all these years. Zohar's space craft contained a series of visual magnification lenses embedded in the outer frame. Zohar tilted the craft to watch through his internal infrared monitor, as he scanned the surface with very faint light from the sunset. Scanning on infrared, he caught a glimpse of the three of them staring up at him. Zohar did an immediate magnification of Andrea with the dimming white light of the sunset. Zohar spoke to himself, "Well now that's a beautiful woman. What's become of this planet? Massive cities. Billions of people. And many very beautiful women. I just can't believe that the humans are still here. Why didn't everyone perish in the cataclysm, like the Big Eyes said?"

Stefano waved to the visitor to come closer. Zohar was fearless and the same fearlessness that had allowed him to cope with the Big Eyes and their far-reaching technologies and concepts--far beyond the scope of any earthling of Zohar's time--led him to bring the craft closer to these earthlings.

He hovered the craft over the water next to the gazebo. The cockpit, so to speak, was at the top of the gyroscope's frame. Zohar popped the canopy on the cockpit. From the light inside the cockpit, Alexander, Stefano, and Andrea saw a smiling silver-haired man who was quite tan and virile in appearance. His vehicle was startlingly identical in design to Alexander's ship.

Alexander called out to him, "Are you from NASA? The German government maybe?"

Zohar tilted his head like a dog becoming accustomed to new sounds, tone qualities; raising both hands, Zohar motioned toward himself which was a request for more speech. Alexander further responded, "You don't speak English?"

Andrea was awestruck, "No, Alexander, look at him. He doesn't recognize our speech patterns."

Zohar climbed from the cockpit. There was a ladder built into the frame of the gyroscope. Zohar descended the ladder and leapt onto the gazebo floor. He reached out his hand in a kind of gesture of blessing; when Alexander reached out and shook it, he seemed delighted to shake hands with Stefano and Andrea. At the same time, they all exchanged hard stares with Zohar as though a deep look might be telling of something-- and indeed it did seem to be a human trait he shared.

Andrea spoke as she stared at Zohar, "I wonder if he knows just where the hell he is?"

Longingly Zohar watched her. He surveyed his immediate surroundings and took a seat at the table and to their astonishment poured himself a cup of coffee. He knew that aroma: the Big Eyes drank coffee because they grew coffee in the biospheres. Thinking that he recognized the sugar, he moistened his index finger in his mouth and dipped it into the sugar. It was sweet. Reaching for a spoon he added some sugar to his coffee and stirred it. Taking a sip, he responded, "Mmmmmmmmmm." Andrea offered him some pastries, which he quickly accepted, again remarking "Mmmmmmmmmmm" with greater enthusiasm.

Alexander sat across from Zohar and stared at the handsome gentleman, "Are we dreaming? Is this some kind of collective hallucination? Too coincidental to be real?"

Zohar wore soft leather boots, burgundy colored pants made of soft cotton (drawn at the waist, and tucked into his boots), and a soft white cotton sweat shirt with a symbol of the sun and the seven biospheres on it.

Stefano responded, "This is strange. Very strange. He's too much like a human being yet speaks no earthly language. Would you please say something, Dad? And look at that shirt. It looks like something from a T-shirt shop at the beach. Who is this guy?"

Suddenly Zohar got up and stood on the banister of the gazebo and jumped over to the ladder to the frame of his space craft. He returned with a map and map light. He spread the map out on the table. It was a large map, about four feet by three and a half, and was a terrain map of what was obviously the Earth. Zohar pointed to North America, quickly zeroing in on the area of Deep Creek, where they were standing. He looked at them and shook his head as if to ask a question.

Alexander interrupted and pointed to the same point on Zohar's map; then, he pointed to the ground and shook his head affirmatively. He was communicating that he understood that this was indeed that very territory. Curiously for Zohar, however, the predicted earthquakes from a fault running along the Atlantic sea board did not represent a cataclysmic end to his people's towns, because the area where he currently stood did not sink below sea level--as had been predicted. Rather now, it seemed that Zohar and his followers had been cast into outer space by the Big Eyes who made Zohar believe, that it was, his, and only his, idea. But why?

Zohar turned to Alexander with an expression of concern. Zohar pointed to his eyes; then with a hand motion, he gestured to indicate much larger oblong eyes that extended from the mouth to the top of the head. Alexander looked deftly into Zohar's eyes; he shook his head negatively at Zohar--who it now appeared used the same head motions to express yes and no. Zohar made the same gesture again about the Big Eyes.

Alexander spoke to the others as he examined the map. "He knows where he's at. It almost seems he has been here before. But look at the rivers on his map; look at the Deep Creek area. There was a settlement here. And look--the Potomac River and Susquehanna followed slightly different routes to the Chesapeake Bay. The terrain has been slightly altered. But notice that the three rivers at Pittsburgh appear relatively intact from his map. The Allegheny mountains which those rivers flow through, are so old geologically that the waters still basically flow the same paths. If he had a star map from the time when this map was drawn we could determine the exact time frame, through the position of the earth to the heavens."

With great surprise and awe they all fixed their gaze directly on Zohar; feeling fearful, feeling intimidated, not taking a cue from each other, they spoke to Zohar in perfect unison, "Who are you?"

Alexander looked quite closely at the white-haired gentleman who was slightly shorter than Alexander. He was five foot ten, very sturdy; he had the physique of a healthy thirty-year-old man. His chest was muscular and his waist was thin. "I do not know. Have not a clue from whence you came, but I've got to know more." Alexander stood on the gazebo banister and jumped on to the ladder to climb into the cockpit of Zohar's ship.

The others, including Zohar, were taken aback by Alexander's boldness. Zohar quickly got back into the ship to protect himself from being stranded. Alexander observed crystals embedded in what he assumed was the control panels for operating Zohar's space craft. "Don't you have a bloody star map? Something to look at? Anything?"

Zohar tried to calm Alexander; took him by the hand, shook his hand and sent him back to the gazebo. Unnoticed by Alexander or Zohar, Alexander's wallet fell to the floor of the cockpit as he exited the space craft. They all waved to Zohar, as he snapped down the cockpit cover. The body of the shimmering sphere rotated at extremely high velocity within the gyroscopic frame. Then, in the twinkling of an eye, the craft arched out of sight and made a spectacular light show.

For a minute or so, the three of them stood in silent awe at this inexplicable phenomenon, and when Andrea spoke first, it was an equally unexpected comment. "Need that stranger say more, Alexander?"

"Say what, Andrea?"

"That you've got to get to work on finishing the certification of your space craft. It's time to really test your virtual particle drivers with actual space flight. Your design and that design appear identical!"

Perhaps because he could not bear to talk about the true significance of what they had just experienced, Alexander continued in this vein. "That takes lots and lots of money. We're so close to the solution. And that's tearing me apart. With Jessica at the helm, how will we ever get the money to finish the job and certify the virtual particle drivers? And how did that ancient earthling ever come in possession of that craft? If he and his kind were here so long ago, where did they go? And what kind of technology did they have? How advanced could they have been? Who was that guy?"

It was Stefano who broke into their pedestrian line of thought. "Alexander, I don't know who he was, but my entire body is shaking with fear. Don't you two realize--we have just been privileged to share an experience in the history of mankind."

Chapter 12
He's No Alien

The following evening Alexander, Stefano and Andrea were still all but in a trance from their encounter with the mysterious individual and his vehicle. Now more than ever Alexander regretted that he had not shown more interest in his father's claims to have had his own encounter with some mysterious vehicle. Alexander wished that he might speak to his father, who was now unable to speak due to his stroke.

As Andrea and Stefano sat in the family room with the fire going, Alexander paced about and eventually spoke. "The anomaly, Stefano. What did you see when you were up there?"

"What does that have to do with this?"

"A lot, Stefano, I suspect. A hell of a lot. Think of the big day- when the others were killed. Before they were killed, did you see anything?"

Stefano stared into the fire. Andrea, her arms wrapped about the front of her body, stared at him expectantly. Stefano looked at Andrea, back at Alexander and said, "My report... well, my report said that we saw what appeared to be terrain inside these massive cylinders, maybe fifteen to twenty miles long...each one. And then--"

Stefano cut himself off. Alexander was impatient. "Just what in the hell else did you see?"

Shaking his head, Stefano proceeded as if dredging up some painful memory. "That some of the scientists lost it when they saw buildings inside some of the anomaly structures."

Alexander was perplexed. "And all these years, you just kept that information to yourself?"

"Hell no, I reported it. But the ICARUS officials decided that, since our rocket planes would never be able to catch up to this anomaly, they would keep it a secret. And what with all the other events during the ensuing weeks and months, the media never thought to pursue this line. Let's face it, no one really wants to know that aliens are living in our own solar system. Hell, everyone fears it."

"Well, Stefano, he was no alien, alien. He was a human being alien. Fears what, Stefano?"

"Culture shock, you big jerk. Culture shock! If you thought aliens were out there, not all that far from us, every day, all the time, wouldn't your head get fucked up once in a while?"

"I do know it and my head is fucked up. You're right--it is culture shock. That's what I'm feeling. But I can tell you one thing, Stefano, that guy last night--he was no 'alien' alien. He was a 'human being' alien. He was a hell of a nice guy. I just felt it."

Andrea had been transfixed by the conversation and was now literally quaking. "It's eerie, very eerie, this culture shock stuff."

Without any of them putting it into words, Andrea, Alexander and Stefano were in fact trapped in the same dilemma as were all their contemporaries when it came to thinking about such aliens. In the 21st century UFO sightings were neither less rare nor more commonplace than in the 20th century. They remained a matter of curiosity for curiosity seekers. It stood to reason that private citizens might find extra-terrestrial contact totally unnerving. Yet for many decades, from the time of the US government sponsored SETI project (Search for Extra-Terrestrial Intelligence) in the 1980's, the US Government scientific-intelligence community had funded a search for extra-terrestrial intelligence.

So there was a dichotomy, even some duplicity, in the government's funding such a venture. Would the authorities keep the knowledge of extra-terrestrials to themselves or share that information with the citizens? But this particular version of culture shock was a theme that was never put to the acid test. With so many people having varying attitudes on the subject of extra-terrestrials, there was no clear cut policy or policies for dealing with extra-terrestrial information, and close encounters. Every situation was unique to itself. Over the decades, then, the SETI people continued to recognize the real possibility of extra-terrestrials and search for them, while at the same time other less open-minded bureaucrats squashed any meaningful discussion or speculation about such a possibility.

Andrea, Alexander and Stefano knew all this in the way that fish "know" the water in which they swim. But what they had not been prepared for was the appearance and behavior of this alien--if such he was. Appearing totally human. Zohar did not engender the kind of concern that would certainly result from directly contacting potentially frightening extra-terrestrials, like the Big Eyes hinted at by Zohar. What Zohar did not, could not, communicate to them, however, was that the Big Eyes practiced stealth, total anonymity: while they lived on earth, no one knew of them or their whereabouts.

In the 21st century, then, as in the 20th, extra-terrestrial beings remained an anomaly to be dealt with the individual encountering them. Which is why Andrea, Alexander and Stefano--again, without putting anything into words--agreed to drop the subject for the moment. None of them was really prepared to consider the significance of their encounter with Zohar. But as they went to their bedrooms that evening, each was clearly unsettled. And each suspected they had not seen the last of this being, whoever he was.

Chapter 13
International News

Once again on a mission to earth for Arlee, Zohar was doing terrain scanning. He was having great difficulty believing his eyes. When he left earth, it was a wilderness, with great forests, where observing bald eagles was his favorite pastime.

But today, in the territories of the bald eagle were sprawling urban centers. He never saw a sprawling urban center like Philadelphia, or Washington DC. His greatest difficulty was accepting the automobile.

"What possible benefit is there to a life of constantly getting in and out of those contraptions?"

He hovered his ship over Philadelphia and watched moving close to houses in the mornings, afternoons, and evenings. There were reports of UFOs all about, culture shock all about. There were pictures of Zohar and his craft in all the national and international news reports, magazines, and news papers. With magnification lenses, they determined Zohar to be -- humanoid? The networks and print media asked the rhetorical question: humanoid, or android? Everyone wanted to know. Yet no one seemed to fear him. He was determined to know more.

Hovering over a school yard in Cherry Hill, New Jersey, he was puzzled by the varied ethnic types. He was in deep concentration observing the children when, suddenly, an armada of heavily armed Air Force ion ram jet helicopters surrounded him. Their propellers had a very short diameter, and rotated at extremely high rpm's; they whistled and whirred. Still Zohar didn't notice them. They formed several circles at various layers parallel to and above his craft. He pulled his head back from his console, when he noticed all of the air traffic about him. His heart pounded. His face turned flush. "Hey, Guys, I'm too old for this stuff. Would you kids get those contraptions out of here?"

They attempted to intimidate Zohar into grounding his craft. Nervously, he put his hands on the crystalline flight control balls. Made from crystal ground into perfect spheres, the balls rolled with his hand and fingertip motions easily in their control bays. With a few zigs and zags, Zohar outmaneuvered them in a moment and arched out of sight. The Air Force gave chase. Zohar reasoned with himself that if he flew low and fast, the other vehicles would not be able to give chase at high terrain speed. Zohar was correct. His ship accelerated so quickly, that the young Air Force kids, most in their twenties, in their modified hovering ion rockets gave up in fear. The chase was too intense, as they maxed out the capabilities of their ion rockets' maneuverability, due to maximum acceleration."

Zohar's craft raced low along the eastern sea coast toward Maine. By flying so low, five hundred feet above the terrain, the craft was not trackable with radar and was also under the clouds free of satellite surveillance.

It was a hot summer day in the east, as he began to decelerate along a deserted shore in Maine, where he set the craft down in a glen surrounded by dense pines. He popped the canopy of his cockpit (where Alexander's wallet still rested on the floor); he jumped from his ship; he stripped off his clothes; he ran through the dense pines, across the beach, and dove into the cold waters of the North Atlantic. The water was as cold as the lakes in the biospheres; he felt right at home in the cold water. He frolicked with a colony of seals. He enjoyed the remoteness of the wilderness. As he was emerging from the water, he looked up to see a bald eagle. "Would you look at that!" he exclaimed aloud. "How beautiful!" It was the first such creature he had seen since he had been removed from earth by the Big Eyes.

Zohar's genealogy, his genetic background was clearly an asset for this expedition. Where did he come from? Prior to the beginnings of recorded history in the Old World, it was reported in Sanskrit folklore, the two major peoples of India were the fair-skinned Indo-Aryans and the dark-skinned Dravidians. About 6,000 years ago, these two peoples, consisting of varied, yet select tribes, came together in a unique alliance.

There were individuals in a few Indo-Aryan tribes who were interested in designing, engineering, and building intricate villages. This led to almost opulent, great wooden prehistoric proto-cities in Northwest India. When certain Dravidian Shamans from southern India came upon these relatively highly developed cities, in the Zagros mountain range, they admired the Indo-Aryans tribes technological wizardry. At the same time, the Indo-Aryans admired the Dravidian Shamans' insights and mastery of natural hallucinogens. For many centuries, they did not commingle their genetic pools. Yet gradually, after centuries of inter-marrying, genetic integration proceeded.

Still over time, the pure black Shamans were more insightful in predicting plagues, diseases, and great freezes which did not permit the Zagros tribes to replenish their human needs in abundance.

While many of Zohar's people stayed in their opulent comfortable, atypical for the Zagros, wooden cities, certain Shamans were respected for their zeitgeist, their vision of the age. There was a strong dependence among the people on hallucinogens which permitted the Shaman's to communicate their zeitgeist among the varied dialects of the prospering tribes within the black and white integrated communities. The message was to prosper. To prosper the Shaman's were urging anyone who was so inclined to migrate westward to lands of dense forests, richer forests, richer lands.

However, the insight was short lived, as more and more Indo Aryan tribes, heading westward, invaded the area of the great Zagros villages, quasi cities. Folk lore in the Zagros region, below the mountain cities, drew savage migrating tribes in search of food and booty. Arlee and Zohar's people suffered an intense cultural stress from on-going sieges of plunder, rape and murder.

As brutal Arctic outbreaks, dips in the jet stream, brought brutal freezing winters to Northwest India, it was even greater toward Europe. Some starving savage tribes, privy to Indo-European hear say, encroached on the resourceful Zagros peoples, Zohar's people, for food and technologies adapted to harsh climates. Some hearty savage tribes, that moved westward, now moved eastward again, finding the staunch Zagros dwellers, and wanting to kill them for their resources.

The Zagros people depended on hallucinogens, provided by the Shaman class, to get them through the stress of hand-to-hand combat engaged in by the men who were led by their matriarchal leaders. The death of loved ones led to unbearable stress and growing social disintegration.

These particular Zagros dwellers, Indo Aryans, aptitude for engineering kept them alive. Their precision wooden cutting instruments. Their precision dwellings. Their precision transport vehicles, often kept them just a step ahead of hoards of invaders, from the flat lands, who sought these notoriously resourceful people in the Zagros Mountains.

Zohar was born, while his mother was on a trade expedition to the Mediterranean in search of herbal medicines. She gave her son the Semitic name, Zohar. When Zohar's mother returned with medicines to treat growing virile disease, a great virile plague exploded onto the scene. There was no guidance from anywhere, Shaman's or Mother Goddess. A society was in peril. Enter the Andromedan Aliens to save the day and offer migration vehicles; near light speed arks, that became the biospheres.

Sitting on the shore in meditation, becoming hypnotized by the waves, he worked at recalling what his father taught him about the use of hallucinogens to learn languages and dialects. It was a method of listening to phonics, syllabic patterns, and observing minute body motions for emotional intent, content and tone; as well as, the tone of voice of the speaker. But obviously, that wasn't enough; he had to live among the people for some period of time and use special hallucinogenic herbs which heightened the sensitivity of various brain centers. Climbing back into the craft, he drew some water from his reserves and mixed the necessary herbs into a heated tea. Zohar believed that his craft was well concealed in that Cape Elizabeth glen, surrounded by dense pines; but, the coast guard knew that he had set down somewhere along the North Atlantic sea coast -- above, Boston. . Getting out of the craft he headed for the road, where he waved down an eighteen wheeler. To the driver Zohar appeared to be a healthy old woodsman, lumber jack, who needed a lift.

"Where are you headed, Buddy?"

Climbing into the cab and sitting down, astounded by the sound of the syllables, Zohar looked at the truck driver in total silence. His eyes were wide; he was dumbfounded. The herbs were taking effect and somehow Zohar understood the intent of the question, not the question itself. Zohar was at a total loss to reproduce anything that might resemble what he had just heard. The root language of English was the Indo European language which Zohar's ancestors spoke. The syllables were unfamiliar to Zohar, but the Dravidian hallucinogens worked a communication link between Zohar and the truck driver.

"Don't give me that dumbfounded stare, Mountain Man. Just tell me in what direction you're headed."

When Zohar spoke in his own language, "I'm lost and scouting the area!"

The truck driver's head snapped back in amazement, "Hey, Fella, have you been sleeping with porpoises? What in the hell did you just say?"

In his Indo--European biosphere dialect, Zohar responded, "I'm a stranger here on my own planet. And I'm seeking the big eyes so that I might employ the will of my people -- The Guild."

"Woe. Woe. No way, Man. I've never heard a human being speak some kind of porpoise talk the way that you speak porpoise, Pal. Are you an animal trainer or something? You're a super trickster. I speak English and you speak...porpoise?"

Zohar was shocked. He remembered speech on earth. Speech from an earlier time. He realized that he and the citizens of the biospheres had altered their speech patterns over time, because there was a time when Zohar sounded much more like this man

The man laughed, "Hahahahahahahahahahaha"; then, Zohar laughed at a more rapid rate.

"Hell, if I couldn't see you with my own eyes, I'd swear you were a porpoise. Now stop the joking and tell me where it is I can land you, Pops? You sure are strong and fit. Silver hared muscle men like you are definitely animal trainers. You're from a circus. That's it!""

Zohar began to get the feel of the speech patterns; extremely slow, deliberate syllables, deliberate speech patterns to deliver slow linear thoughts. Zohar turned up the stereo in the truck and listened to the country music station; the speech patterns were slower yet.

The truck driver responded, "...sure love this, love song, great music; the woman's telling her man to be more in tune to her needs; the man's telling the woman the same. And they just can't resolve their... dilemma."

Zohar repeated the syllables slowly, "Di lem ma?"

"You burned out on drugs or something, Buddy? You sure are some kind of strange. "The truck driver pulled into a truck stop off Interstate 95 at Portland, Maine. Zohar got out of the cab and followed the driver into the truck stop, a veritable world of gadgets, video technology, and had the strong aroma of freshly brewed coffee. This stop was quite large with specialty stores, arcades, and several restaurants.

Chapter 14
Learns To Speak

Several days later, Alexander received a call from a special government agency which was a department of ICARUS/NASA. They secretly maintained interest, vis-a-vis Stefano, in Alexander's private research. However the consensus was that no researcher, including government researchers, had perfected the virtual particle driver due to the need for a clean method of producing virtual wave effects, which were in the field of negative physical energy, graviton-like waves--a spectrum of particles and waves that are never directly detected, isolated, but whose existence have measurable effects.

In the 21st Century, Hawking's Virtual Effects were theorized by researchers to be the binding forces that bind atoms, aggregations of quarks; the binding forces produced in the center of stars where all of the elements, including the heavy elements, are metabolized by the active negative forces bending and warping the energy field of the positive forces. Hawking's Virtual Effects, a set of discrete mathematical formulas, originated after the year 2000, by other astrophysicists, opened certain scientists' mental conduits to isolating and controlling the tachyon wave. But to the layman, the tachyon wave was generically discussed as a virtual particle; quantum, tachyon waves behaved as waves, but were discussed as particles for the general public. When the general public asked how a particle was capable of exceeding the speed of light, wouldn't it be pure energy? Scientists scratched their heads at creating such an obviously rhetorical question. Yet, they persisted in calling it a virtual particle for the time being.

To measure something believed to be the binding force of an atom by creating a controlled atomic explosion, or controlled fission, as in fission reactors, was difficult to contain without the controlled containment vessel of a nuclear reactor. The virtual particle driver was the embodiment of a new technology to take men to the stars. Essentially, tachyon like waves (created through controlled nuclear fusion, not fission) were focused by the virtual particle driver at angles of attack on the immediate space around the virtual particle driver. The fabric of space, the harmonics of virtual waves, particles, moving faster than the speed of light, contained the gravitational field. Alexander's nuclear fusion wave/particle driver was a black box producing a field of virtual waves, including tachyon waves, moving faster than the speed of light and negating the effects of the weak force graviton waves -- pure energy, theorized, observable, yet not capable of being isolated; referred to as Hawking's Virtual Effects in the twenty-first century.

* * *

"Hello, Alexander, this is Doctor Charley Tong from ICARUS/NASA. Do you have a minute?" Alexander answered the telephone at Deep Creek. With all of the chaos caused by the inter networking computer virus Stefano and Alexander held off the inevitable -- eviction, from the facilities.

"Oh, yes, Doctor Tong, I thought you were on the entrepreneurial path, that you finally struck out on your own without any help from your ICARUS support group, family so to speak. Or the free consultations of our sales engineers. Stefano's men and women."

"Come on now, Alex, this is a friendly call. It's about you and your new ship. We looked it over and can't say that we really understand your proprietary technology, not standards based, like your drawings and CAD engineering..."

"Oh. I see. The work of Stefano maybe?" Alexander was infuriated with Stefano but powerless to say anything for the time being.

"Stefano? Ah yes, he works for you, I remember now. No! Our best minds can't make heads or tails out of your innovative design. And the use of hybrid heavy elements in your virtual particle drivers are something that only a scientist like you understands. Who was flying your ship? And why did he leave your ship...just, sitting up in Maine?"

Alexander followed UFO reports, but this report did not compute. There was a long silence, while Alexander composed himself He thought about the stranger, whom they had met. "My ship? My ship? My ship is up in Maine? Yes--my ship is up in Maine. But no one knows that I've assembled a second more sophisticated ship." Thinking quickly, he said that because his ship's technology could be nothing like Zohar's.

"Listen, Alexander. Since you do virtual effects research and your wallet was inside the vehicle, we're calling you. Now do you want us to return it to you? Confiscate it? Or meet us up in Cape Elizabeth where the vehicle is?"

Alexander felt compelled to take the offer; his wallet. "Mm ahhh oh well, of course, of course, yes, yes I do want my second ship back? You said my ship, Tong, correct? Cape Elizabeth? What state?"

Stefano chimed in, "Hey, Alexander, a CNN news report said Cape Elizabeth, Maine. Lately you're oblivious."

Doctor Tong continued with Alexander on the telephone, "Well, Buddy, I wouldn't expect to find your wallet in a ship that arrived from another star system--unless, you were out shopping there. Now quit sounding so damned confused. Or we'll confiscate it. Enthusiasm for your secret projects are rampant around here. You're what folk lore is made of. And this is a second ship? What about the first?"

Alexander was barely able to speak, "Ahhh...enthusiasm, yes that's what's important. How about we set up a meeting and pick up the vehicle together? Could you arrange to have it transported back here? it's just that we're having some severe navigational problems and don't want to fly it anywhere. Yes--those navigational problems caused us to leave it sitting in Maine. We hoped it wouldn't come to this. Embarrassing. You know?"

After scheduling a meeting in Portland, Maine, to decide how to transport the vehicle back to Deep Creek, Alexander and Doctor Tong signed off. Immediately Stefano and Alexander plunged into a discussion of the phone call. Stefano was unable to understand why Alexander made a pretense of the ship being theirs.

"Because, Stefano, I saw it as an opportunity to leverage my sisters. Publicity of the right kind. We've got no money. I had to do it. And worst of all--actually no, best of all, my lost wallet is in the vehicle. I have to admit that I was suspicious of you there for a moment, Stefano."

"And how quick you were, Alexander to tell a great...fib."

"Fib my ass. Major lie. How do I certify my vehicle? Then explain a second vehicle with an alien propulsion system? Stupid is more like it!" Alexander felt the total absurdity of his deception, but he was compelled to see it through.

Sitting in their office, each on his own swivel chair, each with his feet on the desk, each leaning back, Stefano got a puzzled expression. "If that space ship's up in Maine, why did that alien pilot just abandon his ship? I mean how stupid could he be...not to know that he was being tracked?"

Alexander stood up and looked down at Stefano, "You know, cousin, I've been pretty stupid lately--assuming, always assuming. So let's not assume why he abandoned his ship. And assume it's the same ship that was here. Because my wallet was in it. So let's just get up there a couple of days early and find the pilot."

"Agreed. But don't permit greed, revenge, recognition for self-redemption to cloud the issues. I'll gladly take those sins. We want that ship here to win this war of wits. Let's get that ship. Bring it back here. And let the whole world wonder."

"That sounds extremely devious to me, Stefano. Let's do it!"

Via Amtrak's new magnetic levitation bullet train, they were in Portland, Maine in two hours--even with transfers in Philadelphia and New York City. Having arrived there two days before the scheduled meeting with the government agents, they searched restaurants, truck stops, hotels, motels. No one fit the description of Zohar, who had by then found a way to learn the language, over the course of six weeks of collecting books and maps -- a lot of maps detailing the rain forests, from Brazil, to Madagascar, to Indonesia. He was in search of The Big Eyes.

* * *

Zohar bused tables at the truck stop. The manager took pity on Zohar; he thought Zohar was retarded -- because, his speech was incoherent and slurred. But the manager soon learned that Zohar was a great worker. He did the work of two or three less motivated younger men. While he was incapable of communication, Zohar understood the manager's orders -- quite well. They gave Zohar a musty old room with a cot in it; at night, he studied the alphabet by watching children's phonics shows on PBS in the employees lounge. When the truck stop manager found Zohar (in, his spare time) absorbed in child phonics, it was a sure sign that Zohar was not all there; apparently, retarded. But Zohar was on the threshold of getting it all together to start speaking English. He continued to drink from the hallucinogenic herbal tea recipe of his Indo Aryan/Dravidian Ancestors. He made daily visits to the Portland Library, where he read the history of Western Civilization up to the year 2040. He read paper back books in mass quantities; magazines, newspapers; especially The Wall Street Journal which gave him the concepts of business and international commerce.

"Come on, Buddy" the manager spoke to Zohar in a fatherly tone, "...it's time to get back to work. Now I'll turn off Sesame Street and you get back to the kitchen and get a cart and start cleaning off some tables."

"Sure thing, Boss. You know I'm kind of getting used to it here. But I really don't understand earth politics. The body politick is so diverse due to the diversity of ethnic groups, nations, ideals, and economic patterns, that I'm totally confused with the entire place. So I still have difficulty. I can't believe that a planet with heterogeneous cultural biases has evolved to such a high level of technological differentiation."

The truck stop manager's mouth hung open, "I thought that you were. That you were. That you are..."

"What? Retarded?"

"That was no act you were putting on for us. Now was it? You've been trying to read. You've been listening to the children's phonics on PBS. Do you have anything to do with the man hunt that's on for a star pilot? or, the owner of a very mysterious interstellar craft?"

"Well, Sir, would a star pilot be a being who's arrived here from another star, solar system?" Zohar asked with enthusiastic innocence.

A Split Second to Midnight

The manager looked Zohar in the eyes. He was totally puzzled by the implication in the text of the question, "From the way I phrased the question...yes. Well are you from another star system?"

Zohar spoke with pure sincerity, "No...no I was born on this earth. In fact I was born right here in North America." And strangely, Zohar pulled out a map of the USA and pointed at Pittsburgh, "I was born at the confluence of these great rivers."

"Hey, Pal, I don't know who you are. I don't know how you got here. But for some strange reason I trust you. And you can work here as long as you want. But no one. No one in their right mind pulls out a map when asked where they were born. Now do they?"

Totally ignorant with the customs of the times, Zohar had to contemplate that question. "Like I said a lot of things are unclear to me, including your customs, your foods, your impersonal manners of dealing with each other. Not that you're mean hearted or anything. There's just so damned many of you that it doesn't seem that people know if they're coming or going. Where I'm from life is leisurely, apparent, beautiful, simple...simply beautiful. And we live a long time."

"Who are you?"

"I'm not sure that I should answer that just yet. But maybe you could help me get back to my ship. Because from watching the news reports everyone's concerned about who I am. And where I'm from. And what my intentions are. And I think that I've learned in the past few weeks that no one on this planet knows who the big eyes are. Do you know who the big eyes are?"

The manager couldn't believe his ears. "Listen, Pal. The more you talk, the more freaked out I'm becoming. You came into my truck stop and hung around the stores and restaurants for days. I took pity on you and somehow made myself believe that you were retarded and needed a job. Now you're asking me to return you...to, your star ship? And you pull out a map, to prove that as a child you spent time in what is now Pittsburgh. Like I said, no one pulls out a map to prove where they're from. Well I'm almost positive beyond a doubt that no one in Pittsburgh designs, builds and sells star ships. If they did everyone in the world would know about it."

Zohar looked that manager squarely in the eyes, "Listen, Friend. I'm no worse than anyone else you'll ever meet. I've never committed a crime. I'm here on a mission. How about if we go to the restaurant, have some coffee, eggs, toast and orange juice. And I'll explain who I am."

"Well I don't know, Pal, it's not good for management to be seen having a serious discussion with the retarded help. Somehow this isn't going to work, if you know what I mean. I'll have some food sent up to my office then we'll head back to your ship. But it's not going to be easy once we get there. There's rumors all about that your ship's going to be loaded onto a huge flatbed hovering transport vehicle...somewhere."

After eating they got in the manager's pick-up truck and headed for Cape Elizabeth which wasn't far. Their timing was perfect. People weren't being restrained from view of the star ship. And Alexander and Stefano were directing the government in the handling of the vehicle. Not that the government wasn't capable of doing an effective job; it was Alexander's way of claiming ownership. Alexander was directing the crane movement, as they swung the ship over a platform truck which drove into the mouth of a hovering ion rocket transport plane.

At that moment, Zohar tapped Alexander on the shoulder, when Alexander turned to look at the persistent tapping; with a shocked expression, he recognized Zohar. Turning in a full open stance to Zohar, with his mouth hanging open, Alexander just stared at the man who said, "Where are you taking the ship?"

Stefano tore across from behind the platform truck, "Hey, Alexander, our pilot's back; he's back; isn't that great?" Losing emotional control, Stefano too just stared at Zohar.

Zohar addressed the two men in a low tone, kind of privately, "We've never met formally. My name's Zohar."

Alexander and Stefano turned to each other with expressions of amazement and spoke in unison--"Now he speaks English?"

"Actually not English I'm afraid. American might be more in order. If you persist in loading our ship onto that platform truck, it's in for a bumpy ride . If your goal is to get to the ion rocket transport system--well, it will never operate again. Unless you know of some big eyed technicians. Its tolerances at the joints and fittings are so critical to flight that you're going to be delivering a hunk of junk back to Deep Creek."

Alexander and Stefano were speechless. Incapable of uttering a word, they turned to each other for help, but they were too emotionally drained to respond to each other. Zohar went over to the crane operator and directed him to, "Lower the ship gently, very gently please and do not bang it on the ground." Zohar climbed the ladder to the cockpit, while all onlookers watched in silence. Zohar popped the canopy and got into the ship. He reached inside a box; he pulled out what appeared to be a weapon, which he aimed at the straps, chains and ropes. They all immediately disintegrated.

Zohar had seen television reports about Alexander Petrov, who was believed to be the designer of the vehicle. Not quite trusting people he assumed were in league with the Big Eyes, Zohar spoke to Alexander, "See you back in Deep Creek, Alexander. We've got many issues to discuss regarding the design of these space vehicles. Not to mention the Technospheres. You must remember that I too have a mission." Closing the cockpit of the vehicle, Zohar manipulated the crystal controls; the ship powered up and arched out of sight.

Alexander stared into Stefano's eyes. Noticing that no one was near them--because all onlookers raced after the ship--Alexander uttered, "I couldn't do that. Could you do that? Who is that guy?"

"I don't know. I just don't know. But sure as hell, we better find out. Let's get back to Deep Creek!"

Chapter 15
6,000 Years Old

Back at the gazebo, consuming the evening meal, Alexander was silent and brooding, as he had been for days. The sun glistened in the clear evening sky over Deep Creek. Andrea in her bathing suit leaned forward to entice Alexander with a glimpse of her voluptuous body. While he slowly chewed his food, she spoke. "How long do we go on like this?"

He bowed his head and rubbed his eyes, "That sun's awfully bright...."

"How long, Alexander? How long do we go on like this?"

"Like what?"

Exasperated she leaned back in her wicker chair. "You're going to lose everything--including me."

Rubbing his eyes, he didn't respond. There was silence. "Now that fits the pattern doesn't it? I guess that you don't understand my pain. I can't quit what I'm all about and go do something else because it alters the tone and the mood of our relationship. Be somebody else to keep our relationship going? What relationship? Be truthful, Andrea. I'm defeated. Because when I lost at LiteWave, I lost myself with it."

"Defeat? No, not defeat. Life isn't what it was...so, you can no longer fight back to be what you were. What you're viewing as a defeat may have some greater significance."

"To whom, Andrea? To me there is no greater significance."

"To the greater realities of personal interaction, love, affection, interest in life. Not your so-called goals and objectives. You've fallen from professional heights that few achieve. Which admittedly required a compulsive person like you. You needed to be in control. But you're proving to be too anal."

"Anal, Andrea? I was fulfilling my destiny and I will continue to find and fulfill my destiny. And these temporary set- backs will not deter my resolve. I'm not going down without a fight."

Stefano interjected, "She's saying, Buddy, the fight is over and you've lost the battle and the war."

Alexander looked at both of them, "Well, once again I made a mistake in assuming something. Assumed that the ship would be returned here. The pilot appears at the last possible moment and takes the vehicle right out from under my nose. Destroys my credibility with everyone. I've lost the battle and the war. But as long as I can breathe. I'll return from this humiliating experience."

"With what, Al," she said tearfully, "With more anal behavior?"

"I don't know. I just don't know."

They sipped coffee on into the evening. Andrea's beauty, for the moment, was of little interest to Alexander.

Stefano continued to present himself as Al's faithful friend to the very end. "Is this the end, Al? If it is, maybe I should be moving on."

Suddenly Alexander was smiling as he peered skyward. "Now don't get too rambunctious, Stefano. I think we've got a visitor!" They all looked skyward and saw an alien ship dancing about the evening sky, as the sun sank on the horizon and dusk turned to night over the area. The ship came down to the shore line of the lake and lazily followed the shore, until it approached the gazebo. The ship was fixed in a hovering mode when the canopy of the cockpit popped open. It was Zohar who smiled at them, and they smiled back.

Andrea stood up and invited him for coffee with obvious gestures, assuming he could not understand her words. "We've anxiously hoped for your return. Come and join us."

Zohar climbed from the cockpit, descended the ladder, and jumped onto the dock. Stefano knew that Zohar knew some English but assumed he would not know anything very idiomatic, so he jokingly observed, "For an old fart, you're very fit!"

Zohar stepped over to the gazebo and took a chair. "Actually, the Big Eyes designed an optimal biological environment for me to live in. And I'm more fit than men far my junior on this planet."

"And what planet are you from?" Stefano asked, somewhat taken aback by Zohar's total command of English.

Zohar was calm, "…my last visit. Don't you remember my map? That map, by the way, has now revealed so much to me about my life that it's difficult for me to comprehend."

Alexander spoke, "How's that? But before you answer, have a chair."

"I estimate my culture to be some six thousand current earth years old. Our customs and technologies were in advance of the time. But from observing what's referred to as science and industry today, we were not sophisticated. Because we lacked the scientific knowledge to create the technology to utilize the natural resources, other than wood and basic metals from crude metallurgy."

"So who invented the technology that you're using right now, Zohar?" asked Alexander.

"The same men who designed the anomaly, Alexander?"

"And what could a stranger from another world possibly know about the 21ST Century anomaly?"

Zohar smiled, "That's where I live. In one of the seven anomaly events, as your ICARUS astronomer friends refer to them. I saw it on Science and Technology Week."

Andrea smiled, "Well, who are those men designing the anomaly?"

Zohar went on. "To repeat myself, men from the Andromedan Galaxy, whom I don't trust. People with a different emotional make up. They're Andromedan Big Eyes who's primary goal in life is to continue their research. You might refer to it as colonialism. They refer to it as research."

Stefano was astounded, "How did you pick-up our language so quickly?"

"Actually it was skill acquired by my ancient race, and the Shamans who led us. They taught us through the use of hallucinogens how to learn languages, dialects. In the biospheres our speech patterns evolved to permit us to communicate simultaneous thoughts. Your human

A Split Second to Midnight

speech, so slow and deliberate, is a lackluster language compared to our newer anomaly based Indo-Aryan language."

"Where do you fit? Why are you here?" said Andrea.

"I'm here on an improbable mission from what is now a highly differentiated culture. The Guild wants me, Zohar, to come back to earth to perfect a technology that only the Andromedans have the knowledge to perfect."

Stefano interjected, "Does this include propulsion systems?"

But Zohar went right on. "...for which, I don't have the knowledge or the skill. But the Guild won't hear of it. They want to take the final step from mortal nirvana to immortal nirvana. By moving Technosphere, a near-light-speed space station to ninety-nine point nine percent of light speed, or as close to light speed as possible before disintegration."

Andrea felt some compassion for Zohar, "And what of you? Where do you live?

"As I said, I live in the biospheres. That great 21st-Century anomaly beyond the asteroid belt. Designed by the Big Eyed Andromedans who schemed to make us believe that a so-called plague would be our ultimate undoing. They used the theme of the invading hoards to create...FUD!"

"FUD?" Andrea replied quizzically.

"Fear! Uncertainty! Doubt!"

"Life in the biospheres?" she said.

"I watched an old movie from your 1930s on a cable channel while I bused tables at the truck stop in Portland--think of me as living in Shangri-La."

"Then why do you seem to resent the Big Eyes?" Alexander inquired.

"Self-determination. Maybe I wish to die a normal death and see what's next. If nothing, so be it. But no one dies in Shangri-La. We're all quite happy--except for me. So they send me out to fulfill some mortal destiny and perfect a newer technology."

Stefano inquired, "How?"

"By tracking down the Big Eyes. Andromedans. They're around here somewhere. Yet no one on this planet knows of their whereabouts? And really after many weeks here, I'm more and more skeptical. But trust me. They're colonialists. My best guess is that they're hiding somewhere in the rain forests--what's left of them. Or the oceans."

"Doing what?" Alexander inquired,

"Doing all types of experiments in genetic engineering and agricultural science. They work silently and they change the environment by creating new species in each of their colonies...your earth, my biospheres."

"Is that bad?" she said.

"I'm not sure. But if you meet them and speak with them, beware. They'll endear you to their point of view, then they'll totally unnerve you. They want us to embody their visions, live out their visions, while they sit back and manipulate us. Total control."

"But no one's got total control," said Alexander.

"Of course not. But you'll find they've got greater control and dominion in all of the dimensions of time and space than we do. It's scary stuff."

Alexander tried a harmonious chord of thought. "Then we might assume that these creatures, the Big Eyes as you call them, are already aware of us?"

"There's a strong probability of that."

"If lots of other people hadn't seen you, Zohar, I'd suppose that you didn't really exist and we were having a mass hallucination. But I did drop my wallet in your vehicle. Let's have a look please. Take us for a ride. Where are the biospheres?"

* * *

Zohar harbored his private anger with the Guild; with the social fabric. While he enjoyed Alexander and Andrea, he resented being on earth. "And what about the emotional content of life here, Alexander? Don't you folks harbor anger, guilt? Aren't you ever angry with the system?" asked Zohar.

Andrea, Stefano, and Alexander all looked at each other in amazement, as Alexander said, "I'm angry, Zohar. I'm blamed for things beyond my control. My life's a mess. I love everyone. And I hate everyone. I love nature. And still I hate nature for the unpredictability of everything; especially, people. I'm on the edge."

Zohar replied emotionally, "It doesn't show. I want to see your anger."

"Anger? An understatement. I can't express the depths of my frustration with my sisters. Icons. Metallic paper-cut-out women. Paragons of business virtue and acumen. I'm angry. And you, Zohar?"

"Anger? An understatement. I can't express the depths of my frustration with the system of things. The Guild have set themselves up as Icons, metallic paper-cut-out women who rule our lives as paragons of virtue with dominion over my world. I'm angry."

Weirdly, Andrea and Stefano were astounded by the repetition in Zohar's reply. "Humanoid? Or Android?" asked Andrea.

Zohar replied, "Human. I'm very human. With sentiments quite similar to Alexander's."

In disbelief, Andrea's head just kept shaking no "More anger, more insanity from you, too, Zohar. Let's see it!"

Alexander responded, "Yes I'm angry. A delusional escape-- that just feels right. So why not be angry with the system? I don't know how to fight back!"

Zohar smiled, "And there's more now isn't there. Like the spiritual wall. We can all experience nirvana in our own delusionary ways. But obsession with nirvana is drowning one's self in delusional bliss. And the wall is never taken away until..."

"Maybe when we die..." interjected Stefano.

Zohar continued, "And isn't that our friend? The End!"

Andrea was tearful, "How can a man born six thousand years ago share the same anger as us? I'll never understand men's inflated egos. What's wrong with more bliss? What's wrong with making everything feel good in time and space. Forget progress! Love life, plants, animals-- or just plain lazy summer afternoons. Progress? Men just piss me off."

Zohar smiled. "If you don't mind me saying so, you're very beautiful in many ways. Like the anger of a mother lion. Like the beautiful blue flash of a meteor."

She smiled. "Zohar, you suffer from a common malady of men much younger than yourself--and only a woman cure that."

Zohar looked in Alexander's eyes, "Alexander? I saw reports about you on television, on cable news. They did in-depth profiles on you. Said that you hold the secrets to the virtual effects drivers."

Alexander lamented, "Do you really want to know my real secrets?"

"Sure," Zohar smiled.

"I blundered. Illusions of success got in the way of reality, people's real attitudes. Consequently I'm nothing without my spontaneous sense of humor and sarcasm--and that's what differentiates me from the rest of the animal kingdom. I've lost contact with my animal nature. And my spiritual nature."

Stefano lost control and yelled, "You're a control freak, Alexander. Who are you kidding? Your nature's been hidden forever."

Alexander smiled, "My animal craving for Andrea...her scent, her beauty, her sensual aura. We once laughed a lot, Andrea."

Zohar looked at Stefano, "And what's your story? I sense hostility."

Stefano snapped, "Hostility? Oh really? Perhaps it's because of Alexander's family. On his mother's side--Colonas. Well, they emptied the Colona legacy, fortune, back in Venice by invoking some little-known estate management loopholes, dating back to the thirteenth century. Maria Colona left my father to be her fool. You just have to know the right lawyers. And maybe become their whores!"

Andrea was appalled, "Is that true, Alexander?"

Hostility and resentment surfaced in Stefano; in Alexander; while Zohar and Andrea felt quite uncomfortable with the clumsily evolving situation

Alexander responded, "Why ask me? He's the expert. Whores, Stefano?"; still, Alexander did not sense the villain at work in Stefano.

Chapter 16
Joy Stick Control

"My father had a vision--to build the virtual effects space craft. And he shared that vision only with me. When he got too old to manage, I took over. But now that I've seen your space ship, touched it, who knows?"

Zohar's vehicle was on the manufacturing floor, (next, to the LiteWave vehicle that only lacked government-certified virtual particle drivers) at the Deep Creek facility, as a favor to Stefano and Andrea who wanted to use it as armor, metaphorically speaking, to stave off more angered backlash from Jessica, possibly Sophia, who barged their way into the facility on that hot August afternoon.

Alexander and Zohar sat in the cockpit of Zohar's space vehicle, while Zohar instructed Alexander on the use of the crystal controls. Simultaneously spinning the two crystal balls to the left turned the ship on, powered it up. The balance of the controls were activated by the touch of the pilot. The pilot, co-pilot, and navigator, when present, sat on a turret in the center of the floor of the vehicle. The turret was elevated three feet above the passengers who sat in captains chairs lining the periphery of the round cockpit.

Having the two vehicles side-by-side lent credibility to Alexander's project, which only required more testing to gain certification. But Alexander's confidence and mental focus were distracted by events.

Sophia and Jessica climbed the rounded ladder to the cockpit of Zohar's vehicle. It had 12 captain's chairs mounted to the floor on the circular periphery of the cockpit, facing outward with their backs to the center of central turret. Each captain's chair swiveled on a three hundred sixty degree radius; each chair was uniformly spaced around the periphery of the floor at the edge of the cockpit. The cockpit, thirteen feet in diameter, usually remained stationary at the top of the gyroscopic skeleton.

In the floor of the cockpit were doors that led to the galley for sleeping quarters, food, and hygiene. At the center of the galley floor, sixteen feet in diameter, was a round table, six feet in diameter; as well as for eating, it was used for food storage, tachyon wave crystal cooking, and food-waste disposal.

Around the periphery of the galley were ergonomically designed, sealed, sleeping chambers which maintained ambient moisture to maintain humans' skin and lungs with 29.86 psi air pressure. Inside each chamber was a zippered permeable body stocking, spring suspended, to hold the resting passenger in place, regardless of speed, gravitational forces and other circumstances. The sleeping chambers also served as hygiene chambers for eliminating bodily wastes. The body stocking also served as a bathing mechanism. The ship's skeleton contained thirty-seven thousand gallons of recycled, constantly purified, water; while maintaining sixty-eight percent relative humidity, there were thirty-seven thousand gallons of condensed water available. The total amount of water and vapor were fixed and did not change. Water was the most critical factor for deep space travel in the spacecraft's closed micro-ecological design. Without adequate water, any space travelers will quickly perish.

This was a vehicle designed by beings from another galaxy, from another planet identical to the earth. Was it so strange that twin planets created twin space vehicles? The difference was that the Andromedan Big Eyes had the advantage of time in developing the more sophisticated tachyon drivers; otherwise, the engineering was quite similar. Zohar's vehicle had the same purpose in mind that Alexander's did -- space travel, possibly interstellar, but not intergalactic.

Zohar's vehicle, a spherical and saucer like object, a shuttle vehicle, came with the Andromedan migration vehicles, which were the mother ships of the Andromedan Big Eyes. The mother ships were transported into the Milky Way Galaxy through an Andromedan technology --

called, Tesserac. The mother ships were designed to maintain the feeling home, while moving through deep space.

The Big Eyes were quite similar in size and stature to humans. They claimed to be humanoid, before they embarked on their voyage to the Milky Way. After arriving toward the center the Milky Way via tesserac, they were mutated by light speed travel while seeking the earth. The earth was designated as their geo-biological twin planet in the Milky Way by Andromedan astronomical teams who studied the earth for centuries in earthly terms.

Zohar's vehicle, an interstellar shuttle craft. based in the biospheres, had food and water in the storage bays. It was capable (with sophisticated tachyon wave drivers) of sustained interstellar flight but had never been beyond trips to Technosphere's artificial orbit about the sun or beyond Pluto. Neither Alexander nor Zohar had explored the possibilities of their individual space crafts.

"Actually, Alexander, at near-light-speed flight, no one consumes food. There's no need to."

Jessica smirked, "Now tell me, Al, just how does he know that? Have you folks been out gallivanting about the galaxy?"

Alexander lost his will to fight. Quietly he looked into her eyes, "Ha?"

Zohar looked into her eyes, "Well, lady, let me tell you that interstellar flight isn't for the weak-minded like yourself. It's for open-minded individuals who have a grasp on themselves. Not for those who just grasp. I'm afraid that you wouldn't last where there's nothing to grasp. Those who seek to hold the world will only lose themselves in the process and are destined to repeat it ...call it Karma."

Jessica quipped, "And who the hell are you, Friedrich Nietzsche? Let me tell you something, Friedrich Boy, the design of this ship is the property of LiteWave Technologies."

(By this time Stefano had climbed the ladder to the LiteWave vehicle. The former ICARUS pilot, Stefano quickly reviewed the information in Alexander's flight manual, a manual with which Stefano was intimately familiar; powering the space craft up was a simple task, and flying the vehicle was as simple as controlling the joy stick and buttons of a Nintendo game. It was straight forward. To climb from a point relative to zero, in small increments, like seventy feet, meant tapping the button on the top of the joy stick; to observe direction, the pilot had foot pedals to control the rotation of the turret -- quite clearly, it was all laid out in the flight manual. To accelerate the pilot squeezed the joy stick; to climb vertically the pilot pushed the button at the top of the joy stick; other variations in the movement of the joy stick, on a 360 degree plane, controlled direction. And the cradle that the pilots hand sat in, while grasping the joy stick and tilting the cradle, controlled the angle to the horizon. However, in space, all of those variables were relative to the perception of the pilot; while flying about the earth, they were relative to the horizon. Stefano had the ship powered up and ready for flight, while the others were focused in and on Zohar's vehicle.)

For a brief moment, Alexander was ill aware of Stefano's intentions to follow in the LiteWave vehicle.

(The bodies of the individual interstellar ships, were near identical. Each ship was integrated into a gyroscopic equatorial outer frame which remained stationary, while the body of the ship spun within the frame; in fact, the physical design was about identical to Alexander's ship. Why? It was more than coincidental. Like disparately, but well, designed basic internal combustion engines, the engineering will always be similar. Form followed function.)

Alexander furrowed his brow and shook his head negatively, when he realized that Stefano was powering up the other ship. Next thing the another sister jumped onto the floor of the cockpit, as Zohar said, "Strap yourselves in, ladies, Al." In a moment, Zohar shut the hatch and hovered the ship over the open roof, seventy feet above the ground. Likewise, Stefano hovered Alexander's vehicle to parallel the other vehicle. Zohar toyed with the controls to give the illusion that the ship might fall, then it lunged off toward a bank of trees, "Watch out and fasten those seat belts."

Jessica loudly proclaimed from her soft leather captain's chair, "My belt's on!" And Sophia concurred, "Me too!" -- and it felt instantaneous, they were off into deep space in a matter of fifteen seconds. Stefano followed their trail in the LiteWave vehicle. They didn't fly straight up, they just raced on a vector right off of the horizon. Beyond earth's atmosphere, the sun appeared to be a very bright star,

With his mouth hanging open, completely surprised, Alexander saw his vehicle racing after them, "God damn it, Stefano, you're not supposed to take that ship out" The LiteWave vehicle was recently tested by Stefano, but not certified by ICARUS/NASA.

Jessica shouted, "Holy hell, we're all going to die," when the ship slowed and landed on the face of the moon. "Jesus Christ, who the hell are you? What in the hell are you doing to us?"

Al's heart pounded, harder, harder, as he took a deep swallow and looked out at the earth. Gathering his wits, he began to laugh, "Now, if the two of you don't leave me alone we're going to leave you both up here without space suits. Let them out, Zohar. Let them out right here and I'll be finished with them."

"Come on, Alexander, I'd rather leave them where no one can find them ever again. How about we just drop them into the storm clouds of Jupiter? And they'll just disintegrate in the heat and wind. Gone in a moment."

Sophia lost it and sobbed openly, "You bastard, Alexander, I'm losing my mind. Get me back to earth right away!" Looking out at the earth, she tore at her hair and screeched, "Damn it, take me back and I promise to stop this charade with Jessica. Please please I just can't stand looking at the earth." She buried her face, "Get me the hell out of here, you bastards, stop this torture. I'm losing it."

"She's losing her grip on reality, Alexander. And look at your other sister; she's come undone." Jessica was in a trance that appeared to be cardiac or breathing arrest. Her eyes were opened wide; she was as stiff as a board in her captain's chair. Frighteningly, her mouth hung open, as if to scream, but there no sound was heard.

Alexander responded, "She looks like she's dead. But did you hear that? She's trying to say something. What could it be?" Incapable of speech, Jessica raised a free hand with her middle finger protruding.

"Alexander, what's your sister saying with that gesture?"

"You wouldn't understand the vernacular, Zohar. Take us back. Wait--look over there! It's my vehicle--Stefano followed us?"

Zohar spoke, "The American language contains a lot of strained syllables. And earth contains a lot of stress with women like Alexander's sisters. I can't just return them. They should learn a lesson for what they're doing to their brother. And I'm just the person to teach them. Look up, girls!" Without warning, they blasted right at the earth and came within ten feet of the surface of the Pacific Ocean, when they leveled off near Hawaii and headed toward Southeast Asia. Zohar eventually hovered over a rain forest in Indonesia. (He was familiar with the locale of the rain forests, because he believed that The Big Eyes may have set up camp in one of the earth's rain forests). He set the craft down near a lake. He popped the canopy. "Now, Jessica, get out!"

Jessica struggled to remain conscious, "Where the hell are we?"

"Find out for yourself. Get out!" Zohar retorted. Zohar by being angry at Arlee, (by extension, irrationally projecting his anger for the moment), was angry with Jessica who mistreated Zohar's new friend, Alexander.

To avoid any further bouts with crippling fear, Jessica struggled to her feet and climbed down the ladder; from a lake, in the middle of a rain forest, she watched the ship disappear, then sank to the ground and heaved up her insides.

Back at the Deep Creek facility, Zohar asked Alexander to remain, while he took Sophia back to find Jessica.

Alexander responded, "Whatever it takes to teach Jessica a lesson. Look, here's Stefano bringing in the LiteWave vehicle."

From the ladder of Zohar's vehicle, Alexander jumped to the floor. A massive shadow from the LiteWave space craft was cast over Alexander. Stefano sat the vehicle down on the manufacturing floor. Incredulously, painfully, Alexander exchanged glances with Stefano who popped the large canopy. Stefano smiled at Alexander, "As always, Alexander, you have what I want! It's charming, beautiful, and quite elegant to ride-- almost better than sex. You know? Momentarily I'm quite confused; sex, space, time, penetration, LiteWave, light waves, light speed, the rush, the triumph, the kill...some day."

Alexander spoke with angered sarcasm at Stefano's vaguely veiled threat, "Is that a tactical, or strategic threat on me?"

Chapter 17
Erotic States of Mind

That night, Sophia accompanied Zohar in his vehicle when he returned to the lake in the Indonesian rain forest, but when they arrived, Jessica was nowhere to be seen. Zohar paced about the cockpit of the craft and spoke to Sophia, "Why don't we get out and go for a swim?"

Sophia felt quite ill from the ride and from the sun beating down on her, and was only too happy to exit the craft. Zohar removed his clothes and waded into the water; it was a shallow pool, several hundred feet in diameter. All types of jungle birds were heard whooping, chirping, cawing, crowing, and yelping. Totally naked, Zohar sank into the water for a cool dip.

Sophia looked at him. Feeling curious about her own feelings toward this virile silver-haired stranger, she removed all of her sweaty clothing-- to Zohar's delight. Gazing on her naked body, he smiled, "The physique of a goddess. Come in, come in, and cool yourself down."

She did. Her thin torso and large, firm breasts shimmered in the sunshine, as she swam a soft smooth backstroke toward Zohar who swam off, then came back underneath her. He surfaced between her legs, facing her; grabbing her wide hips, he pulled her closer. Their bodies met.

She ran her hands across his hard chest, when she felt his erection in her crouch. "What are you doing to me, Silver Fox?"

"What you want, Sophia. I can give you what you need. Take away all your stress, return you to your naturally erotic state of mind."

"And how do you know that?"

"It's evident in your every expression. I've known a few women like you. It was in their every expression. They didn't love one man. They loved men."

She was aroused to the point of feeling extreme sexual anxiety, anticipation, as her insides quivered. Losing control to his strong but gentle touch, she slowly inserted his phallus and shimmied on him. Moaning and groaning, she cried out, "Oh god, not in my wildest fantasies, not in my wildest dreams, has there ever been a moment like this. Don't stop! Just don't stop!"

With his strong firm hands grasping her hips, she rode up and down on him. She lost all sense of inhibition, as she moved him down into the shallow water and thrust herself up and down. She grabbed his hair and pulled herself up, then she thrust herself back. "Oh god, this is incredible! I could go on forever like this, I love it."

For his own reasons, Zohar was careful not to ejaculate into her but withdrew at precisely the split second after she was in full orgasm.

She then collapsed on him, and they kissed and frolicked in the water. Suddenly they stopped when they heard distant screams of terror. The screaming seemed to be coming toward them.

They looked up and saw Jessica running toward the water and shouting, "Oh god, someone save me! Help! Help! I'm being devoured!"

Zohar instantly got up and ran toward her, as she rushed into the water. Her clothes were covered with thousands of red fire ants and she dove entirely under water. When Zohar pulled her face from the water, she was close to losing consciousness. He ripped off all of her clothing, every stitch; then, he pulled her to the shore and covered her with mud to stop the ants who continued to ravage her. Quickly he scampered about the rim of the small lake in search of something. Sophia could hear him revert back to his biosphere manner of speech. After a few minutes, fortunately for Jessica, he found what he was looking for. It was a type of fungus that grew under the bark of a certain rain forest woody plant. He stripped the bark from the plant; under the bark grew a fungus that mixed with the plant's sap like secretions to be used as a natural medicinal ointment. It had a surprisingly fresh aroma. Zohar came back with the bark but seemed unable to speak English to ask

Sophia to help him, so active was his adrenaline flow. He dragged Jessica back into the water and washed all of the mud from her body, every crack and crevice; then he dragged her back to the shore, where he laid her naked body on the sand and began to apply the natural ointment. Jessica was covered with red welts and was unconscious. With gestures Zohar directed Sophia to help in the application of the moist fungal ointment; they covered her face, hair, under her arms, the entire front of her body; then they applied the ointment to her back. Zohar then picked her up and laid her on a warm rock, "Give her an hour, Sophia; the application will neutralize the venomous saliva of those insects. It almost always works. She's in shock right now."

"Almost always?"

"Yes, Sophia, almost always. It also has psychedelic qualities, like mescaline. When she awakes she'll be quite relaxed and probably feeling quite...amorous, quite possibly not be herself."

"Her? Horny? I can't wait to see it. Why don't you apply some of that stuff to my skin? I want to experience what you're talking about. And I want to feel your animal touch--that's the only kind I like!"

With his fingertips scooping the natural ointment from the bark, he applied it to her nipples which grew erect as her head sank back with pleasure. He spread it across her back; then she lay back on the warm rock as he spread it across her long lithe legs. Then he applied it to his own legs, chest and face. They basked in the hot jungle sun; already each of them were tanned to varying degrees.

"It's marvelous to lie naked in the direct sun light with no transparent shields like we must have in our orbiting biospheres."

"Zohar, are you an ICARUS scientist or something? What biospheres are you talking about?"

"Sophia, I would love to take you there. They're breathtaking in their beauty and ecological design. Each has developed its own character through the use of hydroponics. There is one with hundreds of thousand of buffalo that roam the low lands while the villages, castles, and cities are built on plateaus."

"I've never heard of such a place."

He smiled, "You will, you will. And once you've left this overpopulated planet, you'll never look back."

"Then tell me, darling--where are these biospheres?"

"Millions of miles out. Far out, beyond the asteroid belt."

Then they were silent for a long while, as the relaxing and psychedelic qualities of the ointment worked its magic on their bodies and minds. About an hour passed when Sophia began to giggle lightly, "Well, Zohar, you magic man, tell me who built these incredible biospheres?"

"Actually, the Big Eyes built them and helped me adapt them to life in our solar system."

"The Big Eyes?" Unable to contain her laughter, she reached for his phallus. "Do the Big Eyes have big dicks?" She touched him affectionately but was unable to contain her giggling.

"Have you ever wondered just how the sun, the moon, and the stars came into being? From a non-material virtual source? A god? What kind of a god can create such a beautiful universe, for the eyes to behold, and fill it with such fucked-up people?"

Just then, Jessica began to awake. She slowly moved her hands across her body, her breasts, her stomach, her vagina. Zohar was lying between as Jessica opened her eyes. Turning her head to the left, she saw Sophia applying oral stimulation to Zohar. "You horny bitch, Sophia, how can you just do that right in front of me? Get away and let me try that."

Leaning up on his elbows, Zohar enjoyed these aggressive females playing with his body. He relaxed and let them have their way.

In a few hours, as the sun began to set in the late evening, Zohar returned with them to his craft. Their erotic state of mind had passed and now they were tripping, mildly hallucinating. Still naked, the three of them sat in the captains chairs of the vehicle.

In her mildly drugged state, Jessica was having a difficult time with her feelings of guilt. As she looked up at the crystal clear night sky with millions of twinkling stars, she spoke in such a low voice that neither Sophia nor Zohar heard her. "Looking out at this massive universe, feeling my lowly being, I realize I've wronged my brother by leading a life obsessed with myself. I had no good reason to treat him so dishonorably and work so assiduously to destroy him. What's wrong with me? I can feel the energy of the stars pulsing. I'm having a great inner vision of oneness with the cosmos. And it makes the I in me feel foolish. How can I ever undo what's been done?"

Chapter 18
Casting Doubt

Back at the Deep Creek site, with twelve hours difference from the Indonesian rain forest, where Alexander permitted the alien, Zohar, to deal with his sister's, Alexander was too wrought and angry with Jessica and Sophia to care. Alexander implicitly trusted Zohar who manifested the purity of human caring which lacked in Alexander's world. Andrea sat in the gazebo with Alexander and ate breakfast. Andrea spoke between sips of coffee, "....regardless, Alexander, no one can undo what's been done, no matter how well meaning they may be or appear to be. Let go of the past. Move on. Forget the money. Let Jessica and Sophia go there own way."

"Andrea, you're so right...forget the past. Let Zohar handle my sisters for the moment. And who's responsibility is to handle our romance. Emotionally my mind feels clear but my emotional responses aren't compelling you. I'm just out of reach, like the climax to this technological quest. Just out of reach."

"But how do you know, unless you keep trying. Stefano took the risk and the vehicle performed quite well. He performed!" "Really," Alexander spoke soberly, "just what did he perform?"

"Oh, you know what I mean."

Alexander gave her a long silent stare, "I know what you mean?"

"He's very attractive, Alexander. And a woman could fall prey to his...his...whatever."

"I neglected you. Yes. But just keep it to yourself."

"Keep what to myself, Alexander?"

"It's too profound for me to engage you regarding, new, recent feelings, about my mother's death. Let the dead rest. Because at the moment you're not looking very well yourself. I don't blame you. I blame myself for everything. Isn't Stefano somehow involved in Maria's fall? You know something don't you?"

Tears streamed down her face. "Alexander, I love you so much. Where did we go wrong? Stefano is less than honorable."

"I went wrong spending my life validating Sergei's dangerous technological ideas? To ever leave you for a moment with Stefano."

"Dangerous? Then be a risk-taker. What do you have to lose? Quit being so scientific! So tedious, tiring, pedestrian, boring, difficult... generally shitty. You created Sergei's compelling technology. Why worry about certification?"

"I am tedious and boring? Worrying about every detail."

"Well how did the Andromedans do it? Certification didn't worry Stefano."

Alexander guzzled down his orange juice. "I don't know, I just don't know. I need to talk to that old stranger and see what he knows. Who knows where he's really from. Jokingly, we say Pittsburgh. But anyway I want to understand their technology." Then, with sarcasm in his voice, he chided, "The Big Eyes. The Big Eyes? Who in the hell are the Big Eyes? Life's surrealistic!"

"Well, Darling, there are even more sobering things to consider, when we look at the events visited on you. Maybe, just maybe, this technology you seek has not yet reached its time here on earth. Maybe you're hundreds of years ahead of your time."

Alexander's expression became somber. "And that, right there, to me that's the worst of all thoughts. To me it seems right, it just feels right. It's *not* a surreal dream!"

"That's the rub! In your mind, it just has to be right. Did you ever consider that your timing's off? What's a couple of hundred years compared to the time that man's been on earth. A split second?"

"Sure, sure, that all makes sense. But I just can't accept that. My father was the intrepid dreamer, not me. These are my times, my destiny."

Andrea was now almost sad. "And there we have it. What is the subjective quality of a dream when life is nothing more than a dream? Sleeping dreams are only mortal interludes denying the painful realities of our conscious dreams."

"To sleep, to dream, only to know that the dream must end. Despair, where Satan gives no quarter, casting doubts on the eternal quality of being, creating deeper despair, where Satan still gives no quarter. Is it nobler to dream of a greater tomorrow? Or live out our hell on earth?"

"So what do we do about this hell on earth, Alexander? Accept it and hope for redemption. What will your space vehicle do for the dreams of mankind? The collective dreams of men? Who is the visionary who understands the collective dream?"

"Who, Andrea?

"What will your dream do for mankind? Very little. It's just that you're caught up in the vision of making it happen, not a vision of the collective unconscious. We all seek that collective vision. Fleeting, ephemeral, a virtual effect of reality."

"Of course, Andrea. My obsession is with dreams...not reality."

"That's right, Alexander, I want to be your reality, that's why I stay with you. In the waning hope that you'll grant me your obsession and be in love with me. We were in love once."

"Quite a dreamy word, love. And whose dream is that? Who can define the vision of love? It's indefinable, like any other passionate dream. Love is a marvelous experience, when you're experiencing it, but when the dream ends, then what?""

Tears streamed down her face, "Then it's over, it's over between us?"

"No, Andrea, it's not over. I'm just very tired and want to get back to work."

"Now that's what a woman needs to hear! Sound work ethics to confirm a relationship. I hate you. Today, I just hate you. What's bothering you, Alexander? Get to the root of it."

"Bothering me? Everything, yet nothing. The universe with so many simultaneous events, varying degrees, natures, contrasted, compared. What? Why? Where? Who is an inventor? Does he get his inspiration elsewhere? Could it be that somebody else is looking into my mind...

from some other place? Somewhere? Some other time? And where will inspiration come from tomorrow?"

"Will tomorrow ever come for us?" Sadly she wiped the tears from her face and walked slowly from the gazebo to the house.

Chapter 19
Big Eyes?

After a day of remaining in geosynchronous orbit, maintaining a position at the same spot above the earth, thirty thousand miles from the earth's surface, Sophia and Jessica were looking for a change of itinerary--and a new agenda.

Looking out at the stars, Jessica spoke. "Are we now your subjects? Or do we have something to say about being held hostage out here?"

Zohar was in a meditative state and chose not to answer. His eyes were fixated on the Andromedan Galaxy, as his mind filled with thoughts of the Big Eyes. He was thinking to himself, "Could it be that someone else is looking into my mind...from some other place? Somewhere? Some other time?"

Sophia went and knelt by Zohar's side. "What's bothering you, Zohar?"

"Everything, yet nothing. The universe with so many simultaneous events, varying degrees, natures, contrasted, compared. We're all quite similar, yet on further inspection we're all quite different, we're individuals...and still, a part of the whole. And when entropy ensues, we become swallowed up by the whole. Curious events, which all play together in this weird synergy of events called life, don't always feel quite by chance?." He now spoke his previous thoughts. "Could it be that someone else is looking into my mind...from some other place? Somewhere? Some other time?"

"Do you mean that in a very literal sense?"

"Yes, Sophia, quite literally." Then he pointed at Andromeda. "Yes, see that galaxy out there, it is our neighbor, yet it is my enemy."

Jessica also came to Zohar's side, "If we were on earth, I'd say that you were one of the most paranoid bastard's alive. But just sitting up here with a view of the universe in all directions, I no longer find your paranoia to be unfounded. I want to know more about these Big Eyes. Who the hell are they?"

"My people lived on earth seven thousand years ago. Yet there are no artifacts, no remains or recorded history of our presence on the planet. The Andromedan Big Eyes came to our great wooden villages and forts to warn us of potential impending disasters about to befall us."

"Disaster, Zohar?"

"Plagues, they claimed. And constant invasions by hordes of conquerors would be our undoing."

"Well," said Jessica, "who in your culture would've understood the full extent of a viral plague?"

"Only one trusted Shaman, Arlee's father, who introduced the Big Eyes to me, because I was considered to be fair and open-minded. A public works engineer, so to speak. I built viaducts and water delivery systems. I knew math, calculus, and trigonometry for engineering. Nevertheless, our people suffered severe emotional problems when they came in contact with the Big Eyes."

"These Big Eyes--they really do exist?" Sophia spoke pensively.

Zohar shook his head slowly. "Not only did the Big Eyes warn us of a devastating plague….they said that we lacked the necessary animal nature to defend ourselves against the invaders from the west. Hordes of mad men, they claimed!"

"So what did you and Arlee's father decide to do?" Sophia asked with eyed innocence.

Zohar went on. "They suggested that we adapt the Andromedan migration vehicles into biospheres to avoid fragmentation, even disintegration, of our social order. Using the migration vehicles we moved from the Zagros range to North America, where, over the course of decades, we loaded all of the things necessary for a prosperous life in space."

Jessica was still her cynical self, "And you bought their bull shit, Zohar? You believed them?"

"I became their student at the urging of Arlee's father who was highly respected."

"And why are we hovering your space craft here in geosynchronous orbit?" Sophia inquired.

"To find them. My suspicions tell me that the Andromedans are still here. They're hiding in the rain forests to continue their genetic and agricultural research. But these people, these beings, practice stealth. They are not easily found, unless they want to find you. Then they're everywhere and you can't get rid of them."

Jessica's shook her head negatively, "Well, these beings, they sound like a group of intergalactic scientists conducting business in our galaxy?"

"Exactly!"

"Quite possibly, Zohar, they wanted to cast your society into space as a biological experiment. If you know what I mean. Maybe you all really were going to die. Then again, maybe not. Still you probably did the right thing by accepting their hospitality," Jessica pronounced.

"They gave us the impression that we were their discovery. But maybe, just maybe, they were the creators of our society, some other place, some where, some other time. Did they create this living earth, so to speak?"

"You're not thinking clearly, Zohar," Jessica snapped.

"The Andromedans, the Big Eyes, who live here on earth today, existed for tens of thousands of years in The Milky Way Galaxy. Transported to our galaxy in some mysterious fashion after The Andromedan Federation of Planets set forth a set of plans to create a colonial biological research lab, the earth, The Milky Way Galaxy. Yet with all of their seeming scientific objectivity, The Bid Eyed Andromedans are always angry. I never realized it until this moment. They're angry with The Andromedan Federation. But why?"

"Why what?" Jessica snapped out.

"Whenever you meet the Big Eyes, whatever you do, don't get them angry. Because that's when you'll get the sense that they own you. They see themselves as our guardian angels so to speak. The Greeks gave them names. Called them gods. And the Greeks prospered thousands of years after my world. Zeus is Andromedan."

Sophia smiled, "Just how, do you know about the Greeks?"

"When I was a busboy unable to speak English--curiously I learned to read before speaking the language. You two are variations of Venus. Very beautiful. The Big Eyes appreciate beauty. In fact they're obsessed with beauty and ingenuity."

"Is that all they're interested in," Sophia inquired.

"No. They've experimented with the human species to get desired results. But they didn't expect the masses to grow, being further nurtured by the teachings of Christ, Buddha, and others. Without some morality, the masses might have collapsed on themselves."

Sophia was aroused by the mere mention of beauty. "My sister's quite right, you know, you're extremely paranoid to believe all of this. What might they want with us?"

"I know that when the Big Eyes meet all of you that they'll be quite enamored with you because you're a highly motivated group of individuals. Andromedans secretly interceding in human genetics can't stomach their human failures on earth. On one hand, the avarice and greed of some individuals, while others display mendacity, sloth and cowardice across great metropolitan areas. Something's gone wrong on this planet but they'll never acknowledge their hand in it."

Jessica was thinking, "...to go along with your paranoia, Zohar?" But what she said was, "Why didn't the Big Eyes eliminate Christ and Buddha?"

"In their own way, they did. But they never interfered directly."

"Except with you. They cast your culture into outer space."

He smiled, "Not exactly. They persuaded me to convince everyone to leave. But they never interceded directly in the process."

Jessica was intense. "Please, let us witness the biospheres!"

Zohar moved his interstellar craft to just beyond the asteroid belt, where they witnessed the biospheres whisking by at ninety-one percent of light speed. They were at a great enough distance to visually make out the biospheres, known to earthling as the anomaly.

Sophia exclaimed, "The anomaly of seven--it's the anomaly!! Unreal! Unbelievable! Stefano's friends died out here."

Jessica, rather frightened, was quite taken by Zohar. As she observed the anomaly passing before her very eyes, she called out, "Who are you? Zohar? Where are your really from? Who in the hell are you?"

Chapter 20
An Emerging Predator

On a hot September afternoon in Deep Creek, Zohar parked his vehicle on the floor of the manufacturing facility. Stefano peered up to view Zohar as he popped open the canopy. The sisters got out first. They wore short tunics provided by Zohar. There was nothing under their tunics as they climbed down the ladder, and Stefano found himself rather disconcerted.

Zohar descended the ladder to be greeted by Alexander. Sophia and Jessica went to Alexander and each gave him an affectionate hug. He was stunned by their friendliness. The sisters found themselves a place to sit, as Andrea, who happened to be there for lunch, was equally amazed.

Andrea said, "My god, Alexander, this Zohar's a magic man." She looked at the sisters who sat, quietly. For once they seemed content.

As Sophia added, "Yes, he's a magic man. He's got magic hands."

Everyone's eye brows raised, as they looked in Zohar's direction, as he scoffed, "Really, it was nothing."

With surprise Stefano shouted, "Who is this guy, Alexander? I couldn't do that. Could you do that? Make those girls smile?"

Alexander and Zohar spent the afternoon discussing virtual wave drivers versus tachyon wave drivers. Zohar quickly grew fond of Alexander and wished to work with him, to learn more about metals, to find a way to build Technosphere II. Alexander grew extremely curious about the tachyon wave driver in Zohar's vehicle and wanted to know how the tachyon driver produced the power to generate the waves.

Alexander knew how to create virtual particle waves, in the negative force, gravitons, via the fusion of atoms. Zohar described tachyon waves, which can be detected but not isolated, a virtual effect, a wave moving beyond the speed of light, as a very effective alternative to the virtual negative force of gravitons. Fusion created too much tachyon energy to be practically harnessed, said Zohar, who described atoms as polarized energy fields which were constantly adjusting their polarity, with spinning sub-particles, to each other with the ebb and flow of tachyon energy. "Alexander," Zohar said. "Sub-atomic energy is a constant. Like high and low pressure systems in the atmosphere, flowing into each other. Yet, they remain high and low."

Understanding this was the secret to understanding the Big Eyes' tachyon wave driver. The earthly approach of the 21st Century was to create the energy by creating something, nuclear fusion, creating atoms--which, as Alexander himself knew, produced harmful side effects to the users. Hence, certification of the LiteWave produced virtual particle driver was a must. Yet, as Zohar pointed out, heavier elements, hybrid elements designed by the Big Eyes, with a crystal-like external structure, were quite capable of extracting tachyon energy from the space in their immediate vicinity.

Alexander shook his head negatively, "As a group, on earth, we haven't gotten to that level. A scientific group experience contemplating the more elegant energy conversion system of the Big Eyes. Tachyon waves converted to the negative force, appearing as gravitons, in a group of elegant virtual effects conversions."

Zohar felt sympathetic to Alexander's disappointment at not living at a different point in history; he felt empathetic with Alexander's inability to match the big eyed technology. "Who knows, maybe a hundred thousand years ahead of you culturally, Alexander? They had to start somewhere, too. Your system works. And knowing the originator is much more exciting than knowing the Big Eyes who probably inherited everything they've got."

"But, Zohar, your task seems quite impossible--to build a sphere that will exist beyond the rim of the galaxy where there's diminished tachyon energy. A nuclear fusion propulsion system may be more in order there. Using the free gases in space, hydrogen ions, to produce nuclear fusion, to produce virtual particle waves and a negative force propelling against the entire energy of the Milky Way Galaxy. A free ride so to speak, until the universe ceases to exist."

Zohar was reflective. "So, we don't use a process called nuclear fusion for our tachyon propulsion system. We capture the tachyon waves right from the immediate space in and around the driver. We warp space, the negative force, gravity, to meet the requirements of the pilot at the controls. There's synergy between my hand and finger movements at the controls and the driver. Synernetics. Synergy with the lattice-network of space. So how in the hell did they get here from Andromeda, if there's diminished tachyon energy beyond the galaxies?"

"Well, Zohar, don't fret over it. They got here some way. Yours is an interstellar vehicle. Maybe they didn't use either propulsion system for intergalactic travel. They performed a tesserac function."

Zohar shook his head negatively. "I think that we're now getting beyond ourselves. Tesserac? I don't know what that means."

Alexander smiled. "Forget it, it's not important."

"I didn't invent the tachyon wave driver. And I've lost sight of exactly how the technology works. I don't know how to create hybrid atoms which are heavier than any elements known to earth. Let alone know the exact sub-atomic make-up of such hybridized structures."

"So let me see if I have it right, Zohar. You came to earth as part of your effort to build Technosphere II. But you don't have the metals, the metallurgical technology, or the wherewithal to design a tachyon wave driver for this new super-duper Technosphere II. And this woman, Arlee, accepts only success."

"I know, Alexander, it's the impossible dream. I told her it couldn't be done. But they all insisted because I was successful at getting the biospheres into orbit."

"Arlee--she sounds like an extremely demanding woman."

"Demanding, Alexander, and addicted to her endorphin-centric view of reality."

"Why is that so negative, Zohar? Endorphins are natures way to... to bliss?"

Zohar reflected before speaking, "Well, has anyone on earth ever been addicted to their own blissful nature for hundreds of years... without change, without mood swings?"

"Now that's addiction!"

As the days passed, Alexander made the effort to train Zohar in chemistry and metallurgy. But from both points of view, Alexander's and Zohar's, there wasn't much enthusiasm for a successful meeting of the minds. They liked each other. They, however, did not feel in concert with each other. Each had his own agenda, each had his individual goals and objectives. For all of the alluring mystery in their coincidental chance meeting, their scientific relationship was not blossoming beyond the seeds of curiosity. Their technologies could not be reconciled to fill each other's needs. But most agonizing to Alexander was how much the technologies, superficially, appeared quite similar.

Zohar had to build Technosphere II. Zohar smiled. "My Friend, rather than agonize over ambient radiation problems with your virtual particle driver, why don't you come to the biospheres and study the writings of the big eyes. We'll teach you a new alphabet, a new language, a new point of view. Together, we'll learn how to produce hybrid atoms, heavier elements."

"And should I accept, should we go to the biospheres," Alexander spoke with tentativeness, reticence in his voice, "then quite possibly we'll lose track of earth time. And when we return, we will return to a different world. Maybe it will be two hundred years in the future?"

Stefano sat on the bird's perch, in a tall leather easy chair, where he spent many hours doing computer simulations, "Buddy, what the hell does it matter? Maybe none of this is really destined to be. Witness how easily those sisters of yours did you in. All over jealousy. Especially their anger that Maria's accidental death is your fault!

"Don't let my sisters know anything about us going to the biospheres. Let them go back to LiteWave enamored with Zohar. And let them know that Zohar and I are friends."

"Alexander, maybe, just maybe, it's the system of things. Maybe it's our Western way of thinking that prevents us from finding the solution to radiation problems in our nuclear fusion driver. You've looked at Zohar's tachyon wave driver. And you're unclear on how the driver feeds itself. We've got controlled nuclear fusion. They've got---?" Stefano, of course, was speaking out of his own selfish concern for his future sale of Alexander's technology to ICARUS/NASA.

Zohar paced among the two young men. "The Big Eyes, they have hundreds of thousands of years of history. The history of Western Civilization, on which I've read volumes, is quite short. And there is little mention of my society. Dwellers in the Zagros range. They have no idea of how technologically advanced we were compared to the tribes in neighboring cities and other regions of the Zagros and Mesopotamia and India."

"Well then, Zohar, our meeting you is just a cruel casualty of fate. And a marvelous experience that just feels right. I felt that I was riding the waves of fate to a fortuitous conclusion. The earth with all of its complexity, cultures, and inequities, was ripe for my style of thinking--solutions for grand international problems, even ecological puzzles of today, transportation for this century and beyond."

Zohar listened intently, as he climbed a few steps of the ladder to the cockpit of his vehicle. "Now you're talking Big Eye talk. Ecology, biology, genetic engineering, horticulture. From their perspective, they lump it all into one category... agricultural science. My guess is that they were an agrarian people who mastered modern technology. They once had massive cities, crime, and disease, in Andromeda. And because of all of the dehumanization and crime in urban centers, they reverted back to the countryside and intellectually retrofitted all sciences into an agricultural model."

Stefano boomed, "Well, don't they have leadership, centers for government? Organizations like ICARUS and NASA hungry for virtual particle technology?"

"Great centers. And each center is a biosphere of some nature. With them, designing biospheres is an art form that creates distinctive life styles for their wealthy bureaucrats."

Stefano was afire with enthusiasm. "To live and die here, Alexander, trying to create user-safe virtual particle technology is sounding a lot less appealing than a scholarly sabbatical in the biospheres. Let's go! Let's see what an advanced culture envisages as high living!"

Alexander's curiosity was also piqued. "For a moment their, Stefano, you sounded like you'd rather privately do your own business with ICARUS. So what of the Big Eyes? You said that they disappeared at some point, Zohar. You employed everyone to help you build the biosphere interiors with sound ecological design and then took off into space. Where did the Big Eyes depart to?"

"When I try to think it through. I get lost. I honestly don't know. I now suspect that they're living in the earth's rain forests. They practice stealth. They're only seen when they want to be seen. They operate continual experiments for the School of Agriculture of the Andromedan Federation."

Stefano got angry. "It's always the same thing, Zohar, you don't know, and they're hiding out somewhere. How might we find them?"

Zohar intimated that there could be a way, a possibility: peruse the National Science Foundation Archives for never-before discovered species of animals. "Probably good ones to look for are fishes. From what I've been reading new species of fish just appear--unpredictably. Assumed to be tens of millions of years old. Likewise for insects. They do it--them, the Big Eyes--to balance the ecology, they create new species. They consider themselves guardian angels and wouldn't permit this planet to just degrade into total chaos, entropy, and cataclysm. They're around. And maybe that's how to find them."

"Find them?" Stefano said quizzically.

"Yes. Where the new species appears. The Big Eyes may not be far away."

"But, Zohar," Alexander insisted, "if a new species is filling an ecological void, the species appears where the need exists, not where the Big Eyes set up camp."

Zohar smiled, "Yes, and that's where they camp, where the voids exist. There may be many camps in the rain forests. Believe me, trust me, they don't wish to be known. We had quite a miserable time adapting to their ways. And they made themselves apparent only because they espoused the belief that my people were all about to perish -- due to purges, pillaging, rape, murder, and the ultimate destruction a bacterial, virile plague."

"Well, I can imagine with all of the work you were involved in, with all the time that passed, with all of the requirements and details that had to be attended to, to get the biospheres into orbit, Zohar, that you would be unclear on many issues. No wonder you speak with so many contradictions! But when I net it all out in my mind, I trust you."

"Thank you, Alexander." Then Zohar looked at Stefano. "Can you trust him, Alexander?"

"Trust? How does anyone trust an emerging predator? But we'll go to the biospheres and I won't complain or worry about you, Stefano. Because, the more and more suspicious I become of you, a blood relative, the more I hate myself. Right now I need more self love, the greatest love of all. Wouldn't you say?

Chapter 21
Finding The Way

Few preparations were required to visit the biospheres. Alexander's primary concern was the passage of time; he feared losing track of earth time. Stefano had no intention of losing track of time. The Andromedans had resolved all of the technological issues of utilizing virtual particles, waves, effects, for anti-gravity propulsion for interstellar travel. Stefano wanted to know everything about Alexander's technology, virtual particle drivers, to sell it to ICARUS.

Before departing, Stefano had a telephone conversation with Doctor Charley Tong, of ICARUS, in Hong Kong. "Listen, Charley. I'm on top of things. I have to take a trip with Alexander to iron out the final details of our transaction...some technological issues."

"Like its so trivial." Tong could not disguise his skepticism. "No I doubt it, Stefano. You've fallen down on the job. I've heard nothing positive from you in months."

"Charley, give it time. You'll hear positive things."

"Caught up in that family web that I warned you about? Off to visit the anomaly?"

"How would you know about that? Jessica?"

"We have intelligence, Stefano. You're treading on very thin ice. And who knows what might happen out there?"

Stefano was bored with the conversation. "Hold tight, give me a few months and we'll have control of the technology to make us both...very rich."

That afternoon, the four of them--Alexander, Andrea, Stefano, Zohar--were climbing into the cockpit of the space vehicle when, to their surprise, Sophia asked to join them. Jessica, having regained her senses (after, her psychedelic trauma in the Indonesian rain forest) remained at corporate headquarters. They all strapped themselves into their seats as Zohar manipulated the crystal controls. They were off! The ship jumped to five thousand feet and hovered.

"Okay, Boss!"

Zohar spoke, "Okay, Boss, would you like to pilot this craft?"

Alexander felt squeamish, inadequate. "Actually, I probably need to learn slowly and now isn't the time."

"No better time than the present."

Alexander's high-back leather chair was on the elevated turret next to Zohar's chair. The chairs were mounted in a tight circle with their backs toward each other The ergonomically engineered pilot control panels faced the outer perimeter of the cockpit.

Alexander got it into his head that something terrible might happen to them all, yet, while feeling concerned, impulsively he felt obliged to take the ship for a final tour around the planet. "Okay, Zohar, let's just enjoy ourselves like one of those arcade games. We're going for a ride. Everyone strapped in?" He pushed down on the crystal controls with excitement, and the vehicle quickly accelerated to half light speed on a vector toward the sun with the impulsive movement of his hands and fingers.

The design of the craft prevented them from instant death from tremendous "G" forces. Accelerating beyond the atmosphere in a moment, the sun appeared to diminish in size and changed in appearance. It was a bright hot star; within ninety seconds, it began to grow more brilliant.

Zohar was sweating. "It's fun now, but in a few more minutes, it will be disastrous. This is not the recommended procedure for approaching a star. Let's alter our course." Zohar leaned forward and made some adjustments that altered their course. "Can you find your way back to earth?"

"Actually, I don't think so," Alexander replied.

Andrea screeched, "Please, please, please take me back to earth. I can't go with you to the biospheres. I'm too freaked out." At that moment, Sophia's chair moved on an arc toward Andrea, when Zohar requested that Sophia console her. Sophia took Andrea's hand and convinced Andrea that her fear would pass.

Meanwhile, Alexander took note of his inability to control the vehicle and started to take instructions from Zohar-- and, so did Stefano. All three chairs were at the control area. "Let's use the earth as our point of reference. First we'll fly side to side, side to side; then, we'll alter our pattern to up and down, up and down." With all eyes on earth, now several million miles in the distance, it appeared to be a bright glittering star, as it moved away from them.

Andrea pleaded emotionally, painfully; "Come on now, let's just get closer to the earth before it disappears. Please I just can't stand it."

"Andrea, dear, I was reacting the same way when it was my first time." Sophia But now this is all strangely alluring. Let the strangeness of feeling infinitesimally small and insignificant go from your heart and the fear will be manageable. Give your mind free reign over your animal nature, subconscious emotional feelings and images that bring security." Sophia's voice was consoling to Andrea who shook her head in agreement and took a deep swallow.

"How come men handle it so well?" Andrea moaned.

After some immeasurable period of time of learning to guide the vehicle, Stefano and Alexander took turns flying back toward earth with strictly hand eye co-ordination; no on-board computer was used; no computerized heads-up display was available to compute an intersect course. Alexander was curious about deep space flight and parallax. How did this vehicle compute parallax, and parallax per second of arc (parsecs), when approaching a distant star?

Zohar laughed heartily, "Come on now, Alexander. I've never left the solar system on my own volition. I just don't know the technology built into this vehicle for deep space flight. I've managed to find my way around the solar system. Locating Technosphere at ninety-nine percent of light speed, beyond Pluto's, my navigational challenge."

Stefano turned his expression quizzically toward Zohar. "But you're admitting that you've left the solar system under someone else's control. Just how far did you go?"

There was something-- mild paranoia-- embedded in that question. Each of them felt some fear about Zohar, now that they were at his mercy in outer space. Was he really from earth? Or might he be a clever visitor from another star? Another galaxy? With an unknown agenda? What was to happen to them, as they accelerated to ninety-one percent of light speed to visit the biospheres? Were they ever coming back? Stefano and Alexander seemed to agree with short glances at Zohar, then back to each other!

"But, Alexander, you only recently said that you trust me."

Suppressing his fear, looking over at Stefano, then back at Zohar, Alexander responded, "Well, of course I trust you. You're being silly, Stefano. Let's keep going with the flow. Let's go for that learning curve and experience operating this vehicle. Let's approach our visit to the biospheres with an open mind."

Zohar got the emotional signal as he responded, "Stefano. That's how I felt about the Big Eyes all of the time. I didn't trust them...ever! So I understand that you don't trust me. Arlee--she trusts them. The citizens of the biospheres never think about them. That's my job."

Andrea felt extremely insecure. "But, Zohar, if the Big Eyes are such benevolent, magnanimous ecologists, why don't you trust them?"

"For the same reason that Stefano doesn't trust me. You just don't know. You just never know. Their history is truly ancient, hundreds of thousands of years old. Exactly how many millennia I don't know. What humans call ancient history, as they await the messiah, is a split second in the ocean of time."

Andrea was surprised. "And you, you know about the messiah?"

"Of course. It makes sense. Especially if you ever meet Arlee, the self-proclaimed goddess of eternal life. And when I came to earth I saw churches across Philadelphia where they maintained different standards of architecture for cathedrals, signaling a common human desire, the coming of the messiah."

"If you truly trust me let's forget your little farewell to earth and let's get to the biospheres. You won't regret it."

Alexander took an eyeball-to-eyeball consensus. With all of their anxiety and fear, there were no negative votes. When, Alexander turned his attention to the controls, "Okay, no farewell to earth today, no showing off, let's just go about our business." Zohar guided Alexander and Stefano toward Jupiter. Zohar used Jupiter to locate the asteroid belt, and once finding the asteroid belt, he sought the biospheres. In about one hundred and seventeen minutes they hovered far above the north pole of Jupiter. Stefano angled the ship in order to observe the surface of the great planet. It was awe-inspiring. Each person's attention was drawn to some feature of the planet. Most notable was a massive storm system on Jupiter that had been visible to earthly astronomers for centuries.

Sophia was awe-struck. "And what's the story behind the endless storms of Jupiter?"

Andrea's eyes watered. "Oh god, this is the most magnificent thing that I've ever seen, beheld. I just can't believe what a massive object it is. And those occasional streaks of light…streaking right by us!"

Zohar spoke in warm sincerity. "Yes, Andrea, space travelers, time travelers. Looks like streaks of light. I know that I'm not ready for that level of existence."

Stefano was impatient. "Don't you know the anomaly's orbit around the sun in relation to other stars, so that we can calculate and intersect their orbit? Can't you calculate an intersect vector? This tin can reach light speed."

"It can fly up to light speed. No, we don't want to get up to light speed. No, I'm not a great navigator. But just a moment while I handle this novice in space warfare." Then Zohar smiled. "We won't miss the biospheres!"

Andrea spoke softly, intimately, "Tell me, is anyone in the biospheres not from earth?"

Himself uncharacteristically fearful, frantic, Stefano worried out lout, "Just who says that any humans lives in the biospheres? Who says? Maybe they just have us out here to kill us. Keep us quiet. What do we really know about you, Zohar?"

"They're all from earth, Andrea. But few of them are as good at calculating numbers, charting navigational vectors, doing quick computations as you current earthlings. In fact, I doubt that the Andromedans are any better at designing and programming digital computers than you current earthlings. If we ever find the Andromedans, you will have a difficult time comprehending their version of patience, Stefano, because you have none."

"What are you so angry about, pal?"

"Right now, Stefano, I am angry. But only for the moment, and for the moment I'm not your pal. One of the reasons that the funding for your project was cut is because of the way you earthlings think. Everything is calculated in probabilities--the probability of profitability, the probability of virtual particle discovery...calculate, quantify. Does anyone from earth have one original thought anymore?"

Stefano took a long hard look at Zohar, "Well, you've got the advantage on us at the moment, Pal."

"And there you go again--Pal! I'm not looking for any greater advantage. Because you've got a collective fear of discovery. Does everyone want to go back? I'll take you back."

Alexander spoke up, "Who wants to go back?"

Before there was a chance to answer, an alarm began to sound. Zohar took an eye-ball consensus of the group who looked toward the biospheres that they were fast approaching. Each of them felt anxiety about visiting a truly foreign culture-- yet they proceeded.

Andrea spoke first. "Well, there really are biospheres! My god, they're huge!"

Stefano chided, "This is a set-up. Those spheres are orbiting the sun about every fifty some days by my calculation. Just how is it that we're up here the day that they pass closest to the earth?"

Alexander spoke to Stefano, "Come on, have some patience. If we had gone off blasting torpedoes at the ICARUS squad, listening to your paranoia, we'd have missed this for another seven weeks."

Zohar spoke, "Yes, yes, we all know exactly what you mean, that none of you trust me. You wanted relief from the stress back 'at corporate,' as you fondly put it. Well now you're going to witness a different way of life. Essentially stress free."

They docked with the lead biosphere of the anomaly of seven. There were docking facilities at the central width axis along the longitudinal plane of the cylindrical structure. During the docking process--opening, moving into, and closing the interlock chambers (that maintained thirty pounds per square inch air pressure)--they were still in a weightless state but remained strapped into their chairs. Their vehicle was maneuvered onto a pedestal where the vehicle locked down. Then the pedestal, with the vehicle attached, sank into a tunnel that terminated at a staging area, where there was beautiful sunlight and tropical gardens. As they finished the entire docking procedure, the passengers were in a nervous sweat but pleasantly surprised at the interior view of the biosphere.

With a diameter of some four miles and a circumference of twelve point five miles, there was room to roam, especially since, the biosphere was sixteen miles wide and offered the inhabitants two hundred square miles of usable space--which were two hundred square miles of lush beauty. There were mountains with stone peaks up to six thousand feet. There were lakes, streams; so, there were fish; many species of fresh water fish. There were agricultural wonders of hydroponics, hundreds of species of edible vegetables, flowers, seeds, grains, and fruits.

Zohar popped the canopy of the cockpit, as each of them, including Zohar, was pleased to be there. They each descended the ladder and followed Zohar down a long path with tall ferns and palms arching over it. They came to a huge square constructed from course white marble slabs; in the fountains, naked women and children played. A beautiful young woman, with no inhibition about her nudity, walked right up to Stefano and smiled. He smiled back.

Zohar smiled, "Alexander, Stefano, Andrea, Sophia--feel free to join them in the fountains. If you're shy about taking off your clothes, you won't be for long. It's just a way of life here. Clothes are for the evenings. And when you're hungry just go into any of the pavilions where there's plenty of food for all. I'll be back."

There were so many pavilions around the square, that they didn't know which to pick. They wondered along the periphery of the fountains, where many young female beauties lazed about and spoke in unusual pitches and sounds. Stefano removed his shoes, his pants, his shirt, and climbed into the fountain, when a few playful kids pulled off his boxer shorts. The four of them were quite a curiosity. They didn't manifest the natural healthy glow which was indigenous to the natives who were curious about these unhealthy appearing specimens. A few young women motioned to Andrea and Sophia to join them in the fountain. Andrea feigned a smile and spoke, "No thanks, no thanks, I'll just keep my clothes on for now."

The young women natives who invited them in looked at each other with surprise, as they mimicked the sound and resonation of the American language. They were appalled by it. With rather concerned expressions, they looked at Andrea--as if they pitied her.

Andrea turned to Stefano. "Did you see how they looked at me? They're all so perfect in physique, proportion, structure, skin tone, skin smoothness, hair, teeth, eyes. They're really beautiful. I feel like a beast."

Stefano replied, "Not you, Andrea, never." Then without another thought, he dove into the fountain and swam among the natives. Alexander, feeling down and distraught, peeled of his clothes and climbed to the edge of the fountain. He dove in and swam among the natives.

Andrea and Sophia now followed his lead. It was glorious. Alexander did a long slow back stroke across a half-mile pool which was filled with breathtaking fountains. Andrea and Sophia followed right along with Alexander, as he shouted, "This is just--is just an architectural feat, stupendous, magnificent, awesome, beautiful! To look up and see mountains is purely incredible! I could stay here forever and never tire of the beauty."

Andrea joined in. "Just the light is breathtaking. Sometimes it's white, then it changes to dancing prisms of colored light through the white light. And it bounces and blasts all about, then it lingers in the sprays of water, then dances through the jets and sprays and splashes. Good, god, I've died and gone to heaven!"

Sophia agreed yet she spoke with an edge of fear and concern, "But Andrea, where are the men? Where in the hell are the men? I don't think that they have day time jobs here."

"Well, dear, get into Zohar, get to know him. He wants to know you!"

Andrea continued her soft backstroke. The water was warm and nudity was not a concern. Eventually the four of them swam back to their clothes. Physically they felt rather inadequate, because every woman was a near-perfect specimen with firm derrieres, firm breasts, firm bodies, firm limbs, beautiful faces, healthy hair, and healthy smiles. Picking up their clothes from the edge of the pool, they wondered to a pavilion at the far edge of the marble square, at the edge of breathtaking stone cliffs. Next to the stone cliffs were raging waterfalls--a mile across and a mile high. Gazing about they realized that they were on a plateau. Somewhat fearfully peering over the edge, they saw stone and marble homes built along the valley's hillsides. And down deep in the valley, there were the men playing water sports. Alexander was totally choked up. "This is...this is, my god, this is the most spectacular place that I've ever seen! Just take it all in. I just can't believe this place. And to think that I mistrusted Zohar for a moment"

"Likewise," Andrea toned in, as they all shook their heads in agreement with glee and awe in their eyes.

Chapter 22
Higher Evolution

Alexander, Stefano, Andrea, and Sophia rested and hibernated for what seemed to be (in earth time) two and a half months. Following their hibernation time, at 91 percent of light speed, when they underwent metabolic optimization, biologically transformed internally, their only external changes were improved skin, improved musculature, improving their features to the human eye. In a Technosphere, at 96 percent of light speed, the eyes began to mutate -- the big eyed syndrome set in, as it had for Arlee. The hibernation period in the biospheres, two and half months subjective time, was fifteen point one eight years in actual earth calendar time.

When they awoke from hibernation, they were initiants into a new life style; they learned from those who mastered verbal communications with simultaneous message content. Verbal communications in the biospheres contained a primary message with words, sentences, and phrases; further, there was a heightened awareness of the emotional subtext. Verbal communication had a feeling of greater emotional satisfaction than it did on earth. To go from English to spoken "Biosphere" was a smoother transition than from Biosphere to English -- variations of vowel sounds connoted present, past, future, future perfect, and pluperfect. Evolving to a higher level of emotional communications, the biosphere method of speech contained a greater range of sound pitches than used by the speakers when they left the earth five thousand years earlier.

Social policies in the biosphere were also at a higher level of evolution--the housing programs, population growth, public works programs, all were more controlled and in harmony with the environment. The inhabitants of the biospheres had learned about marble as a building material in addition to their traditional use of wood. A palatial white marble building was erected in honor of Alexander, Andrea, Sophia, and Stefano; it was their residence for as long as they chose to remain residents of this first biosphere. The oak wood floors and handsome light pine furniture were imported from the seventh biosphere--the one that contained all of the industry required to support the eight million inhabitants of the biospheres.

The first four biospheres contained most of the inhabitants of these space colonies; the fifth in orbit supported the extensive grasslands and forest that were the preserves of wild life of all sorts, including buffalo, and their natural predators, mountain lions, jaguars, wolves and panthers; the sixth in orbit contained the various educational institutions and sports facilities; the seventh in orbit contained all the manufacturing facilities--saw mills, pottery kilns, candle making, tanneries, garment manufacturing, stone cutting, glass making, rubber processing, and a modest metallurgical installation for processing iron and rare metals--as well as advanced research laboratories for projects such as tachyon wave crystal research.

Tachyon wave crystal processing was the most notable feature of their technological development. As a result of the writings and teachings of the Andromedan colonists, this space-born culture never developed a need to invent devices that utilized electricity. It was a profound difference from earth cultures. Hybrid heavy element crystals were used for lighting and generating energy, a variation of their tachyon wave driver; their crystals generated energy without an external source. Their perception of energy consumption was quite different from earth's inhabitants in the 21st Century.

Also tachyon wave crystals were engineered, by the Andromedan Founders of the biospheres, to maintain the ambient weather patterns in each biosphere. The crystals could create and control, in their limited space, high and low pressure systems for maintaining rainfall; this meant that no irrigation was ever necessary for growing optimal crops in their hydroponics pools.

The second biosphere maintained a climate and ecology similar to that of New England's; it's ambient temperature was cooler than the first biosphere's. All plants, including oak and maple trees had curious growth patterns, because the light came from the sides of the biospheres and not from overhead. This biosphere contained pine, birch, maple, and oak forests with homes nestled among the unusually shaped trees. It was densely populated, but nothing like an earthbound city--there were no roads, only trails for walking and bicycling. They had invented their version of bicycle tires, with Andromedan rubber processing; they had not discovered rubber on their own--this was a different kind of rubbery compound.

The third biosphere had a greater variation of terrain than the first or second with a greater array of wooded forests and rain forests. The rain forests, which had unusually shaped trees and plants, existed in the low lands and contained creatures found in the Amazon and North American sub-tropical regions. The fourth biosphere was an urban center for commerce, science, and technology. There were some buildings as high as ten stories; the architectural style tended toward multi-angled granite walls forming buildings like earth's great cathedrals--some had large rooms with high domed or angled wooden ceilings.

In order to procure all of the necessary raw materials necessary to support this way of life, Zohar had been assigned to co-ordinate their acquisition before the biospheres' inhabitants migrated into space. He had spent more than two decades on this task.

"How did they persuade you to co-ordinate this massive undertaking and load the biospheres with all of the millions of tons of materials necessary to sustain not only life, but an opulent life style?" Alexander asked Zohar.

They sat at the gazebo on the square, near fountains that overlooked Alexander's new home at the base of the falls. Zohar explained. "The Andromedan Big Eyes had the technology to load the biospheres with heavy natural materials. Arlee's father was believed by the people. He was our Dravidian prophet leading us out of the plague to a promised land. The Adromedan's Big Eyes appeared in our colony when I was a young man. They found Arlee's father who guided them to me, an architect, mathematician and teacher. I wasn't the only engineering type--there were many. I compare our culture to ancient Greeks. We developed Hellenistic ideals after many long internal struggles of the heart and mind. Yet Western Historians knew nothing of our cultural advancement to a Hellenistic stage. It's endemic to the Western ethnocentric bias. I see now why the American Indians learned to hate contemporary white men who can be so damned self-centered, self-serving, and painfully narrow minded."

Alexander nodded, "How have your learned so much, Zohar? But remember, your culture pre-dates our detailed historical knowledge; records. Don't be angry. No one knew, or still knows of the Indo-Aryans of the Zagros to this day. Still I see your point..."

"I've returned from my visit to earth with many books on the ancient Greeks, the Chinese Dynasties, Hinduism, Buddhism, and many treatises on the body politick of the earth...today. But mostly I love Greek tragedy and mythological variations of Zeus."

Alexander smiled. "This is all too fantastic, too difficult to believe. Why did these Andromedans choose to avail themselves of humans--if, as you say, they practice total stealth?"

"I really don't know. Certainly it was not a chance meeting. Their culture is hundreds of thousands of years old. Most likely, earth has a very special place in their research and in their hearts."

"So how do you feel about that?"

"Awful! For me, to live and die on earth was sufficient to my view of human nature. Arlee's an egotistical bitch who's addicted to her private blissful visions, her spiritual nature...to the loss of her animal and human natures. And if you ask me, all she's addicted to are her own endorphins!"

"My god, man, how did you learn about endorphins?"

"Alexander. I've been alive for five thousand earth years. Who knows? Who's counting? I'm their student--of those men from Andromeda who are bio-engineers, medical scientists, although as always, the bastards refer to themselves as agricultural scientists."

" Bastards? Why?"

"You'll see, you'll see. You want to design a tachyon wave driver? Help me design one that will burn perpetually without Andromedan intervention."

To understand the Andromedan Tachyon Wave Driver, Alexander had to learn the Andromedan alphabet; so, he spent long relaxing afternoons studying at the fountains in the square with Andrea, who learned the customs of the natives.

Finding him totally irresistible, Sophia went to live with Zohar; she temporarily changed residence, to the academies and sports centers biosphere, where Stefano was enamored with a sport, that recently developed in their sports world, snow wing competition. The snow wing was fabricated from light weight materials into a delta wing shape, a basic triangle. From the top of the triangle, the front of the snow wing, to the back of the snow wing, the base of the triangle, the distance was eleven feet; the base of the triangle was nine feet. At about the mid-point of the wing, from the base to the apex of the triangle, there was a wire stretched across two posts which ran parallel to the base. The wire was stretched three feet above the standing surface; the wire gave the snow wing operator something to grasp in case he or she lost their balance in a swift descent down a snow-covered mountain slope, or during microtachyon wave propelled flying turns. The standing surface of the wing was covered with a gritty material to give the feet a good grasp on the surface. In the center of the wing, toward the rear, there was a stick that pointed to the front, the pinnacle of the triangle. The operator lifted the stick in order for the snow wing to become airborne, to lower the ailerons. The stick also moved from left to right, right to left, to guide the snow rudders that guided the wing through the snow; right to left, left to right. The stick controlled the snow wing, when airborne, for in-flight turning and banking.

A snow wing rider's bent leg posture and sideways stance appeared quite similar to a surfer on a surf board; as the snow wing charged down a steep snow covered mountain side, the rider sometimes grasped the three foot high horizontal wire during his surfer like foot movements to maintain his balance. At some point in the descent down a snow-covered slope, with ground speed reaching ninety-nine miles an hour, the rider pulled up on the stick and the snow wing became airborne. Freely rushing through the air, the rider used his body weight and the control stick to guide the snow wing to the lake below. The waves on the lake, which was ten miles across at the shore, were in the range of twelve to sixteen feet high. The goal was to guide the snow wing down the slope, become airborne and ride the wing to the lake to catch a wave in mid-flight and surf the wave to the shore. It was extremely exciting to watch and extremely intense to perform. It took months and months of practice to be able to operate the snow wing efficiently enough to catch a wave on the lake. Most performers leapt from the wing, before crashing it into the lake to avoid personal catastrophe!

Yet there were other profound problems associated with manipulating and maneuvering the snow wing.

In reality there was no gravity, only centrifugal force; therefore, if the snow wing did not continue on its downward momentum, the rider might get caught in the swirl, updrafts associated with the biosphere rotating on its longitudinal axis. The rider might never come down; in order to circumvent this event, the designers added micro tachyon wave drivers at the tips of the wing to drive the wing down in case of an unavoidable updraft, that might cause the ailerons to be ineffective. The micro drivers were controlled by a button on the control stick which was used to provide lift off from the snow; once airborne, pushing the button would propel the snow wing down toward the lake. Like most overconfident sporting enthusiasts, eventually with practice, the riders pushed the snow wing to higher speeds, when catching a wave was an art form. They risked life and limb. With great speed, agility, an enthusiast could ride the pipe of a wave for miles, if he caught the wave far enough from the shore. Hundreds of thousands of people came out for the day, when the snow wing competitions were on. It was a great spectacle judged on balance, style, performance, precision and speed.

Some super enthusiasts wanted to create a new competition, where the rider drove the snow wing into the updrafts, doing a three hundred sixty degree ride through the sky, then came down again on a mountain slope to eventually lift off again to ride down to the lake to catch a wave.

In his collegiate days, at CalTech, Stefano did some surfing; the Pacific Ocean waves occasionally had the height, curl and pipe of these biosphere waves which were like the waves of Hawaii and Australia. (The Andromedans created these artificial waves, and ambient snow conditions for their own sport, back in their ancient time frames). Stefano enrolled with the snow wing contingent. He was a novice. Stefano wore the swimwear of the day that was quite similar to American swimwear in variation, style, and color--bright, baggy multi-colored trunks.

Many of the experienced snow wing enthusiasts, who did many rides per day, wore wet suits, because the lake temperature was never above sixty-five degrees. At the top of the mountain peak, in the staging area, about seven thousand feet above the lake level, Stefano spoke with his coach who suggested more aerobic training for Stefano. "Listen, Son, your cardiovascular development program will improve your performance. For now just get used to the feel of the vehicle and we'll be getting you into better physical condition. Caution for now. Don't emulate the tricks just yet because there's a lot of agility and strength involved." Stefano didn't like the assessment, but reality was reality; and through enthusiastic continued participation in the program, his physical stature improved, and he became very tight, cut, toned. His body developed its own exterior armor, as his deep sub-conscious mind wanted to go to physical war with Alexander; beat Alexander; physically punish and humiliate Alexander.

Chapter 23
Sibling Rivalry

Several weeks later Alexander and Andrea took a shuttle to the sixth biosphere, where Zohar and Sophia were staying. Stefano was enamored with all of the beautiful women--from his perspective, one more beautiful and exotic than the next.

They attended a class in theater and life styles, modeled after an Andromedan precedent. Alexander, Andrea, Zohar, Sophia, and even Stefano, went to the event. They sat in body-molded oaken marble-based chairs which formed a theater in the round; it was open-air--no roof; the seating sloped down to the stage bowl at the bottom. The seating capacity was two thousand people. Alexander, Andrea, Zohar, Sophia, and Stefano sat in the front row.

The instructor took the stage and gazed at the four visitors from earth. The instructor suffered a great curiosity about the four and their perception of life in the biospheres; more intense was the instructor's curiosity about their personal lives. Until Zohar returned to earth at the orders of Arlee, earth was believed, by the biosphere inhabitants, to possibly be void of people due to plagues.

The instructor a tall slim man, graying at the temples, appeared anguished, "For those of you who don't know me, I'm Malzon. And today I possess an infinite curiosity about our home planet for which we've developed all types of myths and folklore. But today the myths are dispelled, the illusions shattered. Earth--as I hear it from Zohar--is a place of great cities, billions of people, a place possessed of high levels of personal stress. At one time we lived through great stress; curiously enough, we're all still here to talk about it thousands of earth years later. It seems maybe a hundred years ago that we left earth."

By this time the theater was full of curiosity-seekers who wanted to hear more, and the instructor motioned to Andrea and Sophia to step forward. Each was reticent about the request. They looked at each other with uncertainty. Wearing short semi-transparent cotton tunics drawn at the waste, the ladies self-consciously came to the stage. The instructor, Malzon, backed away from them, as he spoke, "Here are two women, visitors from earth. Each of them was nurtured under stressful conditions--life on earth! Do you agree, Andrea, Sophia?"

Andrea looked toward Sophia; in a moment, through a series of uncomfortable gestures toward one and other, Andrea agreed to speak first. "Well it seems that we are a great curiosity to all of you.. And I'm quite uncomfortable about this because I worry that we might be judged before we're known to all of you. But I feel quite comfortable with your hospitality and friendliness. Compared to life on earth, life here in the spheres would be described in earth terms as…Shangri-La."

Nervously, she looked toward Sophia who spoke. "Well, they say that confession is good for the soul. And I'll confess to you that the primary reason that we're here today is because of a sibling rivalry. A rivalry between my brother, Alexander, who sits there, and my older sister and myself. Had this rivalry not led to a complex unresolved situation, the untimely death of our mother, we wouldn't be here today. So while earth is quite different from these spheres, I believe that sibling rivalry is something that we can all relate to…both you, citizens of the spheres, and us from earth. We all deal with our familial pressures in different ways. And moreover manifest those same problems, differently, within our peer groups."

Malzon nodded in agreement, "Indeed, Sophia, child development is critical to the success of any society. And what we observe here in the spheres are the possible emotional blocks to varied areas and regions of the mind through emotional trauma, misplaced anger, mixed emotional symbols, mixed emotional metaphors, as the result of confusion in our early lives. Let's do a little exercise in life styles and theater, if you would? Let's test our psyches for conflicts; if not obvious conflicts, problems. Explore our animal, human and spiritual natures…"

Zohar smiled and intoned, "From what I've read, on earth, they call this type of exercise 'thematic apperception,' of a sort."

Sophia looked toward Andrea who shrugged her shoulders; why not? Sophia responded, "I'll do my best to participate, and 'apperceive.'"

"All this exercise requires is a response. It does not have to be the truth, in any way accurate. It must be spontaneous. Without precognition, please don't think about my questions, just respond. You can fabricate answers as much as you please. So, Sophia, I saw you at the library of the academies today. And I was enamored with your beauty. However, I was amazed at your surprise to see your father in the library. You appeared anxious and tried to avoid him. Why?"

"My father?"

"Well, not actually. Of course, Sophia, he wasn't there. This is just an exercise in spontaneity, responsiveness. So. I noted your surprise at seeing your father in the library today. You were anxious. Why?"

She smiled, "Well, you see…ahhh….my father doesn't approve of my relationship with Zohar…he was nearby in one of the aisles scanning biosphere literature. I didn't want dad to make the association."

"Of course. When I spoke to your father he was quite thrilled with the idea that Zohar and your sister were kind of a…thing, Dad thought that Zohar and your sister were in love."

"It doesn't surprise me that dad would respond that way. Know something that I didn't and never communicate it to me in small talk. Dad was like that. He preferred that I learn the lessons of life, and painful ones at that totally…the hard way. He was like that with my sister and I, yet he engaged in elaborate explanations, and discussions, with his eldest child, Alexander."

"Why is that? Did he favor your brother?"

"Of course!"

"Your father and brother? Does that relationship disturb you?"

Sophia looked at Alexander, "It was a relationship based on pride. Father was an inventor. He didn't believe that women could suffice as inventors, only men. And worse, Alexander is a spitting image of my dad. Dad owned a major corporation that developed technology. Father did preliminary, missionary, work on virtual wave drivers and passed the project on to Alexander. My sister and I never knew of the research.

Of course our jealousy was fueled by the attitude that women are less competent than men. A Russian sexist attitude."

"Funny, Sophia, but your father and I discussed that very attitude. He felt that you and your sister possessed too frivolous of natures to pursue such intense technological endeavors. How do you feel about that?"

"Angry. We were never given a chance. And now due to twists of fate, due to my own indiscretions and stupid pride, I find myself here. A visitor in a strange and beautiful world. But my anger is fading. I want to know more about living here. It's a beautiful and meaningful life style, one that seems to stimulate and preserve the best in people."

Malzon was amazed. "Well. That was an exercise with a very honest woman. Is the misplaced emotional symbol here...pride?"

Sophia nodded affirmatively, "Yes, of course, me a proud woman versus family pride. The symbol of a confused family relationship."

Malzon came closer to the women and motioned to Sophia to be seated, as he turned his attention toward Andrea. "After I left the library today, Andrea. I saw you with Stefano. You were holding hands--which surprised me. I thought I saw you kiss Stefano. Isn't that unusual under the circumstances?"

"I felt very lonely today. Like always, Alexander hasn't been paying much attention to me and spent most of his time with Zohar who seems to have a place in Alexander's heart. I'm quite lonely. I'm totally in love with Alexander. And he's got his vision of the world. The world according to Alexander is a place that needs to be conquered, in a self-styled disciplined way. Not outright conquered, just certain things. And maybe I wanted to make him jealous. I want to motivate him to conquer me, if I choose to be conquered."

"So in this case, while Alexander and Stefano are cousins, you found it personally acceptable to use Stefano to your own ends?"

"Actually it's more complex than that. I'm also in love with Stefano. If I hadn't met Alexander first, I could permit myself to fall madly in love with Stefano. And it has occurred to me that Stefano is the better choice. But I'm obsessed with Alexander. And obsession is a difficult thing to conquer...territorial, animal in nature."

"Another emotionally mixed symbol here; obsession? Confusing, difficult to deal with, emotions are unable to find free expression; locked into one confusing driven obsession." Malzon motioned to Andrea to have a seat, as he beckoned Alexander and Stefano to the stage.

Alexander and Stefano were bolder than the women who were the pioneers for the apperception exercise, as Malzon continued. "Life styles. Conquer obsession? Not too likely. It's something that needs to be unconquered. Funny, that word, 'conquer,' Alexander, I just heard someone mention today that you were conquered by your sisters in a struggle for pride? The person I spoke to shall remain nameless. This person intimates that pride is at the very core of your nature."

Alexander's head snapped back, "Well, Malzon, your exercise in spontaneous life situations takes on a tone of instant relevance. You've gotten right to the core of our natures. But you didn't develop that pride is my problem the way you developed the problems of the ladies. You just assumed it. What's that a product of?"

Malzon smiled at Alexander, "Yes, Alexander. Then explain this to me if you would. Someone observed you studying one of the shuttle crafts. It seems that only certain things interest you. Can I assume from that, the grander scope of curiosities escape you?"

"No, Counselor, you shouldn't assume anything. Form a hypothesis-- maybe. But that's as close as we come to assuming. Assumption is prejudicing any situation by assuming one's correctness."

"And in science and technology, Alexander, after many years of research, hypothesizing, postulating, theorizing, testing the theory-- don't we still assume. Don't we assume our character and personality as deep internal spontaneous beliefs? Our innate human natures?""

"Maybe, well yes...we do. The life of a scientist should purely entail the scientific method. But I would be a fool to say that anyone can always recognize when he's assuming something...based on, of course, his deepest spontaneous beliefs. No one can claim to have never assumed, for that would be...inhuman. We assume more than we can ever scientifically prove. And we all assume much more than we'll ever admit to. Because we'd go insane having to prove everything before taking action. And I like to take action more than I enjoy scientific endeavor. And isn't that the crux of the weakness of humankind...impatience, a strong desire for action overrides even the most mindful reflective individuals. I want action. I want change. I seek to empower change and that's what really makes me human. And when things don't go my way, when I implicitly believe that I'm right, which is only an assumption...then, and only then, am I truly showing my human nature."

"But were you empowering your will when you came to the spheres? What could you hope to accomplish in scientific endeavors by coming here?"

"I thought that I knew why...why I decided to come here. To study the teachings of the Andromedans. But when I was removed from my environment, I realized that my beliefs are trivial. That my life is trivial. That I'm only an organism within a species. Before the biospheres I only saw myself and my ambitions. Here I'm starting to see my animal nature--and it's closely tied to my spiritual nature...my sense of freedom."

"So what of ambition, Alexander? Is that an honorable motive?"

"Honorable? Ambition is the driving force behind any organizer. I'm not a scientist. I'm an organizer who does research to support his ambitions to organize. That's what I failed to realize on earth. Sure, to the unambitious, ambition appears to be a self-serving, self-gratifying motive. But ambitious individuals ultimately serve the greater needs of the species. Yet the ambitious ones find great gratification in their success. Being in concert with my ambitions is the essence of my emotional being. It gives me great ego gratification to succeed...a uniquely human trait."

"Then, Alexander, when your ambitions are stifled by others, what becomes of your egotistical human nature?"

"You ask tough questions, Malzon. Am I here to bare my soul to strangers?"

"Respond as you will. Your exposition of this point is of your own free will. And we appreciate your candor. We're here to heighten self-awareness through apperception. It's the purpose of this course in theater and life styles. What's to become of your egotistical human nature?"

Alexander walked about the periphery of the round stage which sat in the bottom of the theater bowl. "Friends of the spheres. I don't know your personal motivations. I know little of your well- balanced culture. But I do know this. One man organized your existence for you and he asked for nothing in return. One man stepped forward in the name of love to spare his friends and loved ones from disaster. He sits among you today. We share humanity in common. So in knowing Zohar, I'm better able to deal with my own egotistical nature. Because only an egotist with vision could have accomplished this tremendous migration of mankind into space. Few on earth have a clue of your existence, your migration into space. The existence of these marvelous biospheres that support your utopian society--that's only a question on earth.

"My egotistical nature led me to become a student of Zohar and the writings of the Andromedans. This will lead me to my ultimate decision, which lies in the focal point of my mind's eye, my existence, my very being. Do I return to earth to complete the work of my life cycle, the arch of my life? Or do I remain in this utopia and learn to savor your stress free life style?

"My friends, earth consists of many societies and life styles. And it is in deep ecological trouble. Things you've never dreamt of cause great pain, anguish, and conflict on earth. Ultimately? Are earth's conflicts a result of familial conflict...sibling rivalry? Is sibling rivalry the basis for the differentiation of business, culture, science and technology-- the result of insecurity that exists within family units? And ultimately transfers into peer pressure? Is the inverse of low self-esteem, egotism? Yet are they one and the same? Do you folks understand me?"

"And, Alexander, my friend," Malzon intervened. "What about obsession in the family unit? What of pride? What about the relationships of the parents to the siblings? What about parents addicted to an idea, trends of thinking."

"Yes, of course, well the possibilities regarding these traits are limitless, due to the almost limitless number of people on earth...ten billion, or more? The problems are countless and too astronomical to consider. Yes, I see your point, of course, yes, my father was addicted to his own dreams and passed his addiction on to me, just another facet of my egotistical bent on life fueled by my addiction for success. And successfully solving complex problems on earth brings the problem-solver on earth the greatest form of ego-boosting praise and adulation from his peers. I was on that path, in the hope of the greater good, when it was stolen from me by my siblings. Leading to my emotional death. Due to the population bomb, earth's ecology and economies are about to undo billions of years of evolution. We now face the physical death of the planet, our Mother Goddess!" "And, Alexander, if you return to earth, will you prevail in the sibling rivalry that exists today?"

"To date, I'm defeated. Worse, the conditions that exist today are too difficult to explain due to the structure of business on earth, which derive from medieval laws of ownership that are maintained in the 21st Century by governments, the legal system and a plethora of lawyers."

"And what is the medieval 21st Century?"

Alexander smiled, "Funny that you should use that phrasing! It is medieval! It means 21 centuries after the death of Christ. Have any of you ever heard of a savior who saves mankind from oblivion by teaching true caring and love for your neighbor? Which of course includes brothers, sisters, mothers, and fathers. Without rivalry. If they had listened to Christ when the population was small, would I be here today? Lost in your utopian world? Losing sight of who I am? Sliding farther and farther from my original goals? Ultimately, will my life have any meaning? I don't know. I just don't know. And even in this utopia, doubt is hell."

Malzon addressed Stefano, "Well now, Stefano. I saw you--"

"Wait, wait, wait! Just stop right there. My personal life is none of your damned business. You can take all your theatrical and psychological verbosity, pedantic insights...and as we say on earth, Stick It! This whole scene makes me sick! And that includes you, Alexander!"

"What?"

"Not 'what,' Alexander. If I ever have to return to earth, I won't be forgiving you. I'll return with a sword to separate my enemies from their thoughts, their pretty heads. Thank you."

"Very urbane," Zohar sarcastically exclaimed before the audience, who were all confused and looking at each other

"No, very urban!" Alexander proclaimed with a laugh and long cynical glare for his angry cousin.

Chapter 24
Idiomatic Expressions

After their playing with ideas of psychology, thematic apperception and theatre in the sixth biosphere, Alexander had a cantankerous exchange with Stefano and returned to the first biosphere to calm his nerves and growing aggravation with Stefano's attitude.

"Alexander, Zohar, and Andrea were at the house at the base of the falls. Alexander was relaxing, Well, Zohar, there's a metaphor on earth for human problems, like your problems with Arlee. The roller coaster ride. The roller coaster has a long struggle against gravity. Then the initial descent comes. You rush down the first hill, usually a long steep hill to maintain your momentum to free climb the next hill. The first down hill rush is exhilarating. And the free rush up the next hill is usually into a sharp turn to keep the stress and exhilaration running high. Yet the entire time you're losing momentum, while you speed up and down smaller hills. After the struggle, human relationships become a rush, then lose momentum."

They sat in the living room of Alexander's new home in the first biosphere, as Andrea served food cooked in the American style--which is to say, eclectic. Zohar came every evening for dinner, as he enjoyed discovering the varied cuisines available from earth. However, one thing that the biospheres, earth, and the Andromedans, had in common was their addiction to coffee.

Zohar complimented Andrea on her coffee, "Awesome brew, Andrea."

"How did you become so Americanized in a few short months? And learn so much about the culture?"

Zohar smiled, "I have quite a few books from the library which I took out--and must owe huge late fees by now."

Taking a seat next to him at the table, Andrea took his hand. "Zohar, you're the most amazing person I've ever met. Things that I've learned during my school days, including a few universities, just lead me to believe that people like you aren't possible."

"How's that, Andrea?"

"Your ability to assimilate a totally foreign culture, language, customs, idiomatic manners of speech and behavior in short order."

He smiled, "No, you don't get it. In the spheres, idiomatic expressions develop daily. More than the syllables and the words--it's the sounds and the delivery of the words. You'll catch on. It's just a more apparent emotional personal life here than on earth. Sure, earth is full of infinite social complexity. Here life is emotional, yet contains subtle complexity. Except for dealing with The Guild. Dealing with Arlee and her quest."

Andrea was perplexed, "Well, can I meet this woman, Arlee, some day? I mean it would be extremely gratifying to meet the princess of light speed, propelling herself to nirvana, ruling the spheres from beyond the galaxy? Creating an oxymoron of sorts...enlightened darkness, happy hell? This dysfunctional bitch has everyone stepping and fetching."

"A role model? No! Addicted to behavior? Yes! Her father was the prophet of doom. And the Andromedans supported his point of view. The timing of their arrival was uncanny. And they wanted us to take responsibility for our migration into space. They came to me because I was the chief architect and manager of public works for the health and welfare of the community. The Andromedans got my attention with all of their super whiz-bang technology."

Andrea laughed, "I love it when you use those clichés."

"No no, Andrea, it's not funny at all. They persuaded Arlee's father to believe his egocentric insights. Well hell! Earth's still there with a thriving, prosperous, international economy. So what was all of that crap they fed us? I really want to know. Who are those damned big-eyed freaks?"

Andrea wore a smile as wide as her face, "Crap? Hell? Damned big-eyed freaks? That's all American shit!"

"That's what's fun about living here in the biospheres. We thrive on your kind of colloquilistic lingo. While earth's similarities to us are gratifying, there's a lot of repressed sexuality on earth. It's crazy...but wearing clothes all day, all of the time, messes up people's minds, not to mention their bodies. There's a lot of fat slothful people on earth. They're a mess, to put it bluntly."

"You know, Zohar, since Stefano's been here, physically he's a new man, totally into snow wing competition. On earth a lot of people preach health, but few live it. Stefano's back to being physically fit..."

"Mentally, emotionally, Alexander?

"He scares me, Zohar. He's an angry man. Who's biding his time."

Concerned for Alexander, for the moment, Zohar chose not to acknowledge the Stefano/Alexander conflict. "What a few months in the spheres did for you sickly earthlings who survive on sheer will power! Your earthly food, the physical environment, your social pressures would put me in the grave. While it's quite interesting, too complex to understand, earth is hell. And I think that everybody there knows it. And by the way, Alexander, I made a point of getting down to an amusement park near Boston. I rode a marvelous monorail roller coaster. Silent, fast, with all its shifting forces, quick fading momentum, I understand your roller coaster metaphor."

Alexander was detached from the conversation; pre-occupied he shifted the conversation, the mood, "Exactly, Zohar. I agree with you. Why are you here? Why did the Big Eyes propel these gigantic spheres to earth and just happen to bestow them on you? So much makes no sense at all. In fact, at the moment it makes very little sense to me. Except to say that on long thoughtful reflections, varying my opinions for weeks, they're into the biological sciences, ecology...agricultural science is the genus of their thinking, their perception, their take on life, their mind set. Just like you've been telling me, Zohar. They were so focused on the well-being of your culture that they gave up their own means of transportation back to Andromeda. How many of them were there? Millions? Like the millions of earthlings here?"

Zohar looked directly into Alexander's eyes. "Exactly. That's been my point all along. Why were the spheres so available for us to adapt to our environmental needs and designs? Our ecology? Which they understood intimately to the minutest details, in ways that we never conceived of?"

Andrea interjected, "Yes, yes, I'm starting to understand."

Zohar went on, "Everyone associated with me during the loading of these spheres with biological specimens, came to hate me. Only after we were in these spheres thousands of earth years did we ourselves become aware of ecology to the extent required to understand our own profoundly complex needs."

Andrea nodded affirmatively, "Without being scientific about it, Zohar, they wanted you to migrate to the spheres. Just another part of their research. But you had to agree to it. So why not take responsibility for it, take ownership of the idea."

"I've thought that through many times. However, the Big Eyes claimed there were catastrophic plagues in the offing, not to mention the invaders from the west. Furthermore, they predicted the plague would leave us in a state of total disrepair and unable to cope with the quickly advancing hordes from the west."

Alexander was somber, "Well? Maybe they were in a state of panic for you over catastrophic events...maybe we ought to go back to earth and find them."

"Well, Alexander, at the moment I have two rather simple choices. Persuade you to help me design a tachyon wave driver that will propel the 'princess of light speed' to her ultimate destiny, 'hell's euphoria'? Or I return to earth to find the Big Eyes. Which is where our relationship serendipitously began. And that reminds me--how did you drop your wallet in my space vehicle? When wallets are so important on earth?"

Alexander smiled, "Wow! Lost wallets? Artificial thunderstorms in this artificial enclosure. Never lose your wallet--because you don't know what you'll find in its place. A torrential downpour? Zohar, how did those Andromedan engineers learn to manufacture all of these weather conditions in such small spaces?"

Chapter 25
Snow Wing

They were enjoying breakfast in Andrea's dining area. The methods of cooking were the same as on earth, but the technology was different. Crystals imbedded in a square plate, like any stove top, were used to heat food in pots and pans. The pots and pans were earthen pottery, non-metallic, heated by the virtual-wave crystals that were manipulated through touch-sensitive, fingertip controls. With the ability to control the output of the heating element, cooking was like natural gas cooking, controlling the flame. And their ovens were similar to contemporary earth ovens, working by convection heating to produce more tasty and satisfying results. But no one in the spheres ever made raised bread, let alone toast. After several months in the spheres--or what seemed like several months, for no one was counting--Andrea got together the equivalent of an American breakfast -- bacon, eggs, toast, butter, orange juice, cereal, and coffee. It took a lot of talking, persuading, and educating, but Andrea managed to develop a reasonable facsimile of bacon; furthermore, she introduced many people to yeast raised bread. They loved bread. And the news about bread spread quickly, and there was a growing focus on wheat --which was available. For now they ate bread from a hybrid flour concocted by Andrea. Butter was a curiosity to the visitors from earth, because it was the same as earth butter. Dairy farming, goats mile, was major component of the economic, non-monetary, infrastructure of the spheres.

"When I think about it, Zohar, I'm amazed at how Andrea managed to get all of the foods together that are necessary for an American breakfast. This is just like home. At ninety-one percent of light speed? Too difficult for me to accept at times. But here we are."

Zohar smiled. "Never, never ever in my wildest dreams had I conceived of buttered toast. I love this stuff. It goes so well with bacon and eggs. I just have to say that I enjoyed breakfast at the truck stop every morning that I worked there."

Sophia awoke to the aroma of fresh coffee. Growing into the cultural ambiance of the biospheres, she was naked at the breakfast table, as Andrea served her and Stefano coffee. "Cover that tool of yours, Stefano. You won't forgive me if I burn it off with hot coffee."

Stefano smiled, "I love it here. I like the casual atmosphere. Acceptance is true throughout the spheres. We're all so up tight on earth. Earth is the social anomaly. I like being naked in the morning, during the day, and it doesn't detract from sensual feelings--which surprises me. Life on earth is entirely too complicated, too painful, too up-tight."

Sophia took a deep breath. "Actually, I'm starting to see things differently. Just as Dad said, we're all born as quite perfect little creatures, perfect entities unto ourselves. With a pure animal and spiritual nature, as the citizens see it here. Right, Zohar?"

He smiled. "But, yes, Darling."

Sophia smiled, nodded affirmatively, politely, and continued on her discourse. "It's when we interact with others that we become lessened by the experience of developing our human natures. Here it's not necessary to pick and choose relationships. Here acceptance brings out the best in everyone. I would never consider being naked before Alexander but now the old ways seem quite inhibited. Earth nurtures inhibitions in all of us...all of us."

Stefano started on his breakfast. He drank a large freshly squeezed orange juice. "Ahhh, delicious, what a flavor. Just how did you get all of this into the spheres, Zohar? There were no oranges around your area of North America."

"Of course we didn't just take things from our immediate surroundings. With the help of the Andromedans, after leaving the Zagros in the biospheres and then settling for decades in North America, exploration teams moved the biospheres throughout the Americas to get things like oranges. Coffee was supplied by the Andromedans. We collected all kinds of sapling trees, medicinal plants--all kinds of things. Not to mention quarries to load ornamental marbles, and some special ores. Those things were already here in some abundance."

Stefano smiled. "It's time for us to stop talking about the Andromedans. No one ever sees the Big Eyes. And life is what it is. It's great. And today I begin participation in the snow wing competition. And, Alexander, you should stay with us over there at the sports biosphere. Stick with the snow wing competition. Forget your cares and worries. Come fly with me."

"Fly with you, Cousin? You know. Back on earth you accused me of sending you mixed signals. But now that we're up here, you're a mixture of euphoria and hostility."

"Alexander, payback's a bitch. What makes you think that I really like you? I don't know whether that's my animal or human nature talking. You know? I can't quite figure it out. But I know that the snow wing competition's what you need."

"For what?"

Stefano stared directly into Alexander's eyes. "Let's just see. It's like the Victorian era when people didn't acknowledge their animal natures. They just challenged one another to duels, to the death. There are no rules up here, Alexander. I'm challenging you to a duel."

Zohar was caught up in the animal challenge. He liked it. It was a stark departure from current behavior in the spheres. "What are you challenging Alexander to do?"

"To get up there with a me in a snow wing competition. I set the pattern. Alexander matches the pattern. He sets the pattern. I match the pattern. Maybe we fly in tandem."

"And?" Zohar asked.

"And we fly dueling patterns. A game of nerve."

Zohar smiled, "Why?"

beings respond to it?"

Alexander was angry. "Okay, okay, you're on."

Alexander and Zohar studied the writings of the Andromedans. They studied together. Alexander was attracted to the life style of the academies and sports biosphere which contained their universities and many sports arenas, as well as natural settings for the snow wing competition. So accepting Stefano's challenge had some merit in Alexander's mind.

Stefano looked up from his bacon and eggs. "Now let's get on with my challenge and stop talking about technology. Our earth works are just primitive."

Zohar sensed an opportunity. "Alexander, while you're defeating Stefano at his own challenge you can live in the academies and sports sphere. The best place to study the writings of the Big Eyes. I'll be your tutor."

Alexander was direct. "Ahhh, for what reason, Zohar? I'm beyond caring about my life. For now I'm focused on the snow wing."

"You're on, Cousin."

Alexander spoke calmly, "Staying here is pure escapism. If I stay, not returning to earth, will I forever regret the decision?" He looked around the table for an answer. They were unanimous -- no, not to be regretted.

Sophia leaned forward in her chair. She was reflective. Her long hair accented her feminine structure. Always sensual, always emotional, always graceful and beautiful, her face reflected an intensely emotional moment. "Jessica and I were the catalysts, Alexander. But other members of the board, and management, once they sensed the opportunity to seize power…they did it! Jessica's leadership wasn't graceful…or effective. Always using mom's death as the excuse for her behavior. Friendships were made. New alliances. She gave up a lot of stock options and almost lost control to other board members in taking you down, Alexander. Returning is only foolishness that will turn your misfortune into a… tragedy."

Chapter 26
Tachyon Power

Several weeks later, with Stefano having more training than Alexander, who dabbled a few hours per day, the jet-ski boys from earth became the snow-wing boys of the biospheres. They were at the staging area for the snow wing competition, 7,000 feet above the lake that had almost perfect ten to fifteen foot waves. The lake shore extended along a ten-mile stretch.

The snow wing itself was extremely complex. There was more to know than required by surfing, wave runners, and jet skis. "This is a profound physical and athletic experience, Alexander."

"There's definitely something mystical about it, Stefano. There's no rush like it on earth. Not sky diving, not bungee jumping, not white water rafting, not surfing the pipe in Hawaii, no winter Olympic event quite matches this..." With that, Alexander suddenly was off down the steep slope. He trained some and read the manuals in detail; practicing snow wing operation in his mind

Alexander's snow wing rushed down a shear-face, sixty-degree descent. His ground speed was soon past one hundred miles per hour. He kept his body close to the surface to remain aerodynamic. He began to panic! His feet became erratic, as he tried to maintain his balance; instantly, he was on course to collide with a giant rock. Instinctively he pulled up on the stick--immediately he was airborne and narrowly missed the rock. Once airborne, he maintained a grip on the stick; utilizing the stick, he banked to his right and swept out over the crowd of observers, then he banked sharply to the left. The snow wing made a sharp yet sweeping turn, as it headed back toward the lake. Alexander maintained a low center of gravity, as his ailerons pushed him down toward the lake. Inexperienced, his chances of catching a wave were poor; frantically, nearing the water's surface, he jumped from the wing just as it made contact with the lake. Both Alexander and the snow wing were unharmed.

The next man down the mountain was Stefano, who kept his center of gravity low as he sped down the same sheer face, that Alexander just sped down. Cognizant of the massive rock, Stefano pulled up on his stick; to get some extra thrust, he pushed the button on the stick. The button engaged the tachyon wave crystalline micro drivers, and Stefano did a three-hundred-sixty degree vertical loop. The observers applauded. Coming out of the loop, he did a sharp right turn and eventually disappeared behind the mountain peak and re-appeared from behind the mountain, where he descended to the lake. Descending rapidly, rushing toward the shore line, he did a sharp left turn and trimmed his ailerons to slow the snow wing, as he skimmed the crest of a wave. Gingerly he sat the vehicle down into the pipe and rode the wave for about a mile, when the wave subsided. There was uproarious applause for the strange visitor from earth. The beach was lined with hundreds of thousands of snow wing enthusiasts.

Observing from the beach Alexander, Andrea, Zohar, and Sophia applauded just as vigorously as the crowd. Stefano was extremely popular with the natives. He was willing to risk more in a shorter span of time than the natives who weren't used to the intensity of a NASA rocket plane pilot. They were slightly reticent about trying the sport -- let alone, doing three hundred sixty degree vertical loops.

Stefano walked up to them on the beach. Beaming, he boasted, "Actually, guys, it's the tachyon micro driver that makes the vertical loop a cinch. I just lift on the stick, start to climb and invoke the micro tachyon wave driver which gives the snow wing additional thrust for executing the loop."

Several of Stefano's new female companions put their arms around him, as he sat between them on the beach. Other residents stood about staring at him.

Zohar, Alexander and Andrea, made their way up the beach to leave the celebrity with his fans. Zohar looked Alexander in the eyes. "You can't be serious about devoting so much time to this frivolous activity, just because Stefano has challenged you?"

"I've been reading, studying, thinking. My work is academic, anticlimactic. There's nothing that I can conceive of that hasn't been thought of by other cultures long before my culture was...a culture. My thinking is a product of my culture. So, what of this marvelous illusion called...individuality?"

"Now wait, Alexander. You're a brilliant engineer. And we all know that."

"Thanks, Zohar. But brilliant is just a word. I don't feel brilliant!"

Zohar shook his head negatively. "Self-deprecation is a real problem with you, the first person in our galaxy to actually apply virtual particle/wave technology on his own. I need you to help me with my impossible task. Please help me? It's the will of The Guild who are too strong for me."

"And what about my world, Zohar? The earth needs my technology."

Zohar was puzzled. He pulled out the stops. "Actually, Alexander, earth is beyond hope. One person cannot manage earth's problems. Earth is not your responsibility."

"It's an impossible situation. But I can't turn away from my home land for a life of...."

"Of what. A life that you deserve? An opportunity to be recognized by others who have earth's problems nearer and dearer to their hearts than you do."

"What are you saying? What, Zohar?""

"The Big Eyes. They're earth's guardians and I aim to prove it to you. First meet Arlee and The Guild. Then we sniff out the Big Eyes to show you just how much they're really involved in earth's problems."

"I still have my aspirations, my company to gain back from Jessica..."

"Never, Alexander. Your selfless aspirations won't help earthlings who are set in their awful ways. Every man for himself. You won't be appreciated...but persecuted, by greed, avarice, mendacity, and jealousy."

"How do you know so much for a person who spent little more than a few months there?"

"Am I wrong? Just tell me that I'm wrong."

"You're not wrong, Zohar!"

"Okay. Let's go and find the Big Eyes. You had some ideas as to how to discover their whereabouts. Let's get an even greater point of view. Where first? Our Technosphere? Or your earth?"

"I've got to resolve my issues with LiteWave Technology. Jessica! The board of directors. They can't get away with what they've done to me. I'm no closer to redeeming myself...from the darkness, encroaching my soul."

"In whose eyes?"

"The most important, Zohar--mine!"

"Let Stefano's challenge go. It's foolishness, Alexander. He showed today that no one can compete with him on the snow wing. And you performed admirably with your limited practice and reading the Snow Wing manual.

Chapter 27
Alien Stealth

Alexander, Andrea, Zohar and Sophia returned to the first biosphere and left Stefano to his private life--so they thought. When Alexander declined Stefano's challenge to the duel by snow wing--simply by ignoring it--Stefano made immediate arrangements through his new biosphere contacts to return to earth.

Zohar felt compelled to fulfill The Guild's edict and implement Arlee's will, yet personally he didn't identify with the needs of Arlee. Why was it necessary to construct Technosphere II so that it could orbit the galaxy at light speed? What was the benefit to the biospheres? Other than satisfying Arlee's convoluted spiritual point of view --what Zohar called "hell's euphoria." Alexander felt the call of his destiny. Zohar felt the call of another's destiny; she, Arlee had to be reckoned with. They had to decide where to go first: to earth in search of the Big Eyes? or to Technosphere I to meet with Arlee? They sat at Alexander's dining table and sipped coffee and ate pastries.

"Earth. Let's go there first," Alexander suddenly blurted out. "There are two possible sites where the Big Eyes might be spotted. Without being too scientific about it, the first place would be the North Atlantic where the Gulf Stream descends from the upper ocean to the ocean floor."

Zohar was as mystified as Andrea by this assured response from Alexander. Almost in unison they asked, "Why?"

Alexander informed them that global warming affected the salination density of the oceans. As the North Pole warmed, polar ice melted, diluting the salt concentration of the Gulf Stream, causing the Gulf Stream not to operate at full efficiency. The Gulf Stream descends to the ocean floor in the North Atlantic off the coast of Greenland at a variable rate, due to the varying salt concentration of the water. Heavier salt water descends with greater rapidity to give the Gulf Stream its momentum all around the planet.

Alexander explained, "The Gulf Stream makes an entire loop around the planet. Since your Big Eyes are basically ecologists from the Andromedan School of Agriculture, they've got to be concerned, at all times, about the movement of the Gulf Stream which is an international standard. All nations live by the health of the Gulf Stream, which affects earth's ecology....hence its agriculture."

"So they might be in the area because it is the most critical aggregate measure of the health of the planet's ecology?"

"Yes, Zohar. Some of these Andromedans are stationed in the area. Can your craft operate under water?"

Zohar snapped away from his intense thoughts. "Well, yes, yes, of course it can--but I don't know how to operate it under water. I never understood why anyone might want to operate under water. But yes.... How interesting!"

Alexander, meanwhile, continued his own musing. "Then again, the Big Eyes may be at the Cape of Good Hope at the tip of South America, where many weather patterns converge. There's synergy between weather patterns and the Gulf Stream. The Andromedans must keep their eyes on the big picture all of the time and sort through the details as variables change throughout the earth-- airborne pollens and insects, for example, can be captured from the upper atmosphere as indicators of the earth's ecological balance."

Andrea looked quizzically at Alexander. "You know, Honey. over the years I've often heard folklore about aliens being spotted around the North Atlantic, Northern Europe, Iberian Peninsula, West Coast of France. Do you think that these Big Eyes might have been the inspiration for these tales?"

"Sure! Two or three hundred years ago. But there're too many people now. Too much commercial and military air traffic. Too many radar networks. Too many observation satellites. Those who practice stealth don't want to be spotted. They're living in the oceans, on the ocean floor."

Zohar nodded in amazement. "Decidedly. You've got the right idea about that. I flew my craft to every conceivable spot that I knew of and there wasn't a sign of them. Not the remotest trace. I thought that they might be seen ascending from the Brazilian rain forests, or the Indonesian rain forests, or Madagascar, the home of herbal medicine."

"Think about it, Zohar. They've probably obtained and categorized every species of plant, herb, and animal on the planet. And they've probably developed rules based on intelligent models of the synergy of living organisms, affecting all life...in other words, the total ecology on the planet."

Andrea mused, "Like the idea that a butterfly flapping its
wings, in Africa, at the right moment, in the right place, can set off a series of events large enough to spawn a hurricane in the Atlantic."

"Yes, my dear, that's part of the story--and that's synergy!" Alexander smiled, pleased that Andrea was finally joining him in his speculations.

"So you're implying, Alexander, that the Big Eyes are in a new phase with their scientific work--monitoring the ecology."

"Exactly, Zohar. Now let's monitor them"; while Alexander and Zohar were off, Stefano wasn't abandoned. He developed his own friends and contacts in the biospheres; when he heard from friends that Alexander returned to earth, Stefano made his own plans to return to earth and left Sophia a message, that if she wanted to return to earth, to contact Andrea.

As fast as they could close out their affairs with the biosphere authorities and submit a flight plan, Zohar and Alexander were back at the controls of the space vehicle, preparing for their return passage to earth. Andrea and Sophia joined them as they headed back to earth. Just in case of any mishaps, their vehicle was loaded with food.

From their subjective experience, they had left earth three months and twenty-seven days earlier; from earth's time line, the had left twenty-three years ago.

They made their way back to earth, with Alexander piloting this time. Through reading the shuttle craft's manuals, Alexander used the navigational facilities which were built into the vehicle. Zohar had never decoded all of their scientific short hand or their operational manuals; therefore, he never utilized the complete navigational and communications capabilities built into the Andromedan interstellar vehicles. At the pilot's controls, there was a round screen that Zohar used strictly for magnification, observing distant objects. When peered into, the round screen gave a spherical view of the outside world with depth perception. Furthermore, by invoking the proper parameters through manipulation of fingertip touch points, the pilot could invoke monitors to communicate with other Andromedan vehicles. The pilot was capable of defining an external physical area through the observation screen; then that physical area was scanned at a predetermined tachyon wave frequency. It was not a frequency capable of being scanned by any earth-based telecommunications equipment, because earth had never made use of tachyon waves to this point in time. The Andromedans used the tachyon waves for all forms of energy based technology, because their tachyon wave technology did not require external power sources. Their tachyon crystals were synthesized from elements heavier than anything found in nature as defined in the periodic table.

Alexander put the vehicle into a geosynchronous orbit at about five thousand miles above the North Atlantic, off the coast of Greenland. Such an orbit was unthinkable with current earth technology, which could only use the balance between gravity and inertia for geosynchronous orbits attainable at twenty-two thousand miles above the equator. Zohar's vehicle could take advantage an artificial geosynchronous orbit above the North Atlantic.

"Alexander, how are you making that display operate?"

"Zohar, I read the manuals."

"How's that?"

"The intelligence built into these tachyon wave crystal computers is astounding. It's just that you had no parallel in your culture for electronic digital computers, Zohar."

"Ohhh. So you're saying that I should've studied the manuals? Broke the code? I guess I've been wrong about a lot of things. Just an old fool."

Andrea and Sophia made a point of reassuring Zohar that he suffered no particular inadequacies, it was simply that he didn't have the benefit of the experience of others building knowledge from generation to generation. Nevertheless, he felt inadequate. Sophia continued by saying, "Actually, Zohar, the more that I know about you, the more that I realize that you're extremely intelligent and courageous. To master technology for the good of your people, you did anything. Everything! Whatever it took! With selfless courage."

Tears streamed down his face. "Well, thank you. Today I'm not sure of anything other than I wish that none of this had ever happened. What's the point of it all? I was happy before I met the Andromedans?"

"I would have died happily 5,000 years ago rather than get taken up by the Andromedans!"

"Who really understands human motivation? For better or worse, you followed your instincts?" Andrea spoke gently.

By this time, Alexander had carefully maneuvered their vehicle into its orbit over the North Atlantic. Utilizing on board communications links, designed by the Andromedans, Alexander began to monitor the North Atlantic, from a high geosynchronous orbit. Several days past, a week past, as they lived off their food supplies in anticipation of making their first Andromedan sighting. Andromedan emerging from the North Atlantic in their anti-gravity vehicles.

As Alexander adjusted his geosynchronous orbit, position over the North Atlantic, northwest of the Iberian peninsula, doing tachyon scanning for ten days, his thinking eventually paid off. They observed the comings and goings of the Andromedans. They didn't have a clue as to which Andromedans were coming and going, because they knew nothing about them. But their initial suspicions were confirmed. Andromedan vehicles were not obvious to radar, nor observation satellites. The only reliable method of tracking them was through the use of tachyon waves, virtual wave energy. For days on end, Alexander read the Andromedan manuals about operating the vehicle under water, while Zohar counted the numbers and types of crafts entering and exiting the surface of the ocean.

"They're all feeder crafts, like ours. There's no mother ship in the immediate vicinity."

Alexander and Zohar felt that the Andromedans would not appreciate their following the shuttle crafts once it exited the ocean's surface. Alexander and Zohar felt more confident in meeting and dealing with whomever was stationed in the ocean. Zohar thought about that concept and he agreed; soon they proceeded to follow a vehicle, that dove into the ocean. Doing all of the touch parameter settings necessary for an ocean dive, without even practicing, Alexander piloted his vehicle right into the ocean. That vehicle, with the magic of advanced technology, absorbed the ocean impact without the slightest jolt to the passengers.

The Andromedan leading vehicle, that dove into the ocean first, was instantly aware of Alexander and Zohar's presence and slowed to lead them to the Big Eyes compound. Sweating profusely, Zohar's heart palpitated. The two vehicles exchanged an interlinking communications protocol; from that point on, they were on automatic pilot. Alexander smiled at Zohar who was ghostly in appearance and didn't feel well. Zohar took a deep breath and swallowed. "Mmm, ahhh, I'll be okay, I'll be okay. Just give me a few minutes. I'll be okay."

The lead vehicle swept through the ocean, a mountain range valley, and did some complex maneuvers that appeared superfluous to Alexander, but he was in awe of the maneuverability and speed at which they moved. Suddenly they dove into the ocean floor. Surprised, spontaneously, they each raised their arms to their heads to protect them from the impact. In a moment, they plummeted through some soft terrain and were inside a receiving chamber. The lead vehicle popped it's canopy, and Alexander popped his canopy.

One Big Eye climbed the ladder to their ship. "Well, now, we've been waiting a long, long, time for a visit from humans. What took you so damn long? Can anyone answer that question? Welcome. Welcome. Come on in!"

Alexander smiled. "Sure, we're following, just lead the way. Hey, you speak English?

"American!"

They walked a hundred yards across the chamber to an interlock door. Standing behind the Big Eyes, Alexander was quite curious about their dress. They dressed like Americans -- jerseys, jeans, athletic shoes. Yet they were quite slim and tall with unusually shaped heads. One of the big-eyed guys turned to speak to Alexander, "I'm going to take you folks to the front desk. You're in for the royal treatment."

They looked at each other with total surprise. They were guests of the Andromedans. Feeling insecure but certain of her needs, Andrea answered, "How about a suite with a Jacuzzi?"

Sophia concurred, "Indubitably!"

"Of course, that's standard with all of the rooms. We all prefer soma beds--that may be the only inconvenience to you."

After passing through the interlock doors, they entered the lobby of the compound. It was a hollowed-out mountain that reached all the way up to the ocean's surface and beyond. Sun- light filled the lobby of the compound. The ceiling tapered up to an eight-thousand-foot peak beneath a dormant volcano floor. The lobby, three miles in diameter, had great similarity to the first biosphere. Alexander, Andrea, and Sophia were unable to contain their tears of awe, while Zohar felt more comfortable. Notwithstanding the similarity, there were no humans to be seen anywhere. There were only Andromedan Big Eyes.

They were led to the front desk and checked in. The front desk clerk said, "You've got the presidential villa, please be prepared for meetings in the morning. You can contact room service for anything your hearts desire."

They made their way across the lobby, through opulent gardens. They got into the elevator to the presidential villa, which was perched on a seven hundred foot high bluff. Adjacent to the presidential villa was a water falls. In this configuration, the falls were a thousand feet high and descended down a convoluted granite face. The falls appeared like long strands of water, elegant. Andrea spoke for the three earthlings when she said, "These falls are utterly beautiful, Zohar. These people have a penchant for natural wonders. Everything they design has a flare for natural art--always so beautiful."

Zohar looked into Andrea's eyes, as they stood on the villa's verandah and watched the falls. "Yes, that's apparent. But what's not apparent is who they are. Be cautious. Choose your words wisely." While Zohar knew some of the Andromedan Big Eyes from previous encounters, he didn't know this group who had chosen to speak English, over their native Andromedan languages.

Alexander spoke softly, intimately. "Zohar, you're such a cynic. Give this experience a chance. They want to meet us."

The eclectic furnishings in the presidential villa gave the guests a view as to the timelessness of the Andromedans presence on the planet. Apparently the furnishings were from all over the planet. Areas of rooms were done in different motifs -- ancient Chinese, Japanese,

French, Middle-Eastern, twelfth-century Venice, art deco, high tech contemporary and many others--while paintings from many periods adorned the walls. The Jacuzzi area was designed with Hellenistic Greek and Roman sculptures. From the design of the presidential villa, it appeared that the Andromedans possessed a great fondness for the cultures of earthlings.

The Andromedans, in adapting their physical surroundings, to utilize earth based furnishings, were quite comfortable in doing so. When they left Andromeda, they were humanoid in appearance, and mutated after entering the Milky Way Galaxy, in search of earth (a twin planet to their own), due to near light speed travel. During near light speed travel they mutated to their current big eyed form and underwent metabolic optimization, once beyond ninety-one percent of light speed.

Chapter 28
One-On-One

    The following day, the humans were given a tour of the compound. It contained everything necessary for scientific research, engineering, and design as well as for the manufacturing of many things--including new space vehicles. There was a facility for processing tachyon wave crystals for a myriad of applications. They were not shown the agricultural and ecological research facilities, which were located elsewhere.

    After the limited tour, their guide took them to lunch. He wore denim jeans, a cotton jersey, and sandals. Alexander and Andrea kept chuckling through the entire episode, because the Andromedans spoke English and adopted manners of speech and posture they assumed to be quite primitive to their own Andromedan customs. Yet the profound difference was in their appearance-- their big eyes. It was disconcerting to Andrea to listen to a voice that sounded American, to see gestures that appeared quite human, all the while looking into their big eyes with no apparent pupils, iris, or other contrasting color. Their eyes were large dark protruding vertical strips, about one and a half inches wide per eye, that reached from just above their mouths to the tops of their heads.

    Their noses were two breathing holes built into a modest bridge. Their upper lip protruded beyond the base of their eyes. Both lips were large, and their mouths were quite wide.

    They sat in a square at an open air cafe next to a large fountain driven by a subterranean river, beneath the ocean's floor. A gushing fountain of water shot three hundred feet into the air.

The Andromedans who lived in this massive undersea compound studied human's civilizations and often adopted the names of their favorite historical figures. Thus their guide, who was enamored with the passage of time and early 20th Century American history, had taken the name of Cronus. He particularly admired Teddy Roosevelt because he, Cronus, considered himself a leader with spirit and flare like Roosevelt's.

They reviewed the menus, which were written in English. The eclectic menu covered seventeen varied cuisine's. For appetizers they chose sushi; for the main course, they ordered a Cantonese sea foods in lobster sauce.

Alexander asked of no one in particular, "Is their dim sum on Sunday morning?"

"Of course, of course, the main course on Sunday," Cronus answered, as he started on the sushi offerings and dipped them in varying sauces. The others did likewise. Cronus consumed great quantities of raw fish, squid and eel. Andrea dipped some lightly battered shrimp as she looked in Cronus' direction; she hoped that he was looking in her direction. There was no telling exactly where his gaze was focused. "So, Cronus, you realize that for us this is culture shock and future shock, all rolled into one curious package."

"Curious, Andrea, how's that?"

"This undersea biosphere is so...so..."

"So? So what?"

"So Americanized? Why isn't it more Andromedan? In fact, what is Andromedan?"

Using his chop sticks, Cronus sopped up a piece of fish in a dark, salty preparation, "Do you know how far away from home we are? Do you know how appealing American things are when you're Andromedan? We're from a planet that's the earth's twin in our galaxy."

Alexander chimed in, "Ahhh, Cronus, how did you pick that name?"

"As your get to know me, Alexander. You'll see my perspective on universal energy, energy annihilation, relates to our temporal perception of time. Still time is a convenient convention. Not real, still we all use it."

"My thinking exactly, Cronus."

Cronus smiled, "I like your Alexander and we need you. All of us here in this little corner of the universe. When I think of your Alexander, my mind goes to Teddy Roosevelt? Quite significant in my opinion, based of the conditions that exist on this planet today. Roosevelt went up against the fortress and won...so to speak. Of course no one ever wins. But when significant elements of the infrastructure were the problem, people like Roosevelt overcame the odds. John D. Rockefeller's fortunes changed and so did the American people, which led to cheap fuel, the burgeoning of the American and European automobile industries. And now we're at today's crisis as a result of those events. Exciting prosperity with deadly ecological consequences."

Andrea and Alexander looked at each other, while Zohar, Sophia, and Cronus consumed greater quantities of raw fish. "Deadly consequences?" they questioned in unison.

Cronus continued, "You're not just here as a matter of pure chance. Sure, you folks sought us. But this is more than a chance meeting. The culmination of a critical phase in human history is starting to unfold here today, Alexander. You're the man of the hour."

"How's that?" Alexander asked tentatively.

"I'm going to let you figure that one out for yourself. But you and Zohar, in an oblique way, remind me of two characters from fairly recent American history. Two major components brought prosperity to the USA--railroads and oil. About that time, at the turn of the twentieth century, E. H. Harriman of the Union Pacific Railroad was having it out with John D. Rockefeller...oh, excuse me, I forget that you earthlings know all this."

Alexander smiled, "Mmm-hmm, sure, sure, to a degree, I'm familiar with that."

"Well are you familiar with Young Woodcock?" The four were startled by Cronus's question. Alexander shook his head negatively.

Cronus continued, "You see, Woodcock is the character from an American entertainment film on the period, Butch Cassidy and the Sundance Kid. Considered by many to be quite entertaining, but also quite frivolous."

Sophia smiled. "Very entertaining! Those two actors are quite beguiling to a twenty-first century woman. When everyone today's so..."

"Anal," Andrea interjected.

Cronus continued, "So. anyhow, young Woodcock was a blind-faith employee. He protected E. H. Harriman's money, the commercial infrastructure. Young Woodcock had no identity of his own to speak of...he, Woodcock, worked for the Union Pacific Railroad, notably Mister E. H. Harriman. Are you getting my drift yet?"

At that moment, the Cantonese food was delivered to their table. Andrea and Alexander were stuffed, while Cronus and Zohar started on the scallops, shrimp and lobster in lobster sauce.

Alexander thought about Cronus's commentary and tried to recollect the movie that he had seen a few times in his home. "Okay, Cronus. It was the end of an era. Butch and Sundance were two mavericks who'd rather die than switch...to a life of conformity like Young Woodcock's who'd literally die for E. H. Harriman's money. The point?"

"Alexander! You're a maverick with character. The polarizing forces of yin and yang are at work here. In Marxist terms--thesis, antithesis. Now it takes a maverick to set the infrastructure back on its course. But in Young Woodcock's day it took a conformist to build the prosperity. Yin, the social binding force of Young Woodcock's era, now requires yang, the social driving force in you Alexander, a techno maverick. Thesis, antithesis."

Alexander and Zohar gave each other long thoughtful stares; each rubbed his chin. Zohar interjected, "Just what is it? What is it you are trying to persuade Alexander to do?"

"Gentlemen, that's for you to figure out. It's up to you to evaluate the situation. Learn the situation as it exists here on earth today. The planet's in intense need of real leadership. To date the Andromedans have not directly interceded in the affairs of any individuals, social or religious organizations, corporations, or countries."

Zohar shook his head negatively. "Cronus--whoever you are, whatever you represent, you have ulterior motives. Why did the Andromedans persuade me to lead my people into the biospheres? When do I ever get that question answered?'"

Cronus went on a discourse about the conditions that existed on the earth in Zohar's time. "The Andromedans, in Zohar's day, were not focused on the tribal and health issues of the planet. We were not experts in human virology. We hadn't focused on the geology of the planet, nor were we prepared to. We did, however, fear that volcanic eruptions in the Northern Hemisphere might destroy many emerging tribal cities, due to disrupted agriculture."

Cronus spoke intently. "We observed many tribes, Zohar. We particularly admired your cities for your creative use of wood and the creation of damns, water distribution systems. Yours was a highly adaptive, motivated, creative people who displayed an ability to deviate from the architectural norms of other cities all about your geographic region. We wanted to preserve the best, because we thought that you and many others could perish. Of course. But planet wide there was a vast array of possibilities. The Andromedan pioneers in those days were agricultural and ecological experts, not geologists, not virologists. We did our best to save you from plagues, invaders, and volcanoes"

Alexander nodded affirmatively, and his approval was good enough for Zohar who said, "There's just so much information today that wasn't apparent back then."

Alexander looked right at Cronus. "Well, Cronus, as affable as you are, as much fun as lunch has been--what are you here to sell us?"

"Sell? Sales? Come on, Guys. I don't like salesmen. I'm not selling anything. Just call me your liaison to the Greater Andromedan Democratic Commonwealths, The Andromedan Federation."

"Okay, so you're Sales Liaison. You're definitely a man on a mission. And you want us to comply with someone's wishes. Whose wishes?"

"Alexander, you must comply with your own wishes. Zohar, as radically against something as he might be, is compliant. He listens to his cultural imperative. His imperative is clearly to...." With those words, Cronus turned in Zohar's direction.

"...to build Technosphere II."

Alexander was amazed. "Well now, that's directly from Arlee, is it?"

Cronus smiled. "He catches on very quickly, Zohar."

"Then where's my imperative from? And just what is it?" Alexander mused.

"Nevertheless. Notwithstanding. Regardless. The fabric is interwoven. One thing leads to another! Alexander! I think that it's time for more introductions. Maybe an ecology lesson will uncover your repressed destiny." Cronus grinned the widest grin.

Alexander lost it! He shouted angrily, "I found my destiny. I found my destiny! My father showed it to me. And others grabbed it from me. I don't know who I am anymore. Lost in this Andromedan madness."

Zohar tried to calm Alexander, "Son, son, you're losing it. Please relax."

"Zohar, save me from this Andromedan madness. Paranoid madness! I can't take it anymore." Painfully, tearfully, he sank into his chair.

Chapter 29
Anthropomorphic Aliens

The Greater Andromedan Democratic Commonwealths were a loose federation of states--the Andromedan Federation of states numbered in the tens of thousands. With its long history, the Federation of States went through many iterations of privatization of industry followed by government control--then back to privatization and on again to government control. Each repetition of the cycle led to the formation of more residual bureaucracy; that residual bureaucracy, in turn, led to a citizenry who were manipulated by the demands of bureaucratic protocol, organizational process, political correctness. A lack of individual influence by the common citizens meant that wealthy and powerful living icons in Andromedan society were the ruling class.

Within the Andromedan superstructure of states, there was a definite plan to have colonies in other galaxies. Eventually, those colonies were to become states. However, sending free- spirited scientists on missions to the closest galaxy, the Milky Way, did not render the desired result. It took a certain type of individual of great intelligence, free spirit, and physical stamina and health to take on the task of intergalactic research. What happened during the course of light-speed travel, in search of the hospitable planet, earth, was mutation. Not anticipated by the humanoid Andromedans were mutations of their craniums, brains, eyes, and bodies.

One state, an individual planet within the Andromedan Federation, had individuals with the necessary qualities for intergalactic research and travel--truly, they were a deviation from the norm of the Federation of States. That planet state, Symbiosa, possessed the quality of spiritual insight into the nature of its citizens. They joined the federation for one good reason: economics. And the symbiotic relationship between that state and the federation led to the first Andromedan exploration of the Milky Way Galaxy. Living icons, wanton bureaucrats, who the big eyes, from the state of Symbiosa, sought to escape, were most powerful in the federation and wanted the "tesserac window" installed on earth so that they could visit earth to persuade its inhabitants to join the federation. Precision was required for the tesserac window, a new technology from an Andromedan corporation, TacTech. The newer perfected window permitted Andromedan diplomats to step through the "tesserac window" directly to earth. When the scientific expedition from Symbiosa launched for to the Milky Way Galaxy, they used tesserac technology. There was no tesserac window established in The Milky Way Galaxy, and the Andromedan scientific team, from the state of Symbiosa, in their seven massive biospheres, dematerialized on the Andromedan Planet State Symbiosa, and materialized toward the center of The Milky Way Galaxy, far from their target, Earth. From their materialized point of entry, toward the center of the galaxy, seven million light years from earth, they traveled at light speed toward the earth at the edge of the galaxy. They found singularities, black holes along the way, which enabled them to traverse great distances by mitigating the normal space topology. Megaparsecs of distance were covered in thousands rather than millions of light years.

Now the bureaucrats of the Andromedan Federation, in Cronus's opinion, wanted a "tesserac window" installed on earth. Before earth was ready for colonization, there was more urgent business at hand: saving the earth from ecological disaster. To the chagrin of the Andromedan Federation, there were few business or governmental leaders on earth who were willing to admit their folly, to admit that earth's ecology was on the threshold of total collapse due to problems of the past and present--political, economic, business, and scientific. The president of TacTech wanted to meet with Alexander; however, the Big Eyes were reluctant to give TacTech contact with Alexander.

Several days later, Cronus and a few other Andromedans came to the presidential villa which had communications with the Andromedan

Federation. Individuals from Andromedan business and government were available for the tesserac three-dimensional video teleconference meeting with earth. Cronus knocked at the door to the main entrance of the villa. Alexander opened the door, "Oh, you, what's up?"

"Now is that any way to treat a colleague?"

Alexander scratched at his face. "Well, Cronus, the scary part to all of this is that you really believe that you're my colleague, don't you?"

Cronus looked at the other Andromedan men, who as yet had not met Alexander, but nodded in total agreement -- yes. Zohar, Sophia and Andrea were having coffee in the kitchen, where they watched the waterfalls through an open French door. Cronus and his fellow Big Eyes followed Alexander into the kitchen where Alexander spoke, "Andrea, Zohar, Sophia--they want to talk."

Zohar angrily looked in their direction. "Really now, the only reason that you ever talk is because...you want something!"

Cronus agreed. "Well, of course we want something or you wouldn't be here. When you followed us into the ocean we locked you onto our signal and dragged you into this place. It wasn't totally by your own free will. Alexander wants something, too, Zohar. So let's get down to business and discuss the issues at hand. Who we are. Who you are. And what we both want."

So, somewhat apprehensively, Alexander, Cronus, Sophia and Andrea followed Cronus and the Big Eyes to the roof, where there was a large crystal sphere, ten feet in diameter. Everyone got comfortable in easy chairs that surrounded the massive tachyon crystal.

The large crystal ball became slightly illuminated as Cronus provided the monologue. The earth was represented three-dimensionally in the huge crystal display; observed from any angle, the earth rotated on its axis.

Cronus spoke. "If we took the entire geologic and biological chronology of the planet, about four point six billion years, and compressed it into one calendar year? By June twenty-first there were the first building blocks of life present in the oceans. By August, simple one-celled plants and animals were differentiating into more complex life forms. By September, living organisms with simple nervous systems like a starfish were present. To move this along quickly, the dinosaurs appeared on December twentieth and were extinct by Christmas. Prehistoric man appeared at about ten o'clock on New Year's Eve. And modern man appeared at about one minute to midnight."

Andrea was mesmerized by the beauty and realistic emulation in the display. "From here, the earth is beautiful and blue and floating softly in a rainbow. But when you touch down things are different here."

Cronus continued, "Yes, Andrea, let's get closer to the shore lines. To the problems that exist in the ecological system. The food chain! Modern man's time on earth, in my earlier metaphor--less than...A Split Second to Midnight! In the cosmic split second of stealing a sweet kiss from your lover, man has soured the planet. Fibroplankton, including a myriad of algae, once considered hearty and impossible to destroy, are being depleted by many toxic waste products including organihalogens--for example, free chlorine radicals. Fibroplankton, including oxygen-producing algae, on a global scale is mutating at an alarming rate, corrupted, and poisoned with organihalogens. We don't know when the end is coming. But it's coming soon, within the split second of the metaphor. Unless these days are shortened man will cease to exist on this planet...through his own volition."

Alexander and Zohar took long deep stares into each other's eyes. Alexander asked with trepidation, "So, how will the end come?"

"We're not sure. We're just not sure. One scenario is that with the depletion of the rain forests, the vast reduction of nitrogen cellulose being washed by the rains into the sea, nitrogen cellulose which builds healthy fibroplankton is diminished, causing chemical imbalances in the metabolic nucleus of each fibroplankton. Due to the lack of nitrogen cellulose to metabolize in mass, fibroplankton mutated by organihalogens are reaching a threshold. And similarly for oxygen-producing algae."

Sophia was wide-eyed. "Once the threshold is hit?"

Cronus painfully, agonizingly worried, said, "Mutated fibroplankton and some algae will emit great volumes of oxygen in an attempt to repair their deteriorating DNA structures...to net it out, the aggregate oxygen of earth's atmosphere will pass the twenty-five percent maximum threshold. Causing spontaneous combustion. The surface of the planet will burn as the mutated fibroplankton and algae keep pumping more oxygen out of their cells and into the ocean and consequently the atmosphere."

Andrea spoke softly, "Unless these days are shortened, no man or living thing will walk the face of the earth again."

Alexander spoke clearly, "Unless--unless these days are shortened? Within a split second to midnight?"

Cronus continued, "Well now, the other scenario is that a large percentage of the fibroplankton and algae will just fade away. Thus less oxygen is produced and earth's atmosphere falls below the twenty-three percent oxygen threshold required to support large mammals like men, who will become extinct. Unless these days are shortened."

Alexander's expression was sullen. "Unless these days are shortened? But how?"

Cronus responded, "We Andromedans, the explorers who settled here, don't want men to become extinct. But we prefer the extinction of man to the total destruction of the earth. If the surface of the earth burns, we all lose."

There was a protracted silence, while everyone thought. After exchanging glances, the Big Eyes sat quietly, appearing to be in a meditative state as their heads turned upward to the natural light through the volcanic mountain ceiling. Alexander considered bringing up "the man of the hour" title given to him by the Big Eyes. What was his role from their point of view? Zohar looked directly at Alexander in an effort to get his attention. Catching Alexander's gaze at that solemn moment, Zohar shook his head ever so slightly from side to side, implying "don't trust them."

Alexander asked Cronus for supporting details. He and his fellow Big Eyes provided statistics on a city-by-city basis of organihalogens being released into the rivers, lakes and oceans, because of a lack of toxic waste treatment. They peered into the tachyon crystal sphere; in it the earth was now enlarged for all to view, and the model rotated rapidly enough on its axis for all to view the hundreds of cities that were fouling the environment. The east and west coasts of the USA were so densely populated that pollution controls instituted at the turn of the 21st Century were not enough to meet the requirements to reduce organihalogens as well as other complex carcinogenic substances. During the late 20th Century, carcinogens were only a concern to wild life, not fibroplankton, especially not algae.

However the continued research of the Andromedan agricultural scientists was proving otherwise. The Pacific rim countries were major violators, due to their continued prosperity and lack of investment in pollution controls. But worse than industrial waste was sheer human waste from consumable products. With free market economies blossoming all over the planet, the standard of living of the West was still a standard to be emulated by competing developing economies.

Cronus shook his head negatively. "You see, Alexander, without a method to distribute pure consumable products, perishables, which now use potentially toxic preservatives in their packaging, the problem of carcinogens cannot be resolved. With the high standard of living which all humans desire these days, there is no solution. This new wave of strange carcinogens is fouling the metabolic process of fibroplankton... in unpredictable ways."

Another Andromedan representative spoke up. "Exactly! Preservatives from food pass into dishwashers and human waste, and when these get mixed together in the sewage networks with detergents, household cleansers, road salts, fossil fuel, acid rain, fluorocarbons--which, by the way, were supposed to be outlawed decades ago--and many newer preservatives for microwave foods--well, it all leads to the creation of what I'll just call 'this stuff.'"

Cronus was passionate. "New--unpredictable--chemical configurations. The task of tracking this...'stuff'...has reached a finite limit. With advanced technology, we're losing the battle. If you could introduce your virtual particle driven vehicles for distribution of fresh food and fresh water, maybe there's time. Remember the metaphor of condensing all of earth's history into one year. The last thousand years are...A Split Second to Midnight, New Year's Eve. But when midnight strikes, the party's over."

"Come on, Cronus. Be realistic. Preservatives in foods have nothing to do with virtual particle driven vehicles."

"Well, Alexander. Something has to be done by earthlings. We will not interfere. Only suggest."

"How do you know so much about me? Who told you? Just tell me that for openers. How does anyone from another galaxy who lives hidden from everyone--how do you know anything about me? About any human beings?"

Another Andromedan, who wasn't so patient, manipulated the control panel of the crystal sphere and suddenly revealed a view of the LiteWave Technology headquarters--into the very office of Jessica! They observed her buried in an issue of *Wall Street Journal* with a stack of papers on her desk.

Alexander commented, "That's not her. Those are the hands of an old woman. Let's get a closer look at her."

The tesserac technology was unspeakably revealing. There she was-- Jessica, a paunchy middle-aged woman with sagging jowls. Uncharacteristically, Andrea snapped, "She...she...she looks awful!"

Andrea and Alexander just kept doing double takes at each other and at the image of Jessica, when Stefano came into her office. As it happened, this was his first time there since his return from the biospheres, the anomaly of seven. They could even here him speak. "Well, Jessica, it's quite a pleasure to be back and too see..." At that moment, she dropped the *Wall Street Journal* from her face.

"Stefano, darling! I can't believe you're back. You were all presumed dead years ago."

Stefano's shock at seeing Jessica's face was an incredibly honest reaction for Stefano, ordinarily a master at controlling himself. "Yes, yes, years...ago...just how many, Jessica...ahhh, how many years ago was that?"

"Twenty-four years!"

Stefano blurted out, "About four months in the biospheres? Each month was six earth years here. And in those four months, Jessica, darling, it seems that my proxy bidders from ICARUS have earned me significant shares of LiteWave through royalty agreements."

"You snake, Stefano. Just how did you gain so much power without being here. Dead. With the rest of 'em."

"Yes, darling," he said, "and how is my friendly proxy, Charlie Tong from Hong Kong?"

"Dead. He died in his late eighties. Not all that long ago."

"I never trusted the man. But he served me quite well. Now I've got the right to sit on the board of directors...shares, and all."

She was astounded. "So now I get it. You sold all of Alexander's secrets to ICARUS. Gave them your power of attorney and in return they bought shares of LiteWave for you. You're the phantom executive.

Hell. You're very famous. Very famous. Brilliant. A master stroke. ICARUS played it for years, guessing that you'd never come back. Because they voted as your proxy--and never let on."

He smiled with glee. "Yes, Jessica, the phantom returns from the anomaly. It was masterful if I do say so myself." He howled like a mad dog, "Twenty-four years?! I've been gone for twenty-four fucking years?!"

Alexander, Andrea, and Sophia looked at each other for a long sobering moment, as Sophia whispered solemnly, "Twenty-four years?"

Andrea was also nearly speechless and squeaked, "Twenty-four?"

Jessica smiled with excitement, "You devil, Stefano, what other nasty things have you done? Confess!"

In his greatest moment of triumph, now his weakest moment, Stefano made allusions to reality. "Made very sure that your brother, Alexander, was blamed for his mother's death."

Alexander and Andrea heard everything through the tesserac three dimensional video spoofing. Saying nothing, they stared at each other long and hard.

Cronus spoke. "Through The Federation's continued research into tesserac transportation technologies, we can do visual imaging across megaparsecs. In fact, we can communicate with the Andromedan Federation who are in artificial orbit about the Andromedan Galaxy at over ninety-seven percent of light speed in a Technosphere."

That comment piqued the curiosity of Zohar, who sat up to stare into the tesserac imaging window, displaying a full-motion three-dimensional image of the tachyon wave driver propelling the artificial orbit of that huge Technosphere from the Andromedan Federation, orbiting the Andromedan galaxy.

Cronus said, "The name of the major supplier of tachyon wave technologies in the Andromedan States is TacTech. But you've got to keep in mind that they aren't too cosmopolitan in their approach to business. They're all graduates of the Andromedan College of Agriculture, which designs Biospheres and Technospheres. They like to think of themselves as teams due to their geographic intergalactic dispersion."

Cronus initiated the communications link between themselves and the Federation's Technosphere, tens of millions of light years away--megaparsecs. Cronus explained that the tesserac communications processors had to perform continual sampling of space topology to sense shifts in the phases of the multi-layered energies of the universe, on a parsec by parsec vector to the Federation's Technosphere, in order to maintain constant communications with it. Understanding tesserac pathing and clocking meant being able to circumvent those great distances, megaparsecs, as perceived when viewed through a telescope.

Cronus explained that tesserac technology was based on the nature of the known physical universe. Based on the concept of matter and antimatter, based on a dynamic (non-static) understanding of energy, based on the uncertainty principal of physics, that one can never be exactly sure of both the position and velocity of an energy particle. In quantum physics, a particle can never be directly detected, but its existence has measurable effects--virtual effects, virtual particles, virtual waves.

"But still, that doesn't explain tesserac," Alexander intoned.

"Of course not," Cronus agreed. He went on to give the metaphor of yin and yang. It starts off with two opposing forces; their origin is an unknown variable. Yang, a virtual effect in time and space, emits pure energy, electrons; yin, emits an equal negative force which annihilates electrons: "But which is which, Alexander?"

"Go on, Cronus?"

Cronus continued that the use of an electron in this discussion was a metaphor for an unknown positive energy, a virtual effect. "As soon as Yang emitted its first effect, yin annihilated it with an anti-effect. Yet nothing was lost; it was a transformation that started spin. A light wave is a hundred millionth of an angstrom. What were the first virtual effects--a billionth of a hundred millionth of an angstrom? How small is small? And what's the shortest time event that a practical Andromedan chronoscope can measure? Ten to the minus billionth billionth billionth of a second? So yin and yang continually annihilated each other, one becoming the other. The energy dance had begun with negative spinning to positive and vice-versa. Mirror images were formed with depth, dimension, and spin. And how long did it take to create enough energy to be the equivalent of one atom--a trillion trillion years in practical terms? God knows? How long is forever? No Andromedan chronoscope can measure that...."

Alexander reiterated, "Sure, a universe fifteen billion light years across, is only fifteen years across if you go a billion times faster than light. And a million times faster than that? Puts us into...hours, minutes, or seconds. I need a calculator!"

Cronus smiled. "Now here's where it gets tricky, Alexander. The universe has never changed its original nature of constant annihilation of matter by antimatter, the energy dance, the spin, the exchange. As we sit here, the known universe is annihilating itself at such a rapid rate, in a billion billionths of a second? Or a billionth of that? Who cares? So if one can exhume the annihilation rate on a measurable, empirical, aggregate scale, from one end of the known universe to the other, the entire energy dance...then, and only then, can one tesserac to his destination on the waves of annihilation."

Alexander said, "But in practical terms, the universe has three dimensions plus time, a four-dimensional analog plane. You're detecting the virtual effects of matter/antimatter, the analog planes of a finite universe, in constant mirror-image reversing, and riding the virtual waves, which are infinitely faster than light speed, to intersect time and distance. From an Andromedan Technosphere to right here?"

In about thirty-seven minutes there was two-way communications, both audio and visual, as the audio-visual communications coder/decoder did its tesserac magic. The distant end, the Andromedan Federation had a three-dimensional crystal sphere display at their end to see six individuals on earth who sat at the base of the hollowed-out mountain. The president of TacTech was a graduate of the College of Agriculture. TacTech's name was not supposed to be involved in the visual teleconference because of the Andromedan Federation regulations and the promise that TacTech was not to be involved. There were three other individuals from TacTech at the distant Andromedan round table.

There was a close-up of the president of TacTech, who referred to himself as-- "Jupiter. Just call me Jupiter. The Roman form of the Greek, Zeus. We all love Greek mythology here in the Andromedan Federation, do we not, Cronus. It's the closest living link to our very distant past. Earth is our friend. We wish to be its mentor. We admire the artistry of the Greeks and the determination of the Romans. And what better name for me--a friend of America, the second Roman Empire--than Jupiter."

Jupiter, as he called himself for now, analogous to the Roman ruling class, wore a navy blue suit with brass buttons to the collar which covered his neck, like a military uniform. His dress appeared quite formal to the Earth-side group. There was a tight shot of Jupiter. Each Earth-side member saw a front view of his face; his eyes were large, yet they were not on the order of the Big Eyes. His cranium was larger than the average human's and he had the appearance of an outer space alien being from an advanced culture. He said, "Again--just call me Jupiter. And we'll dispense with protocol today because our friends from Earth are not familiar with our social customs."

Cronus responded, "Yes, Jupiter. It's good to see you today. You appear quite well. And today we wish to introduce you to our friends from earth...Andrea, Zohar, Sophia, and her brother Alexander, Andrea's husband."

"Let me compliment you, Zohar, on the fabulous job that you've done with your biospheres. The standard of living there is the highest that I've ever witnessed. But of course, the limited nature of that environment makes such a high standard of living possible. You are the envy of trillions of Andromedan citizens who only hope for a chance to live in a biosphere...let alone a Technosphere. We knew of you Zohar, through our advanced technologies, because we've monitored the scientific expedition from Symbiosa since they arrived in your galaxy."

Zohar, who was not used to business negotiations, was vulnerable to a sincere-sounding compliment. Zohar responded enthusiastically, "You must come and visit us in the biospheres when you get an opportunity."

Jupiter wasn't expecting an invitation and tried to hide his intentions of visiting the Milky Way Galaxy, Earth, the Big Eyes. "Well, of course, when it's technologically feasible. Today, the tesserac imaging window; tomorrow a tesserac transport window that can intersect time and distance...precisely, within an angstrom."

Were they intending to invade earth in peaceful ways--through the use of commerce and technology? Colonize the place? "Seems to me, Jupiter, that you've got to transport the technology here in order to affect its use? Transport yourself here?" Alexander commented.

"Really, we're getting way ahead of ourselves. Since we're being so open in our questioning, let's get to the point, Alexander. We're looking for you to apply your virtual wave ships in your new transportation age, to reorganize the living habits of earthlings before...the clock strikes midnight."

Cronus interrupted, "Good use of earthly colloquialisms, Jupiter!"

Alexander looked Cronus's way with disdain and muttered under his breath, "Good job, Young Woodcock. E. H. Harriman would be proud of you. Is this the case in Andromeda today? Business runs government?"

Jupiter did his best not to lose his composure while showing his aggressive nature to Alexander, Zohar, and Andrea. "Yes, yes, earthly colloquialisms are effective in making the point...A Split Second to Midnight, Alexander. We want, I mean wish, you to resolve this impending tragedy. You were the chief officer of a successful company. You and your father pioneered virtual wave technology in the colonies-- I mean...your home planet, of course. That technology puts Earth on the threshold of a transportation renaissance."

Zohar chimed in, "It seems that the Andromedans of earth have emulated many things at home. The biospheres. Technosphere. You're operating at what percentage of light speed?"

"Ninety-seven!"

Zohar continued, "Arlee, who you must be aware of by now, operates Technosphere at ninety-nine percent of light speed and is addicted to endorphins, a hellish euphoria, which only feeds her delusional spiritual nature."

Jupiter had a perplexed expression, a twitch, "Well, sir, ahhh... we avoid endorphin addiction at all costs. Ninety-seven percent is the maximum speed. As we creep beyond ninety-seven, we lose sight of practical realities."

Alexander interjected, "There's so much that we here on Earth aren't privy to. As to the origins of life on earth. And our intimate similarities to Andromedans. Oxygen breathing, carbon- and nitrogen-based cellular structures. The DNA helix. It's common to Andromedans and earthlings. Coincidence?"

"There's so much to know. So much to learn about the synergy between our galaxies. This is not the time or the agenda for that discussion, Alexander. We need you to empower new technologies for your new world order. And we'll assist you. We need your contacts on Earth."

Zohar interjected, "Forgive me. I'm not educated in the contemporary ways of earth as the rest of you. But to ask Alexander, one individual, to lead a place as complex as earth with its myriad of problems is not in order. Regardless of how profound his managerial and engineering skills might be. It seems like always, you Andromedans have your hidden agenda. What is it that you really want, Jupiter?"

"Now, that's a brave man, Cronus. Now I understand why he was chosen for the job of migrating the Zagros people."

Zohar interjected, "Were you alive when Cronus and his accomplices arrived here ten thousand years ago?"

"Of course I was."

Alexander interrupted, "So therefore, Jupiter, these ecological problems have been around a while, and you've certainly been aware of them. Why do you seek us now with only...A Split Second to Midnight?"

"I've discussed my proposal with the Andromedan Federation. We are willing to endorse a technological exchange program with earth. We will come to ratify a technology treaty. And pass the necessary technology to you, Alexander. To clean up the mess, before the cataclysmic end of this grand experiment."

"Jupiter, the tesserac transport window has not arrived on earth. How are you going to get here...to ratify anything? After you've left us here to dangle until A Split Second to Midnight? Or is that all rather intentional?" Alexander asked with a smile.

Jupiter smiled. He sat up in his chair and leaned forward, making his face larger on the crystal sphere. The genesis of man was a question, among many, in today's subtext. Jupiter attempted an answer. "You see, it wasn't our idea to create this grand experiment, Earth. Look around your solar system. Earth is quite different than any other planet. The chemistry is different. Where did the water come from? Giant frozen planetoids, comets, composed of water, crashed into the earth...long before, it orbited your sun."

Jupiter responded, "Earth was created in six phases, not including the first phase: the creation of energy, the energy dance. The Earth today is the creative vision of those who lived in Technospheres for billions of earth of years. Passing into the immortal state of nirvana, they carried their vision with them and the ability to move as angels, freely, through the astral plane. They are the angels who focused the forces of your dark star, Nemesis, that created the planet of super temperamental beings, earthlings. And with the earth came Mercury, Venus, and Mars. Your mercurial nature, Alexander tells you what?"

"Tells me that metaphysical coincidence, synchronicity, doesn't exist. Mercury is the symbol of quick wit and lightning human thought, intimating that while things appear coincidental, like life on earth, coincidence doesn't exist. Things are as real as they seem to be."

"Earthlings?" said Jupiter. "Ultimately, one day, destined to be angels themselves by the nature of their DNA structures. Earth's position is neatly focused at a point in the topology of space to be effected by the energies of the great local constellations--Gemini, Sagittarius, Capricorn, Cancer and so on. Why in the hell has it all gone wrong?"

Alexander spoke up. "Jupiter? Really? Come on--give us your real name, your management title."

"Insolent One--mind your manners. One thing that we cannot tolerate from our leaders, Alexander, is impertinence"

"Strong words for a man literally millions of light years away!"

"Oh, ye of little faith. You will become my son on earth. You are the fulfillment of my dreams. The resolution, the denouement."

"To what?" Alexander asked with an angered tone.

"To the end. The end of your world. You will be the savior."

"Those are big words. Too big me for me. I'm too humble for your needs."

The room resonated with Jupiter's rage. "Humble? Humble? No, not humble at all. Let's trace a few events in the history of your Western Civilization--which, by the way, to use your colloquialism is well...a month or two, in my subjective technosphere time, four hundred to five hundred months in biosphere time."

"Alexander blurted out, "About four months in the biospheres? Each month was six earth years here." Your entire history, since the Old Testament, is just a few years here in an Andromedan Technosphere. Now are you ready to listen?"

"Absolutely not. I've had it with The Andromedan Experiment. I'm out of this meeting."

Jupiter, from megaparsecs of distance, through the miracle of technology , looked deftly into Cronus's eyes. "Tell him, tell him it's time to listen. It's time to face reality."

Alexander was enraged, "You feeble excuse for a leader. Look over here and address me."

"You're addressed. You're a Roman. At the Council of Nicea, Rome nationalized the church, which started the metamorphosis of the West. The beginning of big time corruption. Which reached well into the Middle Ages. Where did Sergei's money come from, Alexander? Not from the Petrovs, who had nothing. It came from the vestiges of the corruption of Venice. Your mother's family was central to it. Maria, as demure and understanding a mother as she was, understood her family tree...intimately. LiteWave Technology was funded by corrupt elements. But the Magna Carta kinda, sorta, set things straight for the common man. And the United States, with its Magna Carta-style government, was the culmination of the British Empire, which was imbued with the Roman imperial ethic: Taxes taxes and more taxes. Get them to pay their taxes. It started with the Christians who would not pay their taxes to Rome. So Rome nationalized the church."

Alexander wore an expression of momentary agreement. Then he spoke, "We don't think that way, Jupiter. Taxes? Taxes are hell. Taxes stifle development. The problem is apparent. Your world is so old, so corrupt, that taxes are the only thing that you understand. We don't admire or revere Rome, the Ceasars, the Vatican. Just a bunch of...who knows what? So, let the world blow up."

"You will all pay taxes to the Federation. It's inevitable. If you wish to save your world. And you will carry the torch, Alexander. You've got the right stuff. You're a leader."

Zohar chimed in. "Taxes? Not in Shangri-La. We don't have a government to collect taxes...."

Jupiter shouted, "You've got another thought coming, Pilgrim. We didn't put you in the biospheres out of pure scientific curiosity. You are emulating the Andromedan system of planet-based beings, biosphere-based beings, and technosphere-based beings. It's the hierarchy of life and government."

With the kaleidoscope of events that unfolded very quickly for Alexander, with his learning of Stefano's guilt in the death of his mother,

Alexander had no time to react to learning that Stefano was a killer. Alexander's distractions with understanding time lines--between earth, biospheres, technospheres, and Jupiter's very condensed view of human history--left Alexander in a numbed state. Learning of the earth's imminent ecological problems motivated Alexander's human concerns, concerns for survival of the human spirit, conserving the earth the home of the human spirit. Yet with all of the unfolding events Alexander lacked a clear sense of feeling; conflicting emotions, with the explosion of information left him -- sickened, worried, distracted, unable to focus, mentally seeking a direction; feeling fear, uncertainty, and doubt.

Chapter 30
Andromedan Federation

Later that night, Alexander and Andrea were in bed. Alexander had decided that he must leave the Andromedan compound based in a hollowed out volcanic mountain in the North Atlantic. The decision still weighed on him, and unable to sleep, he lay brooding, his head resting on the pillow with his hands behind his head. He stared at the ceiling containing an Italianate painting--cherubs and gargoyles encircled the central subject, a couple who were making love.

Andrea was the first to speak. "What are you thinking, Al?"

"Just how much I love you. That I can't live without you in this world gone mad. See those cherubs? They represent my sweet love for you. And the gargoyles represent the nastiness in my heart."

She reached beneath the sheet and touched him. "You're all that matters to me, Darling. You're all that matters to me. But I fear that I'll have to give you up. And I can't live without you"

He jolted his head up. "Give me up? Never, that's not in the plan."

"Don't you see that the handwriting's on the wall? The Andromedans trust you, need you."

He smiled. "Mmmm...so that's what you think? You haven't been exposed to enough business negotiations. Jupiter was very clumsy today. And I don't understand why. Actually he was desperately clumsy."

"Don't you get it?" Andrea retorted. "Didn't you listen to Cronus? They're just not cosmopolitan--urban, or whatever you want to call us. They may have evolved to a higher level, but they're still very direct--"

She actually winced before she finished her thought. "Colonialists. The earth's in deep trouble. And they're asking someone whom they trust--you--to guide them and the planet through a critical period."

"Of the Andromedan experiment?" Alexander chided, "There's more time in the 'Split Second to Midnight' metaphor than they're letting on. They're leveraging us into colonialization. Cronus and the boys aren't so willing to help them colonize the earth. Cronus and the boys want to keep things cozy, just the way they are. They know that TacTech of Andromeda hasn't been listening closely to them. There's a coup forming. And I'm not going to be anyone's fool."

"But what about your goal to build your virtual wave vehicle?"

"Goals? Objectives? What I wanted to do was to go back to Deep Creek and continue with my life's work, right where I left off. I've changed. Screw the job, the research, the grit, the angst--yes, and the ecstasy! Let's have kids as an affirmation of the future. This is the new Alexander. I'm tired of worrying about...what I've lost, what I can't control. If the world blows up, it blows up."

Andrea shook her head negatively. "Well, at a time of crisis, you sure are the calm one. Marry me again?"

"Who said that I married you?"

"Alexander?"

"Yes, Andrea?"

"Kiss me?"

"Gladly!"

With that, all thoughts of the Andromedans or virtual wave vehicles were banished as they sexually indulged themselves as they hadn't in years.

Chapter 31
A Wanting Egotist

In the morning, Alexander and Andrea collected their belongings in preparation to leave. Zohar brewed a pot of coffee and they sat down to take their breakfast. Alexander stepped out onto the verandah to watch the waterfalls that fed a fountain below, and Zohar followed him. "So what do you think of all of this, Kid?"

"Zohar, I want to go back to the biospheres. Rest up, then head back to Deep Creek. If you would just drop me off there, I'll never forget you. You can come and stay with me any time, for as long as you like. I'm going to my life's work."

"And what about Jupiter's offer?"

Andrea smiled and did a friendly negative nod; so much for last night's promises of a family and marital bliss. "Back to the grind, Alexander?"

"Zohar, leave me out of this intergalactic fiasco. Jupiter wants to get his tesserac transport window set up here so that hordes of Andromedans can come in and create mass confusion in an effort to colonize the planet at…A Split Second to Midnight. At which time they will resolve all of the ecological problems. My life won't change all that much."

Andrea smirked, "…come on, Alexander. If Jupiter and company take over. You don't think that they're going to make themselves visible. Life will change. Trust me!"

"You don't get it, Al. The Andromedans are not a forgiving people. They'll find you and punish you for not accepting their offer. That's the way they are."

"Punish me? How? I believe you. But a man's got to do what a man's got to do."

Zohar shook his head negatively, "Now that they've met you, they'll find your rejecting them extremely distasteful. Their egos are huge. Their minds resolute. Jupiter's coming. I'm convinced of it."

Alexander turned his gaze from the waterfalls and looked directly at Zohar, "I don't give a damn. They can all go to hell. Because I'm not going to make it easy for them. Let them find another fool who loves their protocol and ceremony. Picking that name-Jupiter! Do you know how much that pisses me off?"

Zohar looked to Andrea, "...the man's stressed. You're just not making sense, Alexander. You do care, do give a damn. And you love your own protocol and ceremony."

Andrea was matter of fact, "...stressed out frustration!"

There was a knock at the front door of the villa. Andrea let Cronus in, and the first thing he saw was Alexander still gazing at the waterfalls. Cronus was six foot three, thin and strong. Alexander was five foot eleven, thin and strong. His head tilted down in Alexander's direction. Cronus spoke in a somber fashion. "You are making a big mistake!"

Alexander, looking into Cronus's face, angrily retorted, "No, you made the big mistake, assuming that I would give in and run to the rescue with you. It's not my problem."

"If not you, then who?"

"The Andromedans. You've been around here a lot longer than we have. You've got squatters rights. You own this planet. Humans? We're just your guests on earth. What can we possibly do that you don't already have the know-how to do?"

"Influence the proper people who constitute the body politick of your planet, the ones who adhere to the notion that time is of no consequence, who believe that things are great."

"Okay, Cronus--and I just now realize that your name is quite apropos for these critical times--not much time left? Give me a number. Not your cornball Cronus expression...A Split Second to Midnight has a range of thousands of years. A real number for the remaining life of the earth...five years? ten years? a hundred years?"

Cronus raised his hand. "Stop right there. Fifteen years at the longest. My prediction is that the oxygen level will soar above twenty-five percent with the damage to the algae and plankton. Causing the surface of the planet to burn out of control. Spontaneous combustion!"

Alexander stared with guilt at Cronus, "Just return home to Andromeda?"

Cronus was quite sad. "We can't do that. We don't fit in there. Jupiter? That arrogant egotist would colonize the universe if he had the time and resources. And we're not going to help him in his quest to set up the transport window to earth. No way. He's out, you're in."

"If you disdain, loathe, your own federation Cronus? And a private corporation TacTech has the most influence over this vast federation. How are we to think that the high levels of corruption there have any interest here? And why do I even know about TacTech? I'm not sure that I get it."

Cronus was quite somber. "We had to show you that we're from someplace real. We were born to wonder. But we're from someplace that's real. Jupiter can't get here from there without our help. He wants to show the Federation what he's capable of."

"Cronus, don't get me wrong. It's not that I don't trust you. It's just that I don't trust you. Jupiter is ready to make an appearance here. I know it. If you don't know it, then the Federation tricked you into giving them your position, a reading on your angular parsec distance from them. My guess is that Jupiter has physically arrived on earth."

Cronus was somber, "Of course, of course, they've developed the technology and we weren't aware of it. Jupiter. Is here? Yes...of course! How stupid of me!"

"So, Cronus, I'm going back to Deep Creek and continue where I left off a few months ago."

"If there was time. Yes, if there was time. We showed you yesterday, when you saw Jessica, that twenty some years have past for you since you went to the biospheres, that your perception of time isn't what it used to be, Alexander."

Alexander expressed concern on his face. His perception of time not what it used to be? And was there only fifteen years left? But why was he chosen to try to right the wrongs of centuries of abuse by the population centers of earth? To Alexander's thinking mind, weighing the implications, he didn't see any way out, regardless of the best of intentions. Baffled, all he could say was, "What, Cronus?"

"Time's not what it seems to be."

Alexander hardly heard what Cronus said, as he pondered the significance of what was going on. There was no human being alive who could possibly mitigate all of the political systems in the world to get them to agree to changing their ways. Again, Alexander could only blurt out, "They won't change their ways."

"Someone needs to persuade them, Alexander!"

"I'm afraid to ask--"

"Ask, Alexander."

"How do I persuade them? With only fifteen years to go? That's how long it will take just to get their attention. And what of time. What's happened to it?"

Confused about his goals, direction, intent, Alexander knew intuitively that he had to leave this underground chamber and face some rather vague yet intimidating circumstance ahead with Jupiter.

* * *

Cronus, Alexander, Zohar, Andrea, and Sophia went to the interlock chamber and then strapped themselves into Zohar's vehicle. Zohar took the controls, and as he busied himself with preparations for the departure, Alexander turned to Cronus to ask some questions that were on his mind. In particular he asked about the Andromedans' ability to genetically engineer new species of plants, algae, plankton, and more complex animals to regulate the fibroplankton and the planetary livable oxygen range of twenty-three to twenty-five percent. As Cronus responded, "We tried every trick that we could conceive of to genetically alter the fibroplankton to save the earth."

"Actually, Cronus," Zohar interrupted, "you're going to have to get us out of here. I don't know the codes or the route."

After a quick touch of his finger, the interlock doors suddenly opened and they burst forth from the ocean floor and straight up. Within moments, they burst forth from the ocean's surface. They climbed to fifteen thousand miles, where looking back onto earth, Cronus showed them the concentration of organihalogens and free radicals in fibroplankton and other microscopic life; from an aggregate imaging tachyon device, the large picture was readily apparent.

Cronus asked them, "How can any group of well-meaning scientists, like us, relatively few in number, correct such a massive problem?"

"But how many came with you in the migration vehicles," Zohar inquired.

"A hundred thousand of us came before your migration into the biospheres, Zohar But most were architects and technicians who came to design structures and do the necessary work of making life here like home. Well, nothing's like home. But this is my home now. And look what intergalactic light speed travel's done to my persona. My eyes. The greatest horror ever visited on a person. My home planet is a twin of the earth--not quite as beautiful, not quite as whimsically wild, the more reflective twin."

"What?" Andrea asked

"I used to be humanoid," Cronus moaned.

Now his big eyes saw many band widths of energy, the entire electromagnetic spectrum. With specialized receptors, he saw several tachyon wave bandwidths, energy faster than light speed; as a result of coming to earth on an extended light speed trip, after materializing in this galaxy, his eyes were profoundly mutated. The eye's DNA helix, in its many chemical configurations, differentiated into specialized retinal receptors capable of sensing band widths beyond light waves, tachyon waves. For the light speed traveler the visible universe takes on a new perception. It appears dead ahead! The brain's DNA altered by light speed travel--physical networking and chemistry--sends signals to the retina in the eyes to mutate, as the eyes orient themselves to a broader visual field, beyond the constraints of light and light speed.

"We see more than we want to see," Cronus exclaimed. "I can actually see gravity waves."

"How's that?" Zohar asked.

"Believe me, if you were me you'd know exactly what I mean. It doesn't require thinking or analysis. It's obvious. It's painful for me to look at many earthlings who lack a clear sense of themselves. They give off all kinds of conflicting energies. Lacking harmony, they're blurred."

Next thing, they left their position from thousands of miles up and headed back to earth and the headquarters of LiteWave Technology. But first Alexander and Cronus navigated their way back to earth and came down to the Sierra Nevada mountains in northern California.

"I've always wanted to do this," Alexander shouted. Then the ship went to terrain run, as they zipped through mountain passes at tree top level, at sixty thousand miles per hour, just twelve seconds. It was frightening, yet exhilarating to the passengers.

"You're an imp, Alexander," Cronus said with a smile.

Alexander responded, "I've seen it simulated in so many computer games. For once, I had to do it myself." In minutes, they zipped around the streets of Los Angeles at a three thousand miles an hour. To ground observers, they were as ephemeral as the wind--gone in the twinkling of an eye. Yet the G forces were mitigated by the design of the craft. It was an awesome experience. Alexander was gleeful and zapped the vehicle right at the Rocky Mountains. It dashed through Rocky Mountain passes on terrain run and corkscrewed upward over the city of Denver to about five thousand miles;. Then it rushed on an angular vector right at the city of Chicago, and streaked over North Michigan Avenue at about a three hundred foot altitude. Gone in the twinkling of an eye. In moments, they were racing around the I495 beltway in the Baltimore/Washington area and headed to the Virginia suburbs, the location of LiteWave Technology.

Alexander landed the craft in the rear parking lot. Popping the canopy, Andrea, Sophia, Zohar, Cronus, and Alexander descended the ladder and went around the front to the main entrance. Of course, all eyes were on Cronus.

The receptionist said, "Who might I say is calling."

"Alexander Petrov and a few friends."

The receptionist recoiled in terror, "Alexander? We thought that you just kind of..."

"Kind of what?"

The receptionist's expression was distressed, her face flush. "Well, that you were kind of--dead? It's been such a long time since anyone's ever mentioned your name. But I've seen pictures of you. How come you haven't... ahhh....?"

Cronus tapped Alexander on the shoulder and leaned over to whisper in his ear, "Ahhh, Al, what the woman's trying to express to you is that you haven't changed--aged-- since you've been in the biospheres."

"What? How old would they expect me to be after a few months. Maybe a year--tops."

Zohar became a part of the caucus. "Actually, Al, you and your friends were permitted to rest and sleep as long as you wanted. Hibernating near light speed your bodies underwent metabolic optimization. You're healthier, younger than ever in appearance."

Cronus continued, "And, Al, metabolic optimization takes a long long time. You just saw Stefano yesterday--when we looked through the tachyon imaging system. Didn't you get it?"

"Come on, now! How long is long?"

The voice of an older woman chimed in, "Try about twenty-four years."

All heads turned to the voice of Jessica who was speechless at seeing Andrea's and Alexander's faces. Jessica stared at them intently. They were equally entranced. They were extremely healthy, quite youthful. While Jessica's portly appearance was affected by twenty-four years of gravitational pull, rich foods, alcohol, and many late night business negotiations at local, national, and international business meeting centers -- otherwise known as resorts. Life styles of the rich and not so famous!

Alexander was speechless. He looked at his hands. He looked at Andrea's face. He looked at Cronus. He looked at Zohar. Each of them varied in age and appearance, yet each was firm, erect, with excellent posture and muscle tone. "Well, it's still good to see you, Jessica. Can we come in?"

"Of course, of course. I've been waiting for your return. Hoping that you might come back some day--especially today."

Alexander suspected the obvious, when Jessica expected them today, after twenty-four years "Well, Sister, were you contacted by a man who refers to himself as Jupiter? And Stefano?"

As they followed her, even Zohar, mentally aware of the time warp, was caught by the emotional confusion in the time warp, as he thought, "Wasn't it just the other day that Sophia, Jessica and I had that little interlude in the Indonesian Rain Forest.

They followed Jessica to the old manufacturing facility. It was large, with the roof open. Alexander's ship had been moved there from Deep Creek, as a kind of a memorial to him. The facility was now used to manufacture space vehicles based on Alexander's initial design. With continued research, the LiteWave scientists had solved the problem of high roentgen radiation from the nuclear fusion used to create virtual waves, gravitational manipulation fields, less sophisticated than the Andromedan tachyon virtual wave anti-gravity drivers.

As they all stood and looked up at Alexander's old ship, there was a protracted silence. Jessica fought the impulse to make comments about their physical differences, age, appearance, body tone, posture, demeanor. But the desire to resist wasn't strong enough. "Actually, Alexander, you look younger than when you disappeared from the face of the earth. But I remember well, the day that I was in Zohar's space vehicle. A little jaunt to the moon. For years I thought that I was hallucinating that day. Now who's this interesting looking character? A friend of Jupiter's?"

"Cronus. My name's Cronus. And as you might have guessed, I'm not very happy today. And I don't have time for social amenities. Is he here?"

From behind them they heard the footsteps of a tall, fit stranger who possessed rather large eyes compared to the humans--still, nothing on the order of the Big Eyes, Cronus. The stranger, Jupiter, dressed in a admiral's styled navy blue uniform with gold buttons, was accompanied by Stefano. They all turned to see Jupiter who addressed Alexander. "You see, the offer was tendered, Alexander, but as always, you had to be in control of the situation. Perception was reality. Yesterday I was megaparsecs away. A distant nuisance whom you chose to ignore. Stefano however is a more reasonable man. He's willing to listen. It seems that he's now a majority stock holder in LiteWave."

Jessica was astonished, unable to comprehend the magnitude of the situation. "Who is this cast of characters, Alexander? And why are you here?"

Alexander spoke. "Cronus is with a scientific expedition from beyond our galaxy. His physical appearance before light speed travel was quite similar to ours. Extended light speed travel caused mutations."

"How interesting, Alexander. Is it time for another Alexandrian discourse on science, business, and industry?"

"Sister. I'm here to bury the hatchet. Smoke the peace pipe. Permit me to get back to my old research with some new twists that I've learned from the Andromedans. Let's build space vehicles to meet the demands of the transportation renaissance!"

"Alexander, there you go again. We've solved the problems in your original design--which, you may be pleased to know, the world marvels at—still. Twenty-five years later you're talking about the transportation renaissance that's already under way. International politics prevented the immediate renaissance to begin while you were here. But Charley Tong from Hong Kong got the ball rolling with Stefano's help."

"Selling my technology, Stefano?" Alexander said angrily.

Cronus interrupted. "Maybe, you're aware of the latest treaties from The Earth Summit. And they're meeting right now in Pittsburgh--the host city. Pittsburgh's now the world's largest biomedical center. Extremely involved in exploring biodiversity. They utilize herbs and natural medicines for organ transplants--big business these days, you might be interested to know-- and picking Pittsburgh is symbolic of the USA's desire to continue to manipulate the biodiversity treaties. They want to show the world that Pittsburgh's medical community can lead the world to new levels of genetic engineering."

"What does that have to do with me?" Jessica asked with a sober expression.

"Probably nothing. However, we need someone influential to get us a forum at The Earth Summit to describe to the world's body politick that current political rhetoric, ideologies, and economic dominance of the treaty by vested interests is going to destroy...this grand and beautiful planet."

Jessica was dumbfounded. "Alexander, why is everything that you're involved in bigger than life? Who are these guys? And where did they get those eyes?"

Cronus lost his calm. "Listen, Jessica, I know that you're a psycho bitch. I know about the insider moves to get your brother ousted from his position as majority stock holder in this company. I'm aware of the fact that you were investigated by the SEC after the fact of Alexander's ouster. You and Stefano, on your own, were great at dirty tricks. A few of them blew up in your face, but you've managed to stay. Further, we know that some of the street names used for the assignments of preferred and common stock issues, for voting purposes, are still fake, Stefano! And both of you still can be investigated by the SEC and prosecuted for antitrust actions...including, statutes that come under the anti-racketeering act. You know it. And I know it. Since we're quietly involved in this planet and monitor event of import. We know all about you!"

Jessica exploded, "Who is this green-eyed monster? And how in the hell do you know everything about us?"

Cronus's head flipped to the side. "Oh, green-eyed monster, is it? That's your attitude? Alexander, inform this psycho bitch who I am. And that I'm not taking any of her back-stabbing crap. Jessica, you've stabbed more people in the back than I've ever had the honor of being friends with. Now, if you want to co-operate with the Federation, let it be. If you don't want to co-operate with the Federation, you're fresh out of a job. Another one bites the dust."

Jessica gave her unsavory look of vengeance to the group. "You come in here, take advantage of my hospitality, try to threaten me with cheap theatrics. Well, actually I have to admit that your intergalactic outfit is pretty convincing. But notwithstanding your theatrics, you can all get the hell out. And for that matter, go straight to hell."

Stefano interceded, "Actually, Jessica, this isn't theatrical entertainment put on for your benefit. Nor is it meant to threaten you directly. These men are on a mission--a way-out mission. They claim that the end of the world is at hand. Jupiter's filled me in. Ha ha! Here we go again. Intergalactic witnesses! And you, Alexander, are you among the holy?"

"That's exactly what we're here to discuss. Unless these days of abuse are shortened, this planet's going to become the biblical hell. I don't have another minute for this self-serving ignoramus--who accuses himself openly of killing my mother." Alexander snapped it out.

Cronus grabbed Alexander, pulled him aside, and whispered in his ear. "Let's get the hell out of here--before Jupiter over there sends in his men to detain us. We'll become their prisoners. We've got to get out of here now. Trust me."

When the loud bantering subsided, Jessica became fearful, "Just, who's making these allegations about street names?"

Cronus the omnipotent, practitioner of Andromedan omnipotent eaves dropping technology, replied, "Your fate's in your brother's hands.

Within one week. I can assure you that the Treasury Department can be here to arrest you and put you behind bars for the rest of your days."

Jupiter abruptly stepped up to the group. "So, Alexander, we agree, after all. Now, to bring this crisis under control I suggest that we set up a corporation to deal with the problems at hand."

"Problems? There're so many problems...injustices." Then Alexander slowly climbed the ladder to his old space vehicle, now a monument. "First, I'll reclaim what's mine."

Stefano stepped forward. "No, nothing's yours, you're legally dead. And that's still my ship. Mine, Alexander. I have what you want. Instead of the reverse."

"Your ship? Somehow, Stefano, I suspect that you always take what you want. Everything's yours. Just like your new intergalactic friend there, Jupiter. Tell him about your corruption. You both share a lot in common--control, controlling everything. I'll deal with you, Stefano!"

Stefano smirked. "Listen to who's talking. The biggest control freak of all times."

While this was going on, Andrea, Zohar, Sophia, and Cronus sneaked up the other ladder and got into the cockpit of the original LiteWave vehicle, where Alexander had already positioned himself.

As the vehicle powered up, Jessica stepped forward. "You can't leave me here in the midst of your latest travesty, Alexander. You just can't take off and leave me here to deal with this Jupiter alien. Who in the hell is he? How do they know everything about me? Alexander--don't go! Take me with you! I can explain everything."

With a burst of light, climbing through the open air ceiling, Alexander's vehicle shot straight away with him and his companions.

Chapter 32
City-By-City

They returned to The Big Eyes headquarters. Alexander and Andrea once again took up residence in the villa. They felt better about Cronus, because he took an emotional stand against Jessica. They met with Cronus on the verandah, when he said, "Help me, Alexander, and I'll help you. Stefano and Jessica can go to jail. And you can have your company back. But first things first."

"Like I said, Alexander, never get them angry," Zohar smiled.

Sitting on the verandah they watched the falls. Alexander had a plan and presented it to the group. He wanted Cronus to produce a report on a city-by-city basis--with weekly, monthly, annual, five year, and ten year projections of organihalogens (fluorine, chlorine, bromine, astatine, and iodine), and free radicals, that attach themselves to the nucleus of fibroplankton cells, affecting their metabolism. Fouling the bottom level of the food chain, the mass of fibroplankton, the mass producers of oxygen in the oceans, was the last act with A Split Second to Midnight. Alexander planned to distribute the report at the Earth Summit in Pittsburgh. It had to get into the hands of scientists, as well as international politicians.

Later that evening, they all sipped an after-dinner liqueur -- Amaretto for Alexander and Andrea, Bailey's Irish Cream for Cronus, Zohar, and Sophia. Alexander felt that it was time for The Big Eyes to show themselves. They and only they were capable of presenting the data to the world.

"But, Alexander, you're the salesman," Cronus said, "Gee, you'll do a hell of a job persuading everyone."

"No one has your intimate knowledge of the data, Cronus."

"Look, we Big Eyes have taken an unspoken vow not to interfere with earth's history."

"Have you ever created a new species of plant, insect, mammal, or other such things?"

Cronus nodded affirmatively. "Sure, that's part of our research and our fun."

"Research or not, your experiments affected the history of the earth. So you broke your vow."

Cronus smiled. "Mmmm, this Bailey's great stuff.... Where were we? Oh yes, once a few years ago, a colleague of mine designed a fish that appeared to be over a hundred million years old. Not so. It was only a hundred days old at the most. We were testing the sense of humor of a certain marine biologist--who, as it happens, will be at The Earth Summit."

Alexander continued, "What we need is some Andromedan communications technology capable of controlling satellite transmissions. We want to broadcast via satellite to all of the cable stations, simultaneously. Every channel across the spectrum."

Cronus responded, "I think that's in the realm of cheap theatrics. Let's just get that report together. Come with me, Al."

In the massive underground compound, a hollowed mountain in the North Atlantic, off the coast of Europe, they left the villa, and descended to an even lower level than the ground floor. They walked to an internal shuttle system. Small vehicles, traveling at forty miles an hour, moved along a conduit track--actually, half a conduit. The vehicle had four seats--two front buckets, two rear buckets. Alexander saw that many Andromedans were busily working in their labs and work areas which were visible from the tram. The wall closest to the tram was glass; the walls forming the rear of the rooms were the granite of the interior of the hollowed-out mountain. They traveled a few miles to a central document processing area and compiled tables of data on a city-by-city basis. The document contained a summary of the condition of the sewage networks, sewage processing, toxic waste treatment on a city-by-city basis--for the entire planet. Each section of the report was in the language of the country being reported. In addition to organihalogens and free radicals, all other forms of pollution were reported for that country and pin-pointed to exact locations and offenders. The technology to produce the reports was not Andromedan, but from Silicone Valley.

"Cronus, just how did you obtain all of this technology? compile all of this information? Survey our cities on a continuing basis? Without being noticed?"

Cronus explained how they learned a lot about how to interoperate with international business and commerce. They built warehouses, where things were delivered and paid for. "We've got a major privately held corporation in Minnesota."

Thousands of copies of the report were printed and hard bound. It was quite an impressive document. Would anyone read it? Alexander observed the compilation and binding of the report. The Andromedan corporation arranged for it to be delivered to the Pittsburgh Convention Center, where they arranged for Cronus to be the guest speaker. While Cronus was a total unknown to anyone, The Big Eyes used their corporate money to make very generous contributions to The University of Pittsburgh Medical Center to get Cronus in as speaker.

"What makes you think that anyone will listen to, Cronus?" Alexander said, as they walked among the fountains in the main lobby of the mountain.

"Well, do I stand any better of a chance than you do, Alexander?

Chapter 33
A Tragic Death

Several days later, there were rumors throughout the USA of Alexander's re-appearance, but all in all, Alexander wasn't a high-enough profile person on the business or political scene for the reports to make an impact. However, Cronus became aware of some facts: that Jessica made a goodwill gesture and transferred some of her stock and other shares with fictitious street names, back to Alexander's name to avoid the unknown--the wrath of the Andromedans. Alexander now had some money.

Alexander and Andrea had checked into Pittsburgh's Hilton International Hotel. Alexander called a local clothier, Joseph Orlando, who had several suits tailored to Alexander's physique; he also bought some shirts, ties, shoes. There were shops in the hotel for Andrea to purchase current fashions. However, due to her extended stay in the biospheres, Andrea had no inhibitions about revealing evening wear. Her once conservative fear of making misimpressions had given way to a healthy expression of her beauty and she revealed her statuesque appearance for all to behold.

Dressed in her evening clothes, she stepped into the room where Alexander was seated in front of the television. He rose to his feet and went to her. "Oh Baby, yes! You're looking great."

"Feeling great, too. It's time to blow off inhibitions."

Her dress was long, lithe, form-fitting, yet it wasn't tight. It hung across her hips in a manner that accentuated her long shapely legs.

It was split up the sides; when she walked, a shapely leg occasionally peaked out. Her long auburn hair was held up on her head. Her deep green dress with gold trim sparkled from every angle to match her green eyes. When she leaned forward to remove her shoes from a box on the bed, Alexander caught a glimpse of her wide set, firm breasts.

"It's amazing how beautiful and healthy the biospheres have kept you. I just have to touch you."

She smiled, "By all means, touch me, kiss me." She let her long dress slink to the floor and stood before Alexander. Smiling, he slid his hands along her thighs and slowly peeled off her panty hose. She pulled his head to her tummy, while he nurtured her love of oral intercourse, not words. He performed the magic that sent waves of pleasure pulsing through her abdomen; she twitched, cried, and sank into his arms.

About an hour later, they were in the lobby of the hotel. Although it was elegant, Alexander observed, "But, Andrea, this lobby just doesn't compare to the lobby in the North Atlantic."

She looked all about. "No no, it doesn't, but we can't have everything, now can we?"

They mixed with the crowd of international diplomats and business people. Picking some sea food from the trays, Alexander and Andrea listened to a smattering of comments regarding tainted sea food--tainted with organihalogens.

Two men were speaking. The first said, "Now, here's another report on organihalogens, fibroplankton. Who's got the time to absorb this kind of information? The money's in biodiversity, biomedicals, organ transplants, genetic engineering. Let those other little countries be distracted by hyperpolitics from nefarious origins. We need to get on track with the right organizations that will help us."

The other gentleman nodded in agreement. "This new organihalogens demographic report's just an irresponsible attempt to create dissent among the countries that continue to profit from biodiversity. Ecological disaster really isn't a cogent topic for this Earth Summit."

Alexander couldn't help but interject, "Well, of course not, what's the sense in returning to the original intent of the Earth Summit? Saving the planet. No no, my friends, what we have here is just one big happy biomedical convention. Just one more trade show."

Andrea looked the two men in the eyes. "Tell me, Guys, who's keeping track of the aggregates in the oceans? Is there an organization responsible for monitoring the health of the oceans?"

The two men looked at them, and one said, "This is reminiscent of the Jacques Cousteau era, the 1980's, when everyone paid lip service to those old timers who glorified and beatified their own thinking. It gave men like him great pleasure to warn everyone of the dangers."

"Is there any greater understanding of the synergy between organihalogens, the depletion of the nitrogen cellulose being washed back into the oceans because of the depletion of the rain forests, and the reduction in the percentage of healthy fibroplankton?"

The two men looked at Alexander, as one said, "Just another wild-eyed pessimist."

Alexander and Andrea stared into each other's eyes. Totally dismayed, they moved to a cash bar for drinks. Drinks in hand, they turned to be greeted by two attractive young men who were taken by Andrea. One of them looked over her back to her backside and said, "Excellent!"

She did a double take at him, "Just what are you looking at?"

"Good looking, Woman!" He leered at her.

She smiled, "Should I smack him, or thank him, Alexander?"

"Thank him! Then smack him!"

"Thank you, Cutey." At that, she noticed that his friend was carrying a copy of Cronus's report. "Pardon me, have you perused that?"

The young man held it up in curiosity. "This? What the hell is this? I tried reading it. It's so dry. But I'm saving it as my souvenir from this Earth Summit. There won't be another summit with this much business opportunity for some time. And I may never be back."

Alexander scrutinized him closely. "Just a souvenir?"

"Okay, okay I kind of read it. It's a lot of exaggerated concern about matters that no one's all that concerned about. If the ecology of the planet were in such a critical stage, folks would know about it, it would be on their lips."

Alexander sipped his drink, "It's on your lips. Let's hear more."

"I'm a marine biologist. And what's curious about this document is that there's no agency, worldwide, capable of compiling this information. So it's invalid, no one's going to believe it. The Andromedan Free Press, with Cronus as the author? Come on. It sounds like an anachronistic sci-fi come-on. Some one compiles this impressive looking document to scare the shit out of everyone. Come on. This is a joke!"

Andrea was intense, "Being a marine biologist, what are your interests here?"

"Hey, lady, come on. Anyone that's at this particular summit is here to parlay their access to different species into money. There's some big scores to be made here. Gigabucks. Smaller deals of megabucks. I'll take a small one. One of these biomedical giants...like Merck, Johnson & Johnson, IBM, Miles...they're here to make contacts with scientific free lancers."

Alexander's head snapped back. "IBM? Did I hear you say IBM. Into the biomedical market?"

"Big time. Where have you been, mister? They're doing quiet research into creating biological cyborgs, you know. And they're betting the farm on it. They're still trying to regain their glory days of the last century."

Alexander smiled. "Sure, sure, biological computers."

"Yea, sure. Hey what's this all about? Come on, Man. Don't act like you're living in the dark ages!"

Andrea stopped them, as they were about to walk off. "Hey, Dudes? What about the political meetings here? Which countries are concerned about our intraplanetary ecology?"

The marine biologist's expression became incredulous, "Come on, what's your problem? Those meetings are all puffery, pomp, and circumstance. Standing on ceremony. Everybody gets up and makes a speech. All their governments make statements about coming changes. Just scan this Andromedan Free Press report here. Nothing compelling's ever came out of an Earth Summit, what with varied conclaves of countries looking out for their own best interests at every summit. As the changing wheels of fortune shift the wealth around the globe. Enough said?"

Alexander looked into Andrea's eyes. "Who's going to listen to this report, let alone believe it? Cronus, where are you now?"

Andrea and Alexander sensed the mood of the earth summit; let's make a deal. While everyone was jockeying for position, Cronus had to get up and deliver the bad news: fifteen years, to the end of the planet? And clearly his source--Cronus's report-- was considered by people in the ecology business to be highly dubious. No one agency, they believed, had the ability to compile conclusive evidence about the state of the entire planet, the failing ecology, the Goddess of Life.

Cronus, at the very last minute, pleaded with Alexander to open the meeting in the ballroom where Cronus was scheduled to speak. There were three thousand seats, but there weren't a thousand attendees, a few hundred at best. The ballroom felt almost empty. Alexander took the podium, in lieu of a nervous Cronus. At the podium Alexander began by introducing the report as a responsible work of research. He then went through a brief, yet analytical, synopsis of the American tax system. He used it as a model for emerging tax systems in free-market countries that needed to use their taxes to clean up their ecological problems, toxic waste sewage processing, sewage disbursements. The American system was not one to be modeled.

He covered the threat of organihalogens and free radicals set loose in the oceans in a geometric progression over the past four decades. That is when his credibility became suspect. The USA, which was supposed to conduct research with the support of other countries, did not support the findings of the Andromedan Report.

Looking out at the ballroom, Alexander noticed Jupiter and Stefano standing in the doorway. Alexander didn't believe that Jupiter had the courage to be seen in public. However, the attendees were clamoring to get close to Jupiter who walked to the podium, while Stefano stayed at the rear of the hall. As Jupiter walked, approached the podium with deliberate aplomb and authority, a crowd clamored behind him. There was growing hysteria in the voices of the growing crowd; soon, it was standing room only. Then there was uproarious applause, when Cronus--appearing quite militant--came in carrying a weapon. This time, he wasn't dressed in his jeans, T-shirt, and athletic shoes. He looked like an intergalactic big- eyed warrior who was accompanied by an awesome beauty in a green and gold-trimmed dress--Andrea.

Cronus pointed his weapon at Jupiter who nodded and moved to the side. Cronus adjusted his weapon, which was strapped to his shoulder, when he took the podium with Alexander and Andrea to his left and Jupiter to his right. Stefano was at the rear of the ballroom.

Cronus spoke. "Well, my friends, there is growing doubt as to the authenticity of The Andromedan Free Press Report."

The applause was thunderous. Each person heard Cronus address them in their own language: French, German, Italian, Portuguese, Spanish, Chinese, Russian, many African dialects and so on, and so on. The crowd was in awe. Now they were willing to listen.

Cronus continued. "Friends, the basic problems in life deal with duplicity; doing it the right way or having it your way. And duality is at the basic nature of every being. If you wish to argue that point, so be it. Duplicity, mans' inhumanity to man, is the manifestation of the forces which drive the universe...yin and yang. I haven't come to argue your religion, nor the source of yin and yang. A great American icon in my mind was Teddy Roosevelt who said, '"Whenever you're asked if you can do a job, tell 'em, certainly, I can. Then get busy and find out how to do it.' Earthlings, your work lies ahead of you! And now I want to turn it back to Alexander Petrov, tonight's keynote speaker."

The applause went on for five minutes. The crowd knew that Cronus was pulling a fast one on them, as they were each hearing him in their own language. Most of the crowd believed that Cronus and Jupiter were fakes--people in special make-up, part of some presentation--and they loved every moment of it.

Alexander continued. Nervously, he cleared his throat; there was dead silence. "Well, my friends. If I may be so bold as to call you that--" The crowd went crazy. They hooted, applauded, and begged for more, as they all looked at each other with great glee. Alexander's eyes and grin grew wider as he reacted to the crowd. He looked at the crowd, back at Cronus, back at the crowd, and back at Cronus. "Is it working for me too, Cronus?" Cronus tried not to give away his position, when the crowd continued to applaud, and stared endlessly at Cronus' weapon?

"Okay, okay..." Alexander intoned, "we're some magicians up here. So hear me out. And please meet Andrea. A living Goddess of Life." The crowd whistled and gave her a standing ovation.

Alexander continued. "There's still hope for us all. It's important that the earth continue, isn't it? When we have to deal with the frustrations of our daily lives, and there are major geopolitical problems looming everywhere, we all want someone else to be responsible for those problems. Don't allow a logical view of everything to block your... your intuition. Most of us are college-trained and have studied mythology and literature that just don't seem to have a real place in daily life. Well, they do! My life had the makings of a tragedy. And now the life of the earth, The Goddess of Life, Gaia, is tragically coming to an end. Why? Because we're all focused on our own prosperity. Our prosperity, our lives, coming from The Goddess of Life. When she dies, we die. There is a profound duplicity here which goes much deeper than hypocrisy. We see ourselves as separate--self-contained, self-sustaining, self-reliant, all admirable qualities. But our lives are rooted in the life of the earth. And we're nothing without her. Each one of you can live without a career. But not without your earth. Take the Andromedan Free Press Report home. And do something about it. Talk to the bureaucrats who misappropriated your money. Make them accountable. Make changes. Make it a great day!"

A fanatical voice was shouting from the rear of the ball room. It was Stefano, who forced his way toward the podium and shouted angrily, "Once again you're in control. That's your game, Alexander. You've set up this platform to be your show. He's the man in control and you're all listening to him. He claims to be Alexander Petrov who was declared dead eighteen years ago. You don't exist! And you're not coming back to take what belongs to me!"

Stefano had by now come up alongside Andrea, and there was a struggle for Stefano's weapon. Cronus had a death grip on Stefano's arm, which was aiming the death ray gun at Alexander. During the struggle, it went off as it swept past Andrea. Her beautiful green dress with gold-trim disintegrated on her body, as her arms raised straight out to form the sign of the cross. Her mouth wore a surprised pained expression, as her naked body burned and disintegrated before all onlookers who were utterly horrified -- shocked, traumatized.

The crowd became frenzied. With horrified anger and indignation, people grabbed at Stefano and disarmed him, while they carried him out of the ballroom, under Jupiter's direction who shouted back the lunging crowd.

As he was taken from the ballroom, Stefano howled with egotistical zeitgeist in his voice that came from the purity of his anger. "Colona money founded, funded, the company, Alexander! It was really my company from the beginning. I fucked your wife! Shoved your self-righteous mother down the steps! Me. I'm in charge now!"

Chapter 34
The Offer

Several weeks later, Alexander sat opposite Jessica in her opulent office. They stared at each other. She preferred to look away, rather than look at his face, his eyes, his pained expressions. "Alexander. I know that I did you wrong. I know that I was unreasonable. But you have to admit early on that you were unreasonable."

Somberly he looked into her eyes.

"Alexander, in your day no one was ready for your vision of the transportation renaissance. If you just hadn't suggested that we get into totally new markets--become Neo-Californians who made all the money! Well, everything would have been okay. And you wouldn't have gotten into this position of the tragic loss of Andrea."

He continued to stare at her sadly.

"Alexander. I protected your interests. Sell your stock. Go start a new company. You've only been on vacation...for the past twenty-four years."

Tears swelled in his eyes. "The Andromedan Federation did me in. I should have listened closer to Zohar. Some Andromedans treachery--can't be trusted. Jupiter gave Stefano that weapon of destruction. Andrea was vaporized. And I can't shake her dying expression."

"No, not Stefano. There were many eye-witnesses. But none could identify him as the perpetrator. You were fooled by someone."

Tears ran down his face. "Too little, too late. I failed to realize Stefano's motivation. Jealousy and greed. Plain and simple. He meant to kill me with that disintegrating gun. And appease Jupiter's anger with me at the same time. How do you kill a man who's already been declared dead? The Andromedans are very cunning. With all of the commotion they thought that no one would identify Stefano. Forgive the pun. They were dead right!"

Alexander sighed, "Jupiter is selling cataclysm. To perpetuate Andromedan rule."

There were no guarantees that the Andromedan Federation would restore the planet, by repairing the fibroplankton/algae problem. It wasn't discussed in detail during anyone's intergalactic teleconference from the underground sanctuary meetings with Jupiter.

"Jessica, Jupiter wants to colonize the earth. His colonial aspirations are tantamount to communism. No one owns anything in the Andromedan Federation. The bureaucrats control everything. They'll confiscate this company for sure. And you'll be out! The gods will come and work their magic on the oceans at the very last moment. Then, Jupiter will rule!"

Unable to focus on his eyes, seeing an urgent message flash at her desk phone that she knew to be from Stefano, she spoke quickly with aggravation. "Alexander, Alexander, who knows when the gods will arrive? If ever. The tragedy is that you've permitted your idealism to dictate the tone of your life. Your untimely choice of visiting the biospheres. The untimely death of your wife. The untimely death of our mother. Just look at you. You're an emotional wreck You've come undone!"

Tears streamed down his face. "Exactly. I've lost my dear wife. And now I'm losing my mind. So I've come to deal with Stefano who was ushered out by Jupiter's men. Now where the hell is he?"

"You don't dictate in here. You can't threaten me with Andromedan rule. Get the hell out of my office. Leave now. And take your stupid fantasies with you. Stefano is innocent. There are no eyewitnesses who will attest to any of your charges. You've lost. I've won!"

He dove across her desk and grabbed her by the throat. "Where's that bastard Stefano? Tell me or I'll choke the life out of you."

"Ahhh, stop! Stop! Ahhhhh, you're killing me! Frantically Jessica grabbed at his hands. Slowly Alexander released his death grip. Almost falling backwards, he fled from the office.

Chapter 35
Goddess Of Life

With intense fear for her personal safety, to repel Alexander's wrath, Jessica had the family compound put in Alexander's name, along with the Deep Creek manufacturing facilities with all of its old equipment and computers. Alexander's father had passed away while Alexander was in the biospheres. Without a clear will from Sergei, with a lot of financial resources, Jessica assumed ownership of a lot of LiteWave assets. She gave the less valuable assets to her brother, Alexander.

"No will. Actually, Zohar, Dad thought that he would live forever. That's just the kind of man that he was."

It was dusk. They sat in the Deep Creek gazebo, which, to their surprise, had been well maintained. From behind them, they heard a voice announce, "And why does that subliminal inexplicable feeling of living forever exist in some people's minds?"

Without looking, Alexander answered, "Actually, Cronus, I don't really know."

Neither Alexander nor Zohar turned their heads to acknowledge Cronus, who said, "You're both looking well."

"Probably too well for as rotten as I feel," exclaimed Alexander. "So, what brings you to these parts?"

Cronus sat next to Zohar. Cronus began an explanation of the origins of his species--not a biological-etiological chronology; rather, he described the spiritual state of the planet of his origin. He estimated that his culture was a million years older than Alexander's.

Alexander and Zohar nodded pleasantly and sipped a strong after-dinner liqueur. Cronus continued. "To permit the destruction of the earth's ecosystem, The Goddess of Life, is to destroy the spiritual system of things. The nature of existence isn't clear to any of us, yet we hold deep beliefs. Like your father, Alexander. Your father believed that he would live forever. Well, I'm not going to argue for or against that feeling of eternal life. But I will say, if this human world is destroyed, there will be no eternal life. To get to heaven you've got to start here. Destroy this temple of life and, trust me, heaven will not follow. That deeply held feeling of eternal life comes from the rhythms of nature. The problem with this planet is its ties to the recent past, existential methodology."

Alexander shook his head in agreement, but responded with a question. "There's no God?"

Cronus smiled. "But there is a Goddess of Life. And the pantheistic nature of the universe cannot be denied. Deify anything, anthropomorphize anything, but few understand and protect the sanctity of nature to assure eternal life to those who seek it. Destroy this natural temple, earth, and anyone alive today who seeks eternal life will spiritually perish forever. Unless these days of ecological abuse are shortened!"

"Is this a Hindu lesson?" asked Alexander. "I'm not ready for this philosophy lesson, Cronus. I am incapable of feeling anything other than grief. Do you understand that?"

"No! Not a Hindu lesson. It's Zen...an integrated view of the whole. The universe and the deity are one and the same."

Through his grief, Alexander mustered up a response, "Zentastic? Zentastic themes for people to be persuaded by. Everyone in search of eternal life can perish with me. I can't save the earth because I'm not the human sacrifice, Cronus. I'm morose over the hell I'm in. An end to all of this is pretty appealing."

Cronus smiled. "Just go and live in the biospheres, Alexander, and your perspective will slowly change to a view of life unbound by hell. The biospheres are heaven. Get into it and forget this traumatic event."

Zohar agreed. "You're becoming a tragic figure, Alexander, because you've totally lost hope. With idealism as your special quarter, your gift is your relentless pursuit of truth. Shine on, you crazy diamond!"

"Shine on!" Cronus shouted

Chapter 36
With Nirvana On Her Lips

On a trip to Technosphere in an interstellar vehicle, after much commiseration, and the exchanging of ideas and opinions, Alexander, Zohar, and Cronus, agreed to agree: certain municipal and environmental bureaucrats (so to speak), world wide, were the primary obstacle in saving the earth's ecological balance. Organihalogens, planet wide, reached critical mass in the oceans from municipal waste. To persuade any politician to change his ways and persuade manufacturing special interest groups to change their demands on the environment was impossible.

Cronus, meanwhile, intimated that Jupiter's coming to earth to effect change was pure wishful thinking. Jupiter was out to build himself a reputation and accrue greater power and influence, by assembling a team who would come to earth and extend Jupiter's influence within the Andromedan Federation.

Cronus smiled. "The primary objective of a bureaucrat is to increase his own job security by hiring more people."

Alexander nodded in agreement. "What benefit is it to a bureaucrat to become efficient and define his responsibilities"

Zohar agreed. "There's no personal benefit to a bureaucrat who's job it is to clean up the environment. He'll becomes obsolete."

"Of course, no one knows the real problems through all of that bureaucratic rhetoric and double-talk," said Cronus, who zapped out beyond Pluto in a matter of seven hours.

Cronus accelerated toward light speed in pursuit of Technosphere. He did some quick fingertip manipulations of the crystal controls and at once had Technosphere imaged on his three dimensional tachyon wave imaging system.

There was no earthly awareness of Technosphere, because of its design; like the biospheres, it was designed for stealth. With opulent personnel quarters, Technosphere was a flattened triangular vehicle in the shape of a pyramid, large enough on the flight deck for twenty individuals to stand in and move about. The shape was excellent for continued quasi-light-speed travel. There were tachyon wave drivers at the three tips of the flattened base of the Technosphere pyramid.

The base of Technosphere did not remain stationary but adjusted to changes in space topology, the aggregate negative force, the warping force, gravity. Due to their near-light-speed velocity, centrifugal force was produced by the orbit. The sun always appeared to be overhead in the vehicle, which created centrifugal force at the base as it orbited the sun. Arlee intended to remain at ninety-nine percent of light speed -- forever, or as long as it took to transform herself from the mortal state of nirvana to the immortal state of nirvana.

In the primary chamber, they stood before Arlee who sat in a high-back captain's chair at the apex of a triangle formed by the rows of the Guild of Women: a row of two women directly behind her, with a row of three behind them, with a row of four behind them. Zohar had already explained to Alexander and Cronus that she was the high priestess of The Guild, The Supreme Goddess, born, in the Zagros range of Northwest India, more than five thousand earth years earlier.

Arlee always wore a slight smile, a sure sign of bliss, nirvana on her lips. Zohar looked into her eyes. The seating chamber was dimly illuminated. Arlee nodded her head affirmatively. "I see that there are several of you. And you've come to seek permission to distribute pure untainted food from the biospheres, to earth."

Zohar with the help of the Big Eyed Andromedans, as a gesture of environmental concern, were going to distribute pure untainted food, from the biospheres, to earth. Food without preservatives; organihalogens. It was a metaphorical gesture to motivate people's environmental thinking, consciousness.

Zohar shook his head incredulously. "Tell me, how did you know? Just how did you know about all the people on earth? About all of the problems?"

"I knew at our last meeting, Zohar. To explain it to you would have been too arduous a task. Your experience in visiting earth was worth an endless number of words. I lacked the patience to explain what you had to see for yourself...and I've never experienced. Yet The Guild is aware of the shortcomings of earth. But when it's all over, Zohar, a deal is a deal. You must build Technosphere II as The Guild has directed."

Zohar was mystified. "Please, a clue, give me a clue."

"Turn and behold," Arlee intoned. And there, for all to see, was a television broadcast from earth, "Zohar, Dear, you were too busy managing the biospheres to learn the Andromedan communications technology which has compatibility with earth side technology, radio waves, microwaves."

Cronus looked at her and smiled. "Arlee, the chances of succeeding are slim. But to invite the Andromedan Federation will accomplish little. They'll just screw things up beyond all recognition. Agreed?"

"Yes, agreed. Jupiter is a political demigod with imperial designs. He will muck it up.!"

Amazed, Cronus looked at Arlee and her Guild. "Well, how could you possibly know about Jupiter? How? Please tell me?"

"A woman's prerogative to have a few secrets, Cronus. You've been on earth too long. You're losing your spiritual nature and its telepathic visions." Arlee paused. "Remember, Cronus, I am the living Gaia. And Gaia is the mother of Earth. So you might say that I'm simply showing a maternal concern for your spiritual health."

Arlee addressed Alexander. "And you, with your special personal qualities, do you expect me to consent to earth receiving the fruits of the biospheres?"

"What?"

"Do you expect me to consent? I can be your ally, Alexander. Your human nature, your ego, says help the planet. When it should be your spiritual nature that says help the planet. Your spirit is overcome with grief over your loss. Andrea."

"And my human nature, Arlee."

"Alexander, your human nature is where all your capabilities are..."

"And what do you suggest to cure my soul?"

"Deal with your thwarted animal nature, Alexander. Kill Stefano, the jackal who will sell us all into Andromedan rule. And Zohar and Cronus will take care of the problems on earth"

Chapter 37
End The Destruction

The Andromedans excelled at creating hydroponically grown vegetable proteins and gave that agricultural technology to the biospheres. Arlee would not deal with anyone until she believed that the Andromedans were dealt with--which came down to dealing with Jupiter. The future gift to earth, from the biospheres governed by The Guild, was to be a meatless regimen of vegetables, grains, and fruits. Unfortunate, because most of the earth daily consumed great quantities of meat, poultry, and sea food. However, dairy products were available.

In anticipation of Arlee's order to distribute pure food, The Andromedans, Cronus and company, built many large cargo ships with great storage bays to be loaded by feeder vehicles, barges, from the biospheres. Alexander anticipated a lot of resistance, anger, even bloodshed, as a result of free food being delivered all over the planet: massive bureaucracies, government agencies, food producers, unions who delivered the food, and retail food chains, all over the planet, were about to lose their market share--simply put, their money!

Cronus designed aerodynamic, free-floating barge vehicles for the purposes of delivering foods from the biospheres to earth. However, evading earthly military ion rocket aircraft, very quick, able to burst to high speeds, quite maneuverable, was Cronus' specialty. He simply neutralized them. As yet, earth side governments had not deployed the LiteWave vehicle, which they purchased from ICARUS/NASA through Stefano. It was still top secret. Cronus devised a method of reducing their ion driver's output, essentially by slowing them down. Cronus also designed smaller vehicles to intercept the earth-based military aircraft. Andromedans didn't believe in destroying their opponents, but at times they enjoyed embarrassing their opponents.

Jupiter called a meeting. He wanted Alexander in attendance. Cronus went for him deep within the hollowed-mountain retreat in the North Atlantic, where Alexander had retreated to study Andromedan archives-- old, very old documents.

"Alexander. There's nothing in those documents that you don't already know."

"Like the Andromedan genesis, for instance? Of course, I know everything about your origins, Cronus. Actually, I don't know anything about you, or your reasons for being here. And why you're oxygen-breathing, cellulose-eating creatures like we are. Really. Can't you understand that we earthlings are mystified by the entire thing. Our genetic and chemical make-ups are virtually..."

"Identical?"

"Thank you, Cronus."

Alexander was puzzled. "So while earthlings search for the missing link in evolution through genetic finger prints, along came the Andromedans who have their own genetic evolution?"

Cronus shook his head in agreement. "So, then, how could there possibly be a match between us? Galaxies apart? The probabilities are astronomically slim?"

"Yes, Cronus. So really how old are you? Just answer that one simple question and I'll stop my research? This entire Split Second to Midnight thing is just a minute or two for you? Now isn't it? You're just toying with Jupiter, aren't you? Even Jupiter doesn't know how old you really are."

"Zohar came at it from a similar point of view, Alexander. So consider this. Zohar is just over five thousand years older than you are. And no harm's come to him or his culture. In fact they have prospered. So does it really matter how old I am?"

"Yes, Cronus, it totally matters. For sure. Who are you?"

"I'm your guardian angel."

Alexander just smiled. "You're a lousy guardian angel."

"Well. You're still here after that fiasco at the Pittsburgh Convention Center."

"And why didn't you use your weapon to save, Andrea?"

Cronus smiled. " Because, Alexander, I'm a pacifist. And that wasn't a weapon. My hobby is linguistic computers. Knowing, understanding, and speaking languages. That weapon was an Andromedan analog crystal computer that took the words from only the podium speaker and fed them to the audience in their native tongues. Everyone knows we were speaking in tongues that night. It was a blast. Everyone had fun!"

"Except Andrea."

Cronus was solemn. "Are you a warrior, Alexander?"

"I could be. But I don't want to be one. Yet I'm not a pacifist."

"Then, Alexander, You've got to go out and win the war of words. The time is upon us. Forget about researching the past. Win this battle. Do the job. Can do?"

Alexander became teary-eyed, "Can do! Angel!"

* * *

Deep beneath the Atlantic, from tunnels leading from their hollowed out underground mountain chamber, they returned to the intergalactic conferencing center on the roof of the villa at the base of the hollowed mountain. Alexander and Cronus had a communications window opened with Andromeda. At once they were in touch with Jupiter.

Jupiter spoke first. "Alexander, Cronus, what have you decided concerning the Split Second scenario on earth?"

Via tesserac communications Alexander looked into the eyes of Jupiter who was back at Andromeda in his Technosphere Space Platform, orbiting The Andromedan Galaxy. Alexander insisted, "First, Jupiter, I must know where Stefano is..."

"What do you hope to do with that piece of information?"

"Show him to me, Jupiter. I want to see him."

"You're a very cunning man, Alexander. Okay, here's Stefano."

Stefano sat on a large green easy chair in pristine surroundings- a background of stark white with beautiful, exotic plants draping the room. Stefano appeared quite comfortable.

"You're an outrageously jealous, cold-blooded murderer who took leave of his senses decades ago"! Alexander could not resist shouting.

"And now you have followed us to the biospheres...for what? To kill us?"

"You think that I had anything to do with Andrea's death?"

Alexander became incensed. "Jupiter. You're taking me for a fool. You expect me to have responsibility...without authority."

Jupiter wore a very broad grin, "My son on earth. Alexander. Already you're playing tough politics. What do I get in the exchange for Stefano?"

"You get absolutely nothing. Not a thing."

"What?!" Jupiter thundered.

"What we have here is a failure to communicate!"

"How's that, Alexander?"

"You're expecting me to become part of your system of things-- taxes, corruption, the whole package. Why not ask me to be a Neo-Californian and pay from the moons of Jupiter? All of those corrupt mining operations..."

"Corrupt? That's such a naive word."

"Is it? You've never defined what the taxes are. What we'll be assessed for being a part of the Andromedan Federation. It seems that we have absolutely nothing that you could want, Jupiter."

"I see what you're thinking."

"So what? What does Andromeda want from us? If we invite you in to repair our ecological problems?"

"Problems, Alexander? Cataclysm is the word. You just don't know what's imbedded in my moons--the moons of Jupiter. Compounds for tachyon technology. You need me to save the fibroplankton--hence, the planet. And we want you and your Neo-Californians to ship us the compounds, from the moons of Jupiter, that we need "

"If not me, then who, Jupiter?"

"He sits here on my right. Stefano."

Alexander could be cunning, but only in the most dire situations. "So, then, Jupiter, you'd assign a criminal, Stefano, to save us from destruction. Isn't that ironic?"

"Ironic? Pragmatic? Those don't constitute an oxymoron. But you'd like me to think that they do."

Alexander shook his head negatively. "This is just turning into idle chatter. Let's get to the heart of this. You send Stefano to us. Here.

At my designated time...oh, say tomorrow at 1400 hours. Then the negotiations will commence. When we have received Stefano."

Chapter 38
Empire? Federation!

That evening, Alexander, Zohar, and Cronus dined in the lobby of the hollowed-out mountain. They all preferred the Chinese Cantonese Cuisine. First came the duck won-ton soup. Alexander took small sips of soup from his large soup spoon. In between portions of won-ton, he said, "You're the genius, Cronus. Think of something. There must be a way to get us out of this."

"Out of what?"

With surprise, Alexander dropped his spoon into that large bowl of soup. "Look, this entire thing's gone far enough. I've had it. My wife's dead. Stefano is Jupiter's man. And the Andromedans' colonial rule is about to have its first seeds planted here. Is that what you want?"

Cronus gingerly put down his soup spoon. "Of course not. We free spirited Andromedan explorers want you to deal with the problem locally, without interference from the Andromedan Federation; Jupiter."

"Well, then, Cronus, between now and tomorrow afternoon you'd better come up with something. I don't care what it is. But it better be something."

"Like what? Alexander."

"Like we neutralize this guy. When we open that window tomorrow, they're not going to send Stefano bearing roses."

"Black roses," Zohar said sardonically.

"Okay, okay. There's not a moment to waste. Let me introduce you to someone who can help us formulate the plan."

"No," Alexander said, "not until I finish my dinner. I haven't eaten in days. I'm starving!" Alexander smiled as the Chinese spare ribs were being served.

"Some people can rebound from anything, Alexander," Zohar said, with an uncertain nod of approval, as Alexander tore into his food.

Alexander explained his position to Cronus. Believing that Cronus was a pacifist, he felt that Cronus had a certain amount of reticence regarding bold and provocative behavior. The very kind of behavior required to deal with Jupiter and Stefano -- now, in the present, before the moment passed. Cronus was unnerved, disquieted, by the prospect of violence.

"So, Alexander, I will help you formulate the plan to deal with them. After dinner. I'll take you to visit The Mule. He's the mastermind of Andromedan technological wizardry."

Alexander was stunned. "And you call him The Mule? Why not Mister Wizard, or something just as frivolous?"

"Obstinate, conceited, headstrong, and lonely. All he's thought about for thousands and thousands of years is his family and mistresses back in Andromeda. He's so stubborn that no one can reason with the man."

"Oh, so you're formulating a plan, Cronus, but we can't reason with the mastermind of a plan that doesn't exist." "Well, you'll just have to trust me."

"And right after eating, they went down an elevator and got onto the high speed tram. They traveled for quite some time, deeper into the earth at eighty miles an hour. In twenty-two minutes, they arrived at the base of another dormant volcano, the dominion of The Mule.

They hastened on foot through several chambers that were all kept sterilized with the use of ultraviolet light. Each chamber was adorned with lush tropical plants. They came to a huge control center. Behind a huge glass wall sat twelve Big-Eyed technicians who weren't willing to deal with Cronus when he requested entry.

"State your business, Cronus."

"You all know my business. I have to speak with him."

One of the technicians in the foyer spoke to The Mule. "Yes, of course, Cronus always has important business. It's his nature."

Cronus was frustrated and embarrassed. "You tell him that he'd better see me. I have colleagues who need to speak to him."

The sarcastic reply came back. "Colleagues? You've taken leave of your senses, Cronus. But of course we all knew that a long time ago."

"Okay. I defer to your technical wizardry. All of you. And that's precisely why I'm here."

The technician in the foyer of the massive subterranean glass palace spoke to The Mule again. "He insists that it's really important. This time!"

Alexander was mildly amused but very aggravated. "Shitheads--can't you understand that he has to talk to The Mule!."

The technician in the foyer spoke to The Mule so that Cronus, Zohar, and Alexander could also overhear. "Listen, these other guys, two earthlings, also want to see you."

The Mule asked, "Ahh, what do they look like?"

The technician answered, "It's uncanny how much they look like the Andromedans of old, from home...up close."

"Okay, send them up," The Mule replied.

They went several hundred feet up an elevator. After stepping out of the elevator they were escorted to The Mule's chamber. Once in his chamber, they passed many full-motion, life-size holograms: Mule art. There were holograms depicting people and scenes from many eras, millennia and centuries past. From the early Romans, there was a scene of people gathering in a public square and shedding their clothing at a fountain. From early Japan, there were scenes of Samurais engaged in sword fights. Most curious to Alexander were full-action holograms of what appeared to be early American Indians locked in a ritualistic spirit-raising dance around a huge night fire in a massive tent village. As Alexander peered into the hologram, the Indians were full- size-- separated only by the glass, the entire scene felt and seemed real. When the Indian chief danced in Alexander's direction, he seemed to stare right into Alexander's eyes. It was unnerving. It captured the mood of the entire chamber: to the senses, real in appearance, yet the events felt ghostly and eerie to the mind. The eeriness was dizzying to Alexander and his head spun.

He complained to Zohar, "No, I don't normally feel this way."

"What way?"

"Spooked," Alexander replied.

They twisted and turned through labyrinth of holograms, stumbling from surprise, at one turn being charged by a bull elephant, at the next turn being in the path of a buffalo stampede, the ground shook. One scene was more incredible than the last. Eventually, passing through all of the hologram chambers, they came to an area of couches and furniture. Sitting in a large recliner that supported his oversized head was -- The Mule.

"Well, Cronus, you've ventured into the outside world. Who are your friends!"

"Zohar, Alexander, meet my very best friend, Mule."

Mule's head was noticeably larger than Cronus's head in proportion to their respective body sizes. "Tell them my real name."

"No need for that! We urgently need your help."

Mule was nervous. "Time is short. We may all have to take refuge in the biospheres."

Alexander snapped, "Fifteen years, at least fifteen years until the ecological apocalypse."

"Son, the apocalypse is now."

Cronus shook his head negatively. "You've got to understand the mentality here, Alexander. No one can tell Mule anything. Every night is our last night on earth. This has been going on for twenty years. Now listen to me--" Cronus raised his voice.

"What now? You know," Mule addressed Alexander and Zohar, "Cronus's our emissary, always trying to smooth things over, always trying to make things right with The Federation. I live every day in a state of fear, like it's my last. Because we're sitting on this time bomb."

Alexander still felt eerie, weird. " So, Mister Mule, you're maudlin over having left your family back in Andromeda. Your eyes are dripping."

The Mule pushed a button on his chair and a hologram appeared, a woman in a flowing transparent silken gown walked toward them, her hair flowing behind her. She stopped about five feet from Mule. The area was dimly lit. Her facial features were stunning with the wanton eyes of a temptress, and she had the body of a goddess. She spoke in soft silken tones. "My love, I pray for your return, the consummation of our love and affection, the conception of our first child."

"I thought he was married," Zohar exclaimed.

Cronus was saddened. "Yes, yes, he has a family. But due to his great achievements in Andromeda he had several mistresses. She was his favorite. And the Federation censured him for his illicit behavior, so then he decided to come on the expedition to earth. No one was able to deal with his impulsive nature. He just had to get away from the oppressive life in our Federation of States. He never listens to reason. He's a mule."

"Oppressive life?" said Zohar.

"As a society becomes more and more differentiated, sophisticated, the people with the most talent and responsibility have no time for themselves," Cronus explained.

"No time for art. No time for love. No time for sex. No time for feasts. No time left for me. Just work. I came here to be an explorer and escape The Federation." The Mule expressed himself in anguished tones.

"Yes, yes, of course," Alexander said.

The Mule lamented, "And now look at us, aberrations of our former selves. Metabolic optimization transformed me from a temporal sexual being to a monster locked in time. Sex is the basis of art and expression. Now I'm asexual. What could anyone want from me?"

"I want to give you an opportunity to help us. To defend us against The Federation. We don't want to be colonized in the name of the apocalypse. We'd rather die than be colonized."

The Mule, with his big eyes, seemed to be looking in Alexander's direction. "You're not coming to ask me to save you from ecological disaster?"

"No!"

Cronus intoned, "Spoken like a true mule, Alexander?"

"We want to have our cake and eat it to. Like you, Mule. We're selfish. We're egotistical. And we want what we want. Want it our way!"

Cronus was amazed. "And what about...A Split Second to Midnight?"

Alexander answered by looking at The Mule. "A man who calls himself Jupiter, and his side kick from earth, Stefano, are coming here to kill me. And that's why I'm here. We don't know how many tesserac coordinates he has on earth...to open windows...here, there, everywhere."

The Mule went on. "But you suspect that Jupiter's coming right into our compound with intent to kill."

"And with my nemesis, Stefano, who especially wants to eliminate me."

Cronus interrupted. "You pioneered the tesserac technology that got us here. Maybe you could work some of your wizardry to stop The Federation dead in their tracks."

The Mule responded, "My oppressors are now your nemesis. Dead in their tracks? I like that. Let me think about it."

Alexander accepted a cup of coffee laced with Bailey's. Zohar had the same. They wondered about the wonders created by The Mule. Alexander kept returning to the American Indian dance, raising the spirits. It haunted him. He felt a ghostly pathos, yet he was simultaneously exhilarated. He spoke aloud, as though no one was listening, "That Indian...his rhythms, his chants, his dance, it's not of this world. For those moments, for that ceremony, he's transformed; he explores his material stream of consciousness for spiritual rhythms and realities... ephemeral, like the wind, gone at sun up. When, he sleeps..."

Zohar intoned, "Really, Alexander, I don't understand you or any of these people. But I support any decision." With tears in his eyes, Alexander turned to embrace Zohar. "You are pure of heart and mind. My best friend ever."

"Thank you, Friend. But I miss the significance."

"Zohar, I'm just as corrupted as these Andromedans. And you'll never understand any of us."

Zohar looked deftly into Alexander's eyes. "And Stefano--?"

"His corruption is so deep that he's become totally evil."

"And tonight, Alexander?"

"Tonight we dream. Tomorrow we act. And when my spirit ceases, I'll sleep."

Alexander and Zohar returned to Cronus and The Mule, who said, "We all feel the pathos, at the passing of the earth. She has a sweet beautiful nature."

"Can the planet be saved?" Zohar asked with a mature innocence.

Cronus interrupted, "Let's say, with all of the spiritual morbidity around here, things aren't getting any better. We can defeat The

Federation temporarily. We may fend off colonization. And we, the Andromedan scientists, are then obligated to save the planet."

The Mule intoned, "Sure, Cronus, you don't have a scientific technological bone in your body. He's our front man, Alexander. A point man, messenger, who reports the news. And makes political speeches. Why did you ever leave The Federation, Cronus?"

Cronus was unhappy with the assessment. "That's why we call you, The Mule, Mule. Your head is so hard that you just don't get it. And I don't want to bicker with you. We make a decision here and now to defeat The Federation tomorrow. Figure it out!"

"Are your ready, Alexander?" The Mule inquired.

"Ready as I'll ever be."

"Now tell me, Boy, can you fire a disintegration phaser?"

"Just show me how!"

"You sure are cocky for a frightened pilgrim!" The Mule lifted his head from his reclining chair; his head was larger than anyone else's in the subterranean colony. "Alexander. It's easier for me to beam you to Andromeda with a disintegration phaser, get you in and out, than any other possible scenario."

Cronus asked for an enumeration of those other scenarios. First, The Mule might try to destroy Jupiter and Stefano during the tesserac transmission -- which would be too obvious to The Federation as sabotage. Second, the Big Eyes might divert The Federation transmission to points unknown -- again, appearing as sabotage. Third, the Big Eyes might try to make it appear that The Federation transmission failed, and that the payloads, Jupiter and Stefano, were accidentally destroyed. Next, they might transmit Alexander to Andromeda with a disintegration phaser as a disgruntled rebel against Jupiter's cause. And finally, they might wait until the eleventh hour to make up their minds -- because none of these other scenarios were really all that great.

The Mule explained that tesserac was a technology that took hundreds of thousands of years to develop and perfect in the world of Andromedan research. Just as it took thousands of years of painful research to develop the capability to electronically store DNA configurations of some host organism; then it was thousands of more years of research to fully recreate the exact host that had been electronically stored. It was the rudimentary step in the tesserac developments to follow.

For millennia, within the burgeoning Federation, there were constant academic arguments about the nature of energy, about the nature of energy annihilation, about how energy regenerated itself at a much faster rate than existing tachyon technologies could explain. The contentiousness of the argument was quite similar to arguments surrounding Einstein's General Theory of Relativity on earth: the speed of light had been an absolute--until the discovery of tachyon waves. However, it was inconceivable to many minds, that annihilation ran at rates which were a billion times faster than the speed of light--indeed, a billion to the billionth power.

The next afternoon at 1300 hours, The Mule had arrived at the conferencing center on the roof of the Presidential Villa. Cronus was there with several of The Mule's best technologists. They had a plan, but Cronus wasn't buying into their plan. It was The Mule's overnight conception. The Andromedans slept very little; they had cerebral natures and this was a cerebral plan.

The Mule held a special tachyon crystal in the palm of his hand. Cronus looked at it with great trepidation before speaking. "You actually believe that this can work? It's never been tried before."

"It has, Cronus. It's just that you've been off in your geopolitical world for decades. We've tried it in the lab."

The plan was to store Alexander's being in the crystal. Alexander would first be reduced to electronic signals, coding, of his DNA structure; then the electronic coding would be translated into tachyon coding; tachyon coding, through their advanced technology, was linked with energy annihilation coding; energy annihilation coding was the basis of the tesserac transmission principle. When The Federation was ready to commence the tesserac transmission, they would see an image of Alexander concealing a disintegration phaser -- clumsy. So The Federation, to protect their interests, Jupiter and Stefano, would annihilate, disintegrate, Alexander, and then commence the tesserac transmission. Of course, Stefano would be transmitted first, just in case there were any glitches in the transmission that day, a safeguard against Jupiter's coming to an untimely ending.

In order to protect Alexander from disintegration, when the earth side technicians sensed a disintegration wave in the tesserac annihilation energy stream, within nano seconds, the Mule's technologists would reduce Alexander to his DNA-coded structure and store him in a tachyon coded crystal. To those at the Andromedan distant end, The Federation, it would appear that Alexander was disintegrated, and they would send Stefano to take Alexander's place on earth to be the earth side representative of Federation colonization--under the direction of Jupiter.

The Federation, since they had the technology to open a tesserac window for transmitting people and solid objects, was able to focus on any individual around the tesserac teleconferencing globe, on the roof of the villa, used in previous conferences with Jupiter. Now that The Mule and his technicians knew that the transmission window was activated, they had a few tricks of their own--ready, and executable.

Just minutes before 1400 hours, The Mule and his technicians were on the roof of The Presidential Villa with Alexander, Cronus, and Zohar. They stood around the table, where the tesserac teleconferences always took place--the massive spherical (globe) crystal display.

The Mule, always struggling to hold up his large head, spoke to Alexander, "Take this phaser weapon and conceal it in your pants. Don't worry--you won't have to use it."

"So what's your plan," Alexander asked.

"Just trust me, Alexander. We've got to make them think that you'll pull the trigger on the visitors. Which will set The Federation into an offensive posture."

"Disintegrate me? Then what?"

The Mule was amazed at Alexander's instant grasp of the risk involved. The Mule said, "Look, from the moment we sense that a disintegration pulse is in the tesserac energy stream, we electronically will snatch you from them."

Alexander's head snapped back. "What? Explain?"

"No time for that, you'll be fine, you'll be in control the way we all want you to be. But whatever you do, give yourself time to adjust."

"To what?" Alexander asked The Mule.

The Mule raised his hands and said, "Okay, okay, just remember this. Avoid looking in the mirror or at your reflection for several days. You'll understand. Just trust me. After that, Alexander, we're all in your hands."

Cronus stepped in. "Ruse and trickery--what craziness have you dreamt up this time?"

"Craziness? Accusing me of craziness at a time like this. Alexander will be in charge of everything. And Jupiter will be satisfied. It can all work out. Just don't look in a mirror, Alexander."

At that moment, the large crystal sphere began to pulsate with sound and light. The Mule motioned to them to take their seats, then he went off with his technicians to operate their control monitors and tesserac sensors.

The tesserac teleconference with the Andromedans was underway. Cronus spoke first. "We're here today as a diplomatic contingency representing the earth and the biospheres. We're here to co-operate fully with The Federation to save the earth from ecological apocalypse."

"Alexander! My son on earth! How speak you?" Jupiter thundered.

Alexander had to straighten up a bit because the disintegration phaser under his shirt was an annoyance. "Yes, I'm in total agreement. We're here to execute the wishes of The Federation, Jupiter. We are all compliant with your directives."

"And how do you speak, Zohar."

Zohar, who had not been kept in the loop on all of the conversations, at least knew that his role was also to agree. "On behalf of the biospheres, in the best interests of the earth and all of its diverse cultures, we will do what is asked to accomplish the will of The Federation."

Jupiter held up a document. "This seals the covenant between TacTech and LiteWave, an intergalactic technology exchange. TacTech will provide LiteWave with the necessary technology to stem the apocalypse--and my boys, Alexander and Stefano, together will execute this covenant with The Federation. Both signatures are required."

Just then, Jupiter was advised of the phaser in Alexander's waist band, "....or the signature of either surviving party will be sufficient. And now for the signing."

The Mule's men sensed the disintegration pulse in the tesserac energy stream just prior to Jupiter's and Stefano's being transported to earth. Instantly they put into action The Mule's shenanigans. What the Federation thought was Alexander being disintegrated were several events--totally simultaneous to the human eye, even a Big Eye. The earth-side big eyed technologists created a disintegration shell. Through the wizardry of electronic and tachyon technology, they instantly decoded Alexander's DNA into electronic signals. The driving force of Alexander's being, his soul, his spirit, was stored simultaneously in a tachyon crystal as a higher spectrum of tachyon energy; then his DNA structure was translated from electronic pulses into tachyon pulses and stored in a tachyon crystal. Those versatile crystals used by the Big Eyes for just about everything that they did. As they stored Alexander through the use of tachyon technology, they created an illusion, like The Mule's masterful holograms, of Alexander being disintegrated for the distant end Federation observers too see.

Very soon thereafter, The Mule's technologists captured Jupiter and Stefano through the same technology and stored them in tachyon crystals. Meanwhile, in all the mayhem of Alexander appearing to annihilate, Cronus went to The Mule and expressed his unmitigated anger. "Whatever you do, don't do the unthinkable. I don't want Alexander's brain mutated to Stefano's body. It's immoral, unethical."

"Then what?" The Mule asked exasperated.

"Okay, a quickie. Just substitute Stefano's facial DNA for Alexander's facial DNA...hair and stuff. Do it! You god- damned Mule. And leave Stefano tachyon stored for later. For Alexander. And save Alexander's facial DNA coding." They tachyon-stored Stefano in a small crystal held for just such occasions; the crystal was mounted on a ring--as jewelry.

The techs listened to the argument and followed the commands of Cronus, approved by The Mule with a quick nod. The technicians raced through several gyrations on their tachyon control panels, as the Federation observers, on Andromeda, saw Stefano and Jupiter materialize. The Federation hadn't categorized or stored information on Stefano, Jupiter's special guest; they only knew him by his face and longer hair.

Jupiter sat in an easy chair on the roof of the earth side villa. "Stefano? Stefano? that must have been a rough transmission for you."

Unable to speak, stunned that he was addressed as Stefano, Alexander looked around the conference table; in fear of speaking, he cleansed his throat. "Oh, ahhh, mmm, well yes--Zohar, Cronus, Jupiter. For my first decision on our technology exchanges, rather than create panic on earth, let us introduce the earth to a sports anomaly from the biospheres. The snow wing. With a proper introduction to the biospheres' favored sports competition, earth can be persuaded to embrace the anomaly.--as non-alien. And I'm sure that Alexander, after making his ill-fated decision to fight back, would agree with me. He won the snow wing competition. But I will prevail in the continuance of the earth, its cultures, its sports, and its competitive nature; a nature bringing it to the brink of apocalypse. Right, Zohar?"

At that precise moment, Alexander winked at Zohar who got the message. It was Alexander, not Stefano, because Stefano prevailed in the snow wing competition, as Zohar so vividly remembered.

Cronus looked in the direction of The Mule, who put a finger to his own throat: the technologists had not forgotten the voice of Stefano, the larynx...in the DNA exchange.

Now, Alexander, wearing a face of evil, materialized as the embodiment of the first covenant between earth and the Andromedan gods.

And Cronus, pro-active in the body politick of earth, presented Jupiter with a speech. He began by kneeling at Jupiter's feet, a gesture of Cronus's wry humor. "We, the faithful scientists of The Federation, in order to form a more perfect union in colonizing space, wish to present you with a ring, a token of our esteem, admiration and support for your wise and noble leadership in picking Stefano to lead us. Stefano. Please present Jupiter with the ring."

Alexander, looked about at everyone; clumsily, he got up and walked about the conference room. They hadn't altered his posture, his stride, his cadence; he looked like Stefano -- but still walked like Alexander.

The Mule gave Alexander the ring of Stefano. The Mule pointed to the ring out of Jupiter's view. "The spirit of Alexander still lives and is symbolized by this ring." He pointed to the small tachyon crystal, which had facets like a blue diamond, where Stefano--form and substance-- was stored. Jupiter loved blue.

Alexander, with the face of Stefano, went to Jupiter. It was his turn to kneel. Alexander had a difficult time kneeling, but Cronus, still kneeling, took Alexander by the hand and said, "Speak, Stefano, of the new covenant!"

Alexander was angry and unable to kneel until Cronus forced him to one knee in a medieval gesture. "The planet Jupiter is the earthly symbol of egotistical man. Each and every man strives within himself to be a god, like you. In honor of your godly qualities we present you with this ring, Jupiter. Always remember the wisdom of your decision... because Alexander has an even greater ego than yours. There wasn't room enough on this planet for the two of you."

"Minions, servants of the empire. You have done well in pleasing me," Jupiter resounded.

"Empire?" Alexander said, "We thought it was a Federation!"

The End

About the Author

He claims his weakness is a vivid imagination which is also his strength compelling Joe to be a tireless story teller. In addition to this book, there are other writing projects under development. He believes that science fiction is the most difficult genre, because SciFi writers must be cognizant of cause and effect in their created domains, causing this work to become the endless editing labor of love.

His undergrad degree is in psychology with many iterations of technolog to follow; first, 1970's Software Engineer, RCA Computer Corp, then IBM Mainframe Systems Sofware Sales; then, 1980's National Account Manager for RCA Global Communications; finally, 1990's to the present an independent internetworking consultant, forming his own business in 1995. To see his latest internet project go to http://www.ipvideos.com.

Printed in the United States
47743LVS00005BA/100-105